NATION

George A. Thorn

Cover design by: George Thorn

For my Mum and Dad, who always pushed me to go further in what ever I set my heart to... even if they found some of my stuff weird.

To all of my friends who supported me, kept me sane and brought insane happiness helping me to express myself more.

I thank and love you all.

CONTENTS

Title Page	1
Copyright	2
Dedication	3
I.	7
II.	64
III.	109
IV.	129
V.	212
VI.	221
VII.	259
VIII.	296
IX.	353
X.	382
XI.	423
NATION WILL CONTINUE...	443
COMING SOON: GRAVESTONED	445
About The Author	447

I.

The carriage was covered in a new coat of paint, which didn't seem new given the wear and tear it had endured. Its back wheels were bolted tightly on, but the carriage still showed a slight sway as it continued down the paved road. Washington, D.C was overcast today. A slight chance of rain in the evening. With carriages like this one, they would be working overtime in the busy towns later on as people would go in search looking to seek cover for the weekend ahead. It was a quiet time in the year. The festivities of winter had drawn to a close and the new year set a new stage in American development. President Theodore Roosevelt was about to have spent one year in office, with his administration working hard to kick the spirit of American pride into highs that would see the country prosper and slowly develop itself into a new global superpower. Given the years America had prior, this was a step in the right direction. America would see more states being created and leave behind less of the native territory. The turn of the century saw the end of the old west. The country's laws on slavery torn up and an industrial revolution spurred on by innovation and confidence. Soon the country's administration would quickly see the importance of land and animal protection, as the president has a big heart for the nation growing up at a young age. The president was sending a clear message of his intentions even before making his way up the presidential ladder. He also showed the importance to young voters telling the nation that preserving the past to a high standard should not occur and that future generations should be listened to, even if some didn't agree. For one man inside the carriage, he couldn't care either way so long as the flag stood flying high. He sat with his legs stretched apart, almost covering the circumference of space on his side of the carriage seats. His beige denim trousers were tucked into his boots neatly with his button-up shirt slightly un-tucking itself near his belt buckle. The buckle was silver with a gold pair of Remington rifles crossing each other over a small vial, slim glass with a cork sticking out from the top; it was half full with smudging fingerprints visible on the glass with a slight shade of colour that could've been soot. A scarf draped down from around his shoulders being held in place by his pinstripe dark brown blazer. His neck resembled that of a turkey, not wrecked but hanging low with a blister red colour. Marked by a vicious attack or caught in the crossfire of something forever leaving a lasting mark to his skin. His face slightly chiselled but couldn't be appropriately shown as it was riddled with unkempt hair. Moustache thick as a rose bush, sideburns beginning to stretch out and curl, ageing gracefully like a wolf's mane. That grey wolf persona was even more genuine when you looked into the man's eyes as you stood face to face with him. Whoever met those eyes didn't know what to think. Those little black dots weren't there. Damaged but still being able to see baffled those in this grey wolf's way. His hat, crushed suede, olive-brown in colour, sat next to him in the carriage. The man had just woken up, the time was 7:36 am. The rain began to fall softly. Grey sky. The street lamps still lit. Washington was soon to be awake. Small pockets of people were already on the streets, waiting for drivers to take them to their jobs. The factory worker's blue denim overalls covered in oil and soot staining them from the heavy moving with the extreme work conditions of an industrial factory that revolutionised the world. Standing side by side with them, the businessmen who're skilled in accounting and finances looked to oversee said factories to benefit the company sustaining these machines. Washington felt clean and tidy in its appearance. Unlike the dusty, hot climate that fell over Texas every hour, the old man felt this to be a much-needed change in scenery. The cold air climbed up through the old man's nose cleaning out his chest. Sniffing up the natural smell of rain on grass felt therapeutic for him. For a brief minute, that is. More pressing matters were soon to be addressed. He reached inside his inside blazer pocket, a crumpled up piece of paper holding an address and message.

1600 Pennsylvania Ave NW, Washington

'The White House'

This message to the recipient has been sent from the office of President Theodore Roosevelt.

Dear Mr Ray William McCarthy.

As president, it is my utmost pleasure to thank you first for your years of service towards the greater good and benefit to the United States of America. A new age is dawning in America, I believe someone with your heroism and dedication should not undergo any more pressure from the all-seeing eye of government officials deciding who you are. I think it is time that an official pardoning is passed to you. The wild west is gone, misinformation spread everywhere. I am here now, and I wish to correct it before we are both gone.

You are invited to my office in the early hours of 6:30am on the 19th of February.

T. Roosevelt.

Twenty-Sixth President of the United States.

A slight raise of the eyebrow. A scratch and sniff of the nose. Ray thought it was too good to be true. The president calling him finally to relieve him of the many accusations that have been swung at him like monkeys with faeces. So much has stuck on to his name, it began to smell. His life before this has been nothing but survival. The wild west was fierce and unforgiving. During his time, he had seen outlaws infamous for their crimes dominate the untamed land, infested with gangs causing violence and disorder, which made any sane person shiver in the hot sun. Texas was a long journey back, but he also seemed frustrated that the government had found him in his time of hiding. Someone like a local could have reported him from his wanted poster. Rats everywhere, feasting on what they can get. That person will have to answer for themselves one day he thought. The carriage driver knocked on wood behind him, signalling that they were just about to stop at his destination. A bar in the middle of the street, situated next to a woman's quilt making store left of a pharmacy on the right. It looked to have been built recently given the way how clean it came off compared to the other establishments in the vicinity. Ray grabbed his hat, placing it back on his head, hiding his silver main, stepping onto the road. His boots both hit the ground, making a small splash. He handed the driver his pay and turned to face the bar as the dark carriage pulled away. A familiar name drew the hatred in his eyes as he stared, dead-eyed at the sign which read:

Bidens.

It stung having to read that. That name he could recall seeing it a dozen times, and almost every time he met it again, things would only get worse. Reaching into his blazer pocket once again, this time pulling out a less torn piece of paper. One that had been neatly folded once. It was a newspaper clipping. A family sat in for a group photo at the top of the article on board the local train. All members of the family were dressed in high-end outfits. The women standing as straight as their unflattering corsets would let them and the men with their collars high up, suits uncomfortably tight.

'Biden family brandishing their newfound wealth and new life.'

Written out eight years ago, Ray moved his eyes around the different faces taking up the photo. Only one had its face crossed off in pen by a large X. Each member had a bottle in their hand, brandishing the alcohol that they intended to serve. Ray knew better than to drink from their distillery. Lowering back the paper away from his pupil-less eyes, he folded the paper back up and moved into the Biden's bar. Slow-moving piano music could be heard by the entranceway, the piano situated near towards the left side window which had red velvet curtains slightly covering the inside of the bar. Two men and women stood talking outside, and a horse stood calmly waiting for his owner to arrive. The rain had drenched him and it gave an almost sad look to Ray as he entered. Extravagant was one word to describe it from the eyes perspective, but a more playful name may have been appropriate for his nose.

The heavy stench of drink, prostitution and other bodily fluids ran up Ray's nose, making him miss the clean air back outside. The piano player was a young boy in waiter garb, keeping his head down, focused on the music with his talented fingers carrying on that sweet sombre track. A massive poker table took up the back, near the stairs leading up to the rooms, with fourteen players around its green-lit table from candlelight. Each man with a good handful of dollars each, ready to play down in the name of the game. Cigarette, pipe and cigar smoke all in one beautiful toxic cloud almost covering up the ceiling. It made going up the stairs a visual representation of what going to heaven might look like to most people who smoked. The bar area, stained. Drink glasses left unattended too, with the barman nowhere in sight. One man sat on the stool with his whiskey glass in hand, moving it around examining the strongly scented liquor which he soon gulped back. Gritting his teeth and with a slight hiss escaping through his yellow stained teeth, he hopped off the stool walking past Ray to the door. Ray stepped away to let him through and lent himself on the driest patch of the bar. Some of the other men sat in the middle of the bar took a quick glance at the old man who had pulled up. Ray knocked politely on the wood to call for the bar-man, but he was not in sight. He knocked again, this time louder.

"Hey! Jerry! You're wanted downstairs!" Said one of the men at the poker table. A faint curse and a slam of the door and the footsteps could soon be heard making their way down the steps. Now in sight past the thick cloud of nicotine, a skinny man with swept-back hair that had been ruffled from shenanigans upstairs, looked onto Ray at the bar. As the piano player, he too was in waiter garb, the classic white shirt and black waistcoat with a black armband. Straightening his vest out, he took huge steps towards the bar before hopping over it to serve. The man was young, mid-twenties. Small patches of stringy hair protruded from his tiny chin. Quite clean, considering the work conditions. Ray zeroed in on the man, with his eyes, he looked up and down, gathering every detail from him as he moved closer towards him. He got everything he needed in a matter of seconds.

"What will it be sir?" He asked with a lack of profession-alism.

"One glass of whiskey, straight. And I'd like to know the

details and price of the rooms upstairs." Ray ordered.

"Sure. Just for the night or a whole day?"

"The night."

The barman poured out Ray's drink handing it to him with a straight look into his pale grey eyes. He winced but did so slightly, so as not to look rude. He went to the room, which led underneath the stairs to find keys for the rooms. Ray put down the glass without a slight hesitation. His damaged eyes still held onto where the barman was, trailing him as he walked on back.

"So we got a room. Ten dollars for the night. If you want a drink or anything your gonna have to speak to my brother Butch who comes in after midnight"

"That's a bit much, don't you think."

"Well, it's the only one left, partner. Do you even realise where you are sitting at right now?"

The barman didn't know where to lay his eyes. They looked up and down the old man's face. Thinking he was blind, the young barman soon had his sights set on the young woman coming down the stairs. Curly red locks with a dimpled face, the young lady gave a small smile, wrapping her finger around one of her locks of fiery hair and her cheeks a light shade of pink. Her pink corset still hanging on with some of the strands keeping it tight around her back unfastened. Her high heels were loud on the wood flooring as she walked over to the door, dishing a small wave to her lover at the bar.

"If you want to lock eyes with her again you'll drop the price right now for me" Ray demanded.

The young barman backtracked for a bit. The old man was not blind at all. The thought of being threatened by, in his eyes, an ancient fossil, was a bit ridiculous. But standing his ground, lifting his chin up, he said: "And if I don't?"

Ray's lips sunk in. He slowly pulled out the newspaper column picture of the Bidens. Flattening it on the bar stand, rotating it so that the eyes of the family in the photo met the barman.

"You're in this picture, aren't you?" Ray asked.

"Y-yes. You some relative we left out?"

"I'm not important. But I may be if you don't heed my words. And this ain't no preacher talk, this is man's talk. Something your grandfather should've done,"

The young man's eyes grew. My grandfather, he thought. Who is this guy?

"Your father clearly didn't tell you about manners. Cause the way you have served me my drink and my living accommodations were frankly, average at best. I can see you were...getting busy upstairs. In fact, everyone here could hear you getting busy. That is no excuse, however, to show pity little attitude to a person who'll pay you your wages. It is that type of pity attitude towards people that have made your family name a sour taste. And from my experience, that taste doesn't go away."

"Mister, I've done nothing to you. If you want the tough questions answered, go speak to my brothers. Just pay and you can have the room."

"Oh, I know you haven't. From what my eyes can gather, you are the spitting image of your dad, and you have the opportunity to not be like your dad. As much as you love him, there is nothing I'd like more than to bring him down for what his father did to the people of Bone-bag. Now I suggest you be a good boy and give me the room for free. If that is, you're certain you're not like your grandfather."

The young barman was now frozen in fear. He didn't know who this slick-talking old man was or what his connection to the Biden name stemmed from, but he was sure that the old man had killed people in his day and that this was a way of leading lamb to the slaughter. That's when the young man noticed the poster on the back behind him. The old man's face was there for all to see. With a small shrug and smile, he then seemed at ease. He placed the keys on the wet wood of the bar stand and politely spoke back.

"Sir. I am nothing like my father. In fact, anything you had with him is none of my concern. In fact, anything you have with him, now or in the future, will also not be of my concern."

Ray slowly nodded in understanding. Playing to the young man was smooth talk for him. He also gave a small smile back to the young Biden. Good things can come from him, he thought.

"Which room am I in, Mr Biden?" Ray asked.

"Room 3."

"Best be clean." Ray joked as he got up from his stool. The floors creaked with every step towards the stairs, another pair of eyes from inside the bar would follow him. Ray held his leg in discomfort as he pushed up the stairs. He was now up in a fog of smoke that had been created by the paying customers below, giving him glaring looks. Room 3, far right of the two other occupied rooms. It wasn't much, four walls, one window, one bed, one desk side cabinet. Candlelit on the opposite side of the wall facing the window. The walls were stained like the bar area downstairs, not with brewed fluids but with bodily fluids. Ray turned his nose up to what the smell could've been. The bed was unmade, as expected from the young Biden son having it for a while. Ray threw back the cover over the white sheet which held sweat marks of the previous people. Lovely imprints to be expected from a randy couple. Ray sat perched on the edge of the bed, plopping his hat onto the small cabinet. Raising his arms, he inhaled deeply before lowering them as he exhaled. Exhausted. He reached into his second blazer pocket, pulling out a soft neatly rolled cigar. His nose ran up its leafy shell, smelling its strong tobacco. It made his eyes flutter for a moment like aged to perfection wine after popping its cork. Ray bit the top and held it under the wall-hung candles orange flame, puffing through to get it going. With a big inhale and exhale, he let the flavours roll around his mouth and again into the air. Rich, heavy tobacco with a slight pine fragrance from the leaves binding the two together. At ease, he walked over to the window to see out to the street. Rain was lighter now than when he arrived but the clouds still looming over with a thunderous presence. A typical everyday city. Ordinary civilised people, more brains than guns which would've been pointing at each other in the heat of a moment or for pride. Washington was different, it had to be. It needed to set a standard. The old dog felt out of place. The President's letter had now made him the last of his kind. Or, he was about to make it so. Back downstairs, Jerry had again snuck away this time around the back into the office area where he himself was the only one inside. Jerry went straight for the phone and began to dial the numbers back.

"It's me. He's here. Made him all nice and cosy for his stay. If he stays longer I'll keep you posted. Let the family know as soon as possible."

Early hours of the morning. Sunrise just a sliver of

the horizon. A knock was made at the old man's door with a voice calling through shouting "Wake up call, Mr McCarthy!" With a creak of his back, he slumped forward like a body rising from its grave. Wheezing, he rotated his hands in clockwork motion, clicking all the bones in his wrist, making them feel loose and re-laxed. Ray then did so with his arms, feet and head. Oiling up the machine for his rounds. He slept in his shirt and slacks for the night, with them both being easily creased for the morning. With his hands, he lazily brushed down on the crease lines of his shirt and trousers. The worn brown blazer would soon hide the creases found on his sleeves. He grabbed hold of his boots from between the bed and cabinet sat at arms reach away from each other and slipped them over his pale ashy feet. With the scarf wrapped around his neck loosely and with a tip of the hat, he was dressed. Very unprofessionally dressed for a meeting with the presi-dent of the United States. Kicking his finished cigar end under the bed which brushed off in the night, he made his way out of the room downstairs. It was clean. Like there was no smokers at all from the previous night. Chairs were all turned upside down resting on the tables with all the broken glass cleared from the floor.

A different worker was behind the bar cleaning up the stains of alcohol, a much broader heavier man with a straggly goatee and crew-cut hair was at the post, donning the waistcoat and armband combo.

"Tell Mr Biden I appreciated the room," Ray said as he made his way out.

"Will do sir."

Crisp morning air with a calmer overcast sky. The worst of the rain was now behind Washington. The dirt ground still somewhat manageable to navigate through if you were a coach driver and you could just walk through it without one leg sinking in further than the other. Ray had just lit up another cigar, gripping it tightly with his teeth while he relaxed his hands on his hips. He began his walk. Not a peep of anyone. Tranquil morning. Trees were waving from the wind with the odd bird flying out from under their leaves. The city had plenty to offer that would tempt a morning person into handing over their hard-earned cents. A coffee shop, bakery and meat shop all had their place nicely tucked away into a small section through an alleyway for those who lived by the road Ray was walking on. A sweet combination of freshly baked goods mixed with the aroma of coffee beans could lure anyone to it.

Ray walked on by. Carrying on further, Ray passed by the newspaper prints pinned on the walls with today's and even yesterday's news. Most of it was damp and tearing up from the rain yesterday. The photograph was just alright to make out if you wanted to get into a story with half the paragraph missing or with your head tilted in an uncomfortable angle. Ray walked on by. Trailing up the road, it started to curve around past a lusciously grown oak tree which sat on the edge of the most prominent patch of an open grass field. A park in which for residents of the area to relax, away from the madness of the concrete jungle. It was one direction now, straight onward, the White House was in clear sight of him.

Oak trees lined up the pathways, dust blowing in the wind to the left side of Ray as he carried on down the narrow path. He could see squirrels emerge in the fields. Alive and well, they sprinted around chasing one another while another collected nuts that had fallen. They scurried around without a drop in speed, carrying this speed over even when they scaled the trees. Crows landed too sharing the field in search of food, squawking as they looked up above to the sky and on their surroundings with the squirrels. Ray walked on by. He started to hunch a little as he continued to walk. Years of trailing down somewhere to the other side of nowhere was nothing new to him. He had seen better sights down south, but this was going to stick in his mind given the circumstances. A presidential pardon was on the way; years of his life spent in hiding was now to be forgotten. His grubby sunken face hid his excitement with a tired, angry expression. Passing by the final line of oak trees, the president's house was in full view. The gates were black, standing taller than the six-foot Ray. He caught sight of the armed patrol. One, two, three, four, all wearing union blue gold button suits with the coat of arms patch on the right side of their uniform with a tinted bronze colour. One followed round the gate fence and soon stopped, before turning around making the length again. Like a caged tiger ready to strike, the guard didn't take his eyes off of Ray who was getting closer to the premises. Each guard was carrying a rifle from the waist up by the butt, pointing the gun barrel upwards. The White House was a remarkable sight, the base of operations was illuminated perfectly with the sunrise. While residents of the area were almost numb to it, almost like a painting, it was too beautiful not to take in even for just a second. Ray followed the fence till he reached to the main gate where a guard stood either side of its panels. Ray stood relaxed with his cigar, puffing away. He eased off the pressure holding his cigar and carefully managed to keep it sat between his lips while stating to them

"I'm here to see the president".

The guards took no notice. Like nothing was said, their trained gaze on Ray remained unchanged. Ray slightly mumbled to himself as he reached into his blazer pocket, pulling out the letter from the president.

"Maybe this might help clear things up?"

The younger of the two guards looked over to the other who was closest to Ray. The elder guard extended his arm to retrieve the letter in question.
Examined, the guard whistled to one of the guards further behind them beside the main entrance. The hustling of equipment was heard as the guard made his way down to the gate. The letter was exchanged again. He gave a quick shot looking at Ray, the guard nodded to

the elder guard as he folded back up the message.

"Ray McCarthy."

"Yeah?"

"You may enter. Mr Roosevelt is expecting you."

A quick turn and click from the key and the gate was pulled open ajar by the two guards. Ray slithered through the gap made before the gate was once again locked shut.

"Follow me." The guard said, tucking away the keys into his deep jacket pocket. He walked stiffly, almost like a march but far more relaxed compared to how he'd be in front of his superiors,while Ray took one step at a time. Relaxed and slow. Lifting his head with eyes in a squint, Ray caught sight of another service guard sat perched at the top of the White House, like an eagle waiting to strike at any given moment. Ray, with another slight smile, nodded to the man up top while he looked on with his rifle in hand, finger just touching the trigger in anticipation. Both men were now nearing the entrance into the most crucial house in the country, the guard already ten steps ahead of Ray stood by the doors while the old man just made it to the giant white pillars of the east side of the house.

Ray's dusty worn away boots stepped through onto the red carpet that lead him into the entrance hall, tracking in the only bit of dirt it looked like it had picked up in its lifetime. Crisp, clean white walls surrounded him with the finest of chandeliers glimmering above him like the sun piercing through tree branches. The guard closed the doors with an echoing slam and a twist of the keys, rattling off as he shuffled them back into his pocket. The guard showed his hand in the direction to go, along to his right, and Ray would follow behind. Resting his hands inside his coat Ray looked on through the hallway, his eyes again skipping the beautiful scenery this time captured in fine painted art hung in golden frames. His slightly arched posture trod slowly on the red carpet, his boots making no sound at all as he followed the path up to the president's room. They came to a stairwell, Ray began to breathe slowly up the white stairway which lead up in a spiral. It showed his age to the guard. Under his heavy breath with a slight one-second pause in between words "Never...again...after...this" he heaved as he made it coming off the final step, he positioned himself facing the hallway. The hallway to the big man's office. The light coming through the slight gap in between the two large polished doors gave a distinct sense of who was behind it. The most important man in the country. And the other side, an outlaw. Ray again brushed off his jacket and rubbed his tired eyes. The crust from the morning still latched on to whatever hair he had left for eyelashes. A lick of a grubby finger, slicking his bushy eyebrows getting them straight. Raising his hand, he wanted to do the same with his beard but again answered himself with the remark "Ah, who cares. The man's got a better moustache than me anyway". The guard simply stared with no expression, nor did he give any fanfare. The door now in his face. He looked down at himself with another worried intake of breath. He knocked on the door and silence met him as he waited. Five seconds, already too long, he thought. Ten seconds, this is awkward. The monotony ended with an "Enter!" from behind the wooden door. Ray turned the golden door handle down and turned his body through the gap he had made opening the door. Slithering through, he shut the door quietly without a sound of the lock clicking back. The room clean. A rich polish smell.

Portrait of George Washington on the left wall next to a commemorative flag of both the United States and it's a military unit. Next to Washington was Abraham Lincoln. Beside him, a landscape picture of the president with a group of young to middle-aged men huddled round together. On the wooden frame, the golden nameplate read out 'Roosevelt's Rough Riders' in deeply engraved writing. To the opposite side of the office a bookshelf, keeping hold of books from animal anatomy to journals. The red carpet had now ended with beige carpet stretching out the whole room with a rug placed just before a person was to sit before the president. The rug, skin from a buffalo. As Ray moved slower into the office, behind the wooden desk, a bull terrier roamed out, staring down Ray before giving a small growl. Ray didn't know what to do, frozen uncertainty to why a dog was with the president at this time.

"Pete! Back here, boy" spoke the voice again from behind the desk.

The terrier turned his head back to his master and walked back behind him, perhaps resting himself by the president's legs.

"You never stare down any animal, Mr McCarthy. No matter how big or small, predator or prey, it will most certainly give the wrong impression. But thankfully with you, I can stare and marvel at you all day. Cause you may be a rare species and I certainly wouldn't want to lose this nor this moment with you." The president closed his journal, putting his pen on top of it before sliding it into a drawer.

His hair swept to the side with a grey and brown colour of which the latter colour was the entirety of his moustache. Glasses sat comfortably on the bridge of his nose with his eyes staring into Ray's. He sat comfortably at his desk with hands locked together. With a raise of them both, he pointed to the chair opposite him. "Please, sit," he said in a welcoming tone. Ray took his hat off, holding it snugly against his stomach as he sat down.

"That's what you wear to a meeting?"

"I wear this for everything. Sir," Ray said, not forgetting his manners.

"Right well, let's get started," the president said, sliding his papers to the left of him. He stood them up, push-ing them down on the desk until they were perfectly straight in his hands before reciting:

"This formal meeting between the two persons presid-ing; The acting president, myself one Theodore Roose-velt Jr and one Ray William McCarthy. The latter being enlisted in the American army in eighteen fifty-five before ranking as a commanding officer to the union army during the civil war between eighteen sixty one to eighteen sixty-four. Ceased all communication and went AWOL, fleeing from his patriotic duty leading to a life on the run which spanned decades with felon-ies such as theft, arson and murder. Yet from what I've heard from a certain individual who shall not be named, you are indeed a special one, Mr McCarthy. Is all that I've listed correct?"

"Correct, sir," Ray answered.

"For what reason?" the president pondered.

"Family needed me."

"Everyone needed their men back, Mr McCarthy, what

gave you the right-"

"Mr President. It was urgent. Like you, I have enemies." Ray said with a trembled voice.

The president's face once again frozen. Staring into Ray's eyes, he could see fear. Slowly putting the notes down, he asked: "Which family was in need?"

"Sir?"

"Like I said, Mr McCarthy, you are a rare breed. And like all the information I have present, I wish to confirm all that is deemed uncertain truth. Straight from the horse's mouth. This family that you said, was it your second?"

"Yes." Ray said, answering this time with no hesitation.

"And was it of native bloodlines?"

"I thought I was here for a pardon."

"You are, Mr McCarthy. But I do wish to go through all that life has bestowed upon you. And being reluctant to share that information now when you have a bounty on your head that has sat on the desks of the secret service and past presidential administrations, it would be quite unfortunate to squander that oppertunity now in these very halls, don't you think?"

Ray rolled his grey eyes with his head tilting down till his chin rested on his chest. Giving a sigh, he spoke again.

"It was the Crows. Before my service, I had helped them set up land territory in the north-west side of the uncharted territories. They were in disarray as they battled the Sioux tribe for ownership of the land. One day away from my duties, I saw it to myself to help them, as I had seen stretches of land that would be perfect from my travels. A feeling came over me that I had not previously felt for them. Instantly when they saw me, the white man, I had a knife around my throat. Hand-carved, silver, the blood of the unlucky few staining its tip. Once I showed them, they gave me mercy...took pity on me. They saw who I am behind the uniform."

"Why do you think they did that?" the president asked.

"They can see more of you in ways you couldn't fathom, Mr President."

"And how do they do so?" Said Roosevelt lifting his eyebrow in curiosity. Ray grabbed a handful of his grey hair and lifted it up high. Doing so, he then swivelled on the chair, turning his back, exposing his neck. Almost like a pin had sunken in, a dark blood spot now dried into charcoal black skin was like a seed in which throbbing veins were seen.

"They prick you. Sample your blood and see if you're worth the time. That's all I figured."

"Fascinating. Almost like marking you as property. That seems to have aged a long time Mr McCarthy."

"They saw me as a survivor. A warrior lying in the wake for the right time." Ray said.

"I'm sorry this I can believe, but you mean to tell me that they are now fortune tellers if they fiddle around with bodily fluids?"

"Like I said. The Crows have ways, Mr President."

"Yes, yes, I see. The better question is, do you believe in these ways? Or was this prediction a gateway into your extreme measures of escape?" Roosevelt said.

"I was not one in the hocus pocus conversation at the local bar, sir. But from what they told me around that campfire that day, much like horror stories, you could only speculate and believe what you want to believe. One of their locals, told these stories in a language I was only starting to grasp. Lean. Strong. Probably their youngest. Akea, his name was. A very positive individual he sat me aside after their chief had enough of storytime. Said to me straight that I am beyond what I claim to be if I do not succumb to what is told of me. Sort of like saying go your own way, and you find true peace."

"And you accepted this as a justifiable reason to act out the way you did in your time after this?" Roosevelt said like a teacher scolding a student.

"Well, it's kept me away from worse things. I think that's what brought me here now. By not succumbing to others who wish to bring me down. Keeping my head high. Now I'm here being relieved of my actions."

"The official report says you sent a squadron of the

unions finest troops to another part of the south in helping your so-called second family which led to bloodshed from all sides." The president said, pressing harder with the facts presented to him. Ray could see the discomfort in his face when discussing this, keeping his composure he continued to explain so his chances of being pardoned could not diminish.

"I gave my word if they were ever preyed upon by worthless scum who kill them for sport or wish to exploit them and their women, I would be there. I gave my word and blood to them. Sir, I don't know what your feelings towards them are, but with past administrations, I have been quite cynical on their stance towards them."

"Now that was only one day, and on that day word got out that you went rogue or were presumed dead. Care to elaborate, which is true."

"I'm more than a uniform. Just like Akea said. I saved them from those southerners who took refuge just west of them. They needed anything they could get their hands on, I saw it in their eyes. I lead my men alongside that same tribe, and yes, bloodshed did happen. Worse than what I could've predicted. But it was not left in vain." Ray said.

"And you justify it with a prophet-like message? Mr McCarthy, your time with that tribe and what you have done in thirty-seven years, has made the country know of your name and the stories that have accompanied your name are now almost folk-law when brought up. Infamy. Like I said, I'm here to hear the truth. Not fabrication. Or perhaps maybe you'd like to tell me about that vial and what it possesses to make a man live through so much that he has to lie about it just to make ends meet."

Ray's eyes widened. The president was not playing games now. He would soon have to speak up. The fear of losing the tribe could be in debate if he didn't.

"How do you know of the vial?" Ray said with a tremor.

"Now that's more like it. The image wiped away, and the true man comes forward. I am like you Mr McCarthy, I too am estranged to the unknown but how can any man live through forty years of protecting a single tribe from scavengers, hunters and any otherworldly threats of the land? All the while causing problems to society that it surpasses any old tale of outlaws and do-gooders? Your pardoning procedures are officially underway if you provide me with your history. What you have told me so far is the truth but one man's account in that squadron reads you took those young boys down to that settlement, aided the Crows and fought off the confederates but didn't end in you just leaving. No, it ended with you, gun in hand pointing at him telling him not to tell a soul of union interaction in the area and why? Because according to him, the words you spoke to him was to tell base camp that only Crows and confederates had engaged each other while you opted to have any trace of your miserable attempts of heroism buried?" Ray was now uncomfortable. The tough persona he showed during his entrance now had his tail tucked between his legs in embarrassment like a scolded dog. It was time for the truth to come out. His emotions ran high as his mind was awash with all the promises about to be broken.

"I couldn't let anyone have it. I was unwise to put that onto the young boy. I thought he would just take his orders and run with it. He was more dedicated to the unions' cause than I was."

Ray had his binoculars up, he could see down from the hilltop the Crows base. He could see Confederate soldiers brandishing rifles with bayonets in the trees behind them, stalking them like a pack of wolves. Bringing them down, his mind raced with ways to go about this, in the end, seeing the odds stacked against him and the Crows, should he brave it on his own. His younger yet not so coordinated mind saw the best way to combat this would be to gather his men to arms and join the conflict. It was the middle of the night, and his squadron was asleep. The group of boys all fit into the twenty to twenty-five category in age. Some looking like it was their first day in wartime as their pretty boy faces would meet the gruelling hardships of war. Ray kicked them all until they were on their feet staggering from being woken at such hours of the morning. Ray signalled them all to keep as quiet as possible and follow him down from their hillside camp. The boys clutched onto their weapons as tight as they could, like kids with their teddy bears as they formed a triangle shape battle line with Ray as the tip. The boys could now see the orange faces sat around the fire, their joyous get together being interrupted as the first set of eyes spotted them, and like deer, they all rose to their feet bringing their bows and arrows up along with their knives standing guard in wide-stretching battle stances. The young men brought their weapons up too, but Ray halted them with a wave of his hand.

"Stand down boys," he said.

"But sir-"

"I said stand down Private!" Ray shouted. The old fox was placed in the middle of it all, unsure of what to do.

"Listen to me. Stand down and move away from this place," Ray said to them in their native language.

"Ray? What are you doing? You're ruining everything." said one of the Crows.

"You can speak their language, sir?" the young man said who had the only facial hair between the other boys.

"Don't draw attention, Private they'll think you're pro-voking them."

"You were supposed to protect us!"

"What do you mean? I'm always there to protect." Ray

said back in English, but it wasn't enough to stop the confusion.

"Protect? Sir, I ain't protecting them, what is all of this?" Now, this was getting worse than what he envisioned it to be.

Come off as a leader to his men or a traitor the Crows. As the bickering soon raised to levels in which words were flung around everywhere, one of the Crows was less impressed and silenced it all. The arrow shot through whizzing past until it landed square into one of the young boys' chests. He stumbled back, shook and shocked yet still trying to raise his firearm up before his legs buckled and his back hit the ground. Dead silence. Then a rifle shot was heard coming behind the tribe as the marksman with the bow, blown away when a bullet connected straight to the back of his head, cracking the skull open. The blood poured into the dirt with chunks of skin and bone sliding down the mans neck. The playing field opened up with bloodshed as the confederacy soldiers charged forward after a line of synchronised shots took place, catching two Crow members and one of the union based boys, square in the head. All three sides yelling cries of war lunged towards each other with knives and bayonets in hand for a close-quarters assault. Fists flying with blood drawing from heads as confederates knocked down their opponents with the butts of their guns before bringing a side-arm to finish the job. Tribal yelling from the Crows terrified the young men in blue-collar coats as they sprung towards them, double teaming them with quick slashes to the legs before eventually dealing the final blow with a slick sound of the knife on his throat. Rifle rounds came from the union boys who were quick to charge their rifles holding them tight as they used them like battering rams. Bayonets piercing the hearts of those defending the south, the bodies soon piled up. Ray, trying hard not to become part of the skirmish, slithered through the fire and fists being flung in battle hid by the Crows tent beside the camp-fire which grew larger from a body now succouring to its flames. As he shuffled behind the teepee trying to figure his way around this battle of three sides, his train of thought was cut down by an unsuspecting attack from one of the Crows. The native threw down Ray with a sweep from his legs, and the two threw down hands, rolling through the dirt and grass as they grappled hold of each other in a test of strength. Ray now in survival mode, got hold of the native member in a headlock, his waist pressing down on his back as his boots pressed down on the hands of his foe. The heels of the boot took effect as the man cried out in pain as Ray held down, wrenching back at the man's neck. Ray's teeth gritted together, saliva dripped from the bottom part of his lip as he took breaths in through his teeth. He wrenched back harder so the native's head was soon nearly touching his chin. As Ray gave more punishment to the Crow, he whispered into his ear:

"Stand down your men, and we can take out the real enemy here."

"How do we not know it's you?" came a calm and familiar voice. Ray froze in place as once again, a cold steel knife tip poked through his hair onto his neck. Releasing the hold, he stood up to see the young man who had not met his eyes in years, Akea.

Same warrior markings as before but with a deeper set of jet black hair.

"What did I tell you those years ago? This, the uniform does not decide for you. Nor does it determine what you think. Look what it has made you do." Akea said.

"I didn't want this to happen. I brought my men to protect you from those southerners! I promised to protect you!"

"Not like this. You would know when we were in true danger. You think those ones in grey scare us? We were leading them here! We had been tracking this group for two days to avenge our women and children. Killed, raped, burnt. We had them, and you ruined it"

"You needed firepower." Ray blurted.

"We needed silence. Then we could attack. Your military may have given you the skills and resources. But did it improve your judgement?!" Akea was now upright in Ray's face. Anger and frustration could be seen in the young Crow's eyes.

"We spent all that time together, where I taught you everything about being a warrior. The lessons needed to survive, and it all seems to have left you. You are now the sheep who pretends in wolf's clothing." Ray had his hand lifted over his revolver with his fingers eager to lift it out from his leather holster, his anger besting him but his conscience telling him not to make things worse.

Steel then soon clicked together, but it wasn't from Ray's doing, shifting the angered eyes of Akea over Ray's shoulder. A confederate soldier welding his six-shooter shot his weapon hoping the bullet would trail through both men standing face to face. Time went slow. Akea had somehow managed to throw his arms into Ray at the right time, pushing him away from the bullet that trailed into only one of its two targets. Piercing into Akea's lung, the large round left a bloody hole from which the red fluid gushed out covering the right side of his rib cage. He fell back from the impact, with his legs buckling from the power of the six-shooter ranger revolver, until his body came down with a thud as the dusty dirt lifted into the air around his body. So did the confederate but at a slower pace. The soldier staggered, gripping his chest from where the bullet had hit before eventually landing awkwardly face-first into the dirt as his blood trickled out from the side of his chest. Ray, with his gun in hand, smoking from the bizarre but impressive shot lifted himself up, jostling himself over to Akea as he laid in blood-soaked pain.

"I...see...your eyesight... has improved," he struggled to say.

"I got him faster than you ever could," Ray chuckled.

"Im-impressive-"

"Impossible," Roosevelt interrupted. "No ordinary man could have made that shot in that small space of time."

Ray smirked. "I thought so too. Even he didn't expect that."

Ray did do the impossible that day. Having made the split-second decision to lift his gun from the holster, with precision, he turned the gun upside down with the barrel facing behind him. He had kept the weapon handle tightly with his fingers in an awkward position with his thumb pushing the trigger at the same time as Akea had moved his eyes in time to the clicking of both Ray and the confederate soldier's gun.

"Usually... it's me who is saving you."

"You still are, Akea."

"Not anymore. It is now... down to you...remember

what I've taught you." Akea's hand shook violently as he reached into his back pocket, adjusting himself ever so slightly so his hand could reach in. Concealed in dark brown parchment paper, Akea handed the small item into his friend's hands, pushing Ray's fingers tighter onto it for it was of great importance.

"Like me...it can make you look...immortal." Akea coughed hard until a little stream of blood started to run down his chin. Ray, with the given gift held Akea tighter than ever. It would be his final words. "The Crow spirit...is...in you, brother." His words got weaker and weaker until Akea slowly slipped away into darkness only to be carried away by his ancestors through the beyond. Ray was awash with emotion. The fighting in the background started to die down, but the noises kept his vulnerability and tears unnoticed. Ray leaned closer, resting his head onto Akea's before, with his free hand, he closed Akea's eyes. Now, there was silence. Ray's eyes shifted away from the body of his friend upwards as he looked both left and right wondering how much time had gone during his grieving. He, without hesitation, unbuttoned his blue union jacket and tucked away the parchment-wrapped item inside it. Turning away to face the teepee that had kept him unseen to all three parties, all he could hear was the roar of the open fire which sat in front of it. It was now louder than when he last saw it and much more uncontrollable. Peering slowly around, he caught sight of it. Now covered in four more bodies the smell of burning flesh soon covered the whole camp-site with its scent. Across from the fire towards the other teepees, bodies laid from the confederates, the unionists to the Crows, their blood almost covering the entire ground. Gunshots, stab wounds, even dismemberment painted a gruesome landscape. Ray trod lightly around with his feet just placing beside the bodies, his eyes searching only in case one was to spring and attack without his notice. No surprise attack would come to pass. Instead, a familiar sound of metal clicking together. Ray turned to his right to see just by the camp-fire of mounted bodies, stood the youngest of his squadron, shaking with fear almost to the point where his knees would give in. Ray saw he was scared, the young man was not holding the gun properly, using it for intimidation rather than direct intent with the tears running down his eyes confirming it. He was trained but had not seen the paintings of conflict before. The whole scene broke him. Ray was more attuned to it and slowly made his way over to his young fighter.

"Put the gun down, son," he called over to him. The young man indeed followed his orders without hesitation, he dropped the gun to the floor with his arms now straight down his sides, standing like an awkward child. A foot away from him, Ray picked up the gun and examined it. With an eyebrow raised, he said "Convincing work, pulling the safety off. But the illusion was lost cause you didn't keep it in your hand. Always keep your gun in hand until you have made a decision son. Cause that what I'm gonna do." Ray checked the barrel of the silver six-shooter to see how many rounds were in the chamber. It was full. Clipping it back in and the safety clicked back again, Ray held the gun to the young soldier's head, aiming straight between the young man's eyes. The young boy was now looking like he could shatter at any minute, he couldn't handle all of this now his commanding officer was holding him at gunpoint.

"I am gonna go away. You make this decision now too. You either hide our boys' bodies away so that the union doesn't know our intervention ever took place, presenting this as a battle between Crows and confederates.

Or I'm gonna blow your head off," the words sending shivers down the young soldier. He asked his high ranking official, "What will I tell them about you, sir?"

"Tell em I'm dead or gone. Your choice, partner."

"He picked the convincing choice, thankfully." Ray said, remembering the event like it only happened yesterday.

"Where did you go from there?" asked Roosevelt.

"Far away. Up north. Basically to relax for the weekend."

"Must've been a relaxing thirty seven year weekend," the President chuckled for a brief second.

"His last words just, changed me that day. I thought that would be the best thing to do. I had no family to go to, no responsibilities and now no job. What was left to lose other than my sanity, right?"

"What about the vial? We now know that was something not to lose" said Roosevelt with a convincing grin.

"It wasn't. But I hardly touched or looked at it until a week of travelling had passed."

Leaving a rucksack down on the ground, Ray stood after dismounting from his caramel coloured steed. Nothing but desert from here until getting further up into the Midlands. He stood basking in the hot sun, which brought the sweat out from his forehead. Ray reached for his flask in his coat which he had taken off an hour ago, laying just tucked under the saddle with his damp sweat showing as a dark stain on the upper arms of his sleeves. He fanned himself with his hat while taking a conserving sip from his water, licking his lips to moisten them. Observing now, around him was the never-ending horizon that started with dry dirt and sand. Green hills off in the far north which harboured the clean air and wildlife. Hoping for a small town to be in distance of where he was. Needing to check his carrying case, he used his compass to double-check where he was. Inside his bag was a sleeping mat, an ageing silver container, a small leather journal and some mints in a copper-tin and just tucked beside it was the vial inside the parchment paper. Ray soon placed the compass back into his army bag before climbing back up onto his saddle to continue north. With no path made into the dirt, he would have to forge his own way up towards greener pastures. On the run from the military, having the loss of his best friend, anything to be isolated. It was needed. His eyes searching the wild frontier while his brain secluded itself in thought at what just happened. Like Akea said, he was always someone who followed the words of others, now was the first time in quite a while that Ray would have to think for himself. Soon he would have to mould himself into a survivor. One that would make decisions on the spot to stay alive. He went slow so as to not tire his horse, the heat venturing up the country would slow the horse, cooler weather up north would be a welcome change. Ray had grown tired of the army, months before the events of last night happened. The position he held bugged him as the civil war generals made the calls while he lead the charge, counting casualties. Fighting his own countrymen was something he wouldn't have thought the country would ever make him do. Escape was paradise, Ray was a union man through and through, patriotic and respecting the president's decisions, but he had friends and relatives who down south who believed in the confederacies values towards the country. Keeping in touch through the post, he would often have letters sent to him in his commander's tent during a time of conflict that high-lighted his friends' concerns with the war. One message that hit him, changing his view of the enemy sup-porters came from his former girlfriend. She wrote:

To Ray McCarthy.

It has been a short time since we talked but a long time in face to face interaction. I am keeping well in these diffi-cult times of division, and I understand and respect your opinion on what is best as an active serviceman to the union. My family has made the matter clear on what they think, but I do not display the anger they possess when talking about it. You would know that very well. It always made me laugh when my father, back then, would not praise a single thing you did to connect with the family but would soon praise to God about you afterwards. You have the brain he never had. Mother is keeping in good health, as am I.

From your last letter, you brought up the past too much from our time together and I would much rather we move on, as it becomes awkward for me to write something to you without thinking about it. Our time was had, and that's it. Much like now with the current times, we need to look forward and better ourselves. Which is why I'm asking you not to reply back to me. We both need time away, and while I appreciate the communication, the trip down memory lane made me feel you were still angry about what you did. I hope your time in service will not make you think differently of me but will serve as a purpose for you to know that not everyone in life you meet will be the same as you. Understand the differences in people and respect them for it as I am doing now for you.

From

Mary Clancy.

Ray was always one to listen when people were part of his life. Being the type at a gathering who wouldn't speak up, still in line but never wanting to be heard. Now, something he didn't know he'd value a lot in his forthcoming years, time away. It was all that he had now. No more following those who viewed the world with him in the same way. Time to see things differently, he thought. The Crows sought to bring that to him, but Ray would not listen. Only through the death of Akea did it make him vulnerable to take it in and look at the world differently. A sombre mood took over as he thought more and more about the people he left behind.

He would soon have to drown it out to stay afloat around the seas of isolation.

As Ray made it into the green plains of the hills, he soon saw life. But not the life he thought he would see first. But that of wildlife. Deer and small creatures such as rabbits and rodents roamed the vast land he was now stepping into on horseback. Deers met him with a quick raise of their heads before bounding away in fear that he was a predator. His horse in focus of the direction they were heading, the top of the hillside. The glare of the sun was brighter now with Ray squinting his eyes tighter, which made his head tense. He and his horse saw out into the land down below, a small mining town with a church. Two farm fields opposite the railroad track. Peaceful, reminiscent of his home back down south, he thought. Well-mannered individuals with no interest in keeping with the theme of the wild west no rules lifestyle.

The rule of law and the constitution held in high standards. Ray made the descent down the hill towards the town where he was greeted by a curved wooden arch with two horseshoes on both columns. Carved into the arch in cursive writing was the word 'Bonebag KY'. Walking through the archway to an unknown part of the state, Ray was not satisfied until a roof was over his head with food to eat. Even the most potent alcohol around was needed to soothe himself from the thought of yesterday. He kept his eyes open for a saloon which had rooms to let, while the busy townspeople looked at him as he walked on through. The curious looks from people as they try to sum up a person and where they have come from and the confusing looks as they try to understand why they are here. A few weren't impressed by what they saw of Ray. He still had parts of his military uniform on, which made them suspect the worst with it being wartime. Ray came across the local tavern and dismounted from his horse, hitching him up outside as he entered. With it being midday there were not a lot of people inside except for one old man in a shirt and suspenders having his lunch. Nothing was too particular about the bar, it was possibly the most generic bar Ray had been into in his life, nothing too exciting but it would do. He noticed the room vacancies sign set up on the wooden counter and approached the middle-aged man cleaning whiskey glasses behind the stand.

"How much for the night?" Ray inquired.

"Two dollars. Just don't be bringing any of your buddies

with you cause that won't swing in here."

"Buddies?"

"From the experience I've had with military boys sir coming in here and starting a ruckus, well it just won't slide anymore in this town." said the barman with a grimace.

"Listen, sir, I've come here to get away from it all. I just want a place for the night. Now you want to take my money or not?" Ray said, placing his dollar on the hardwood. As he slid the paper note toward the barman, the shotgun slowly went back under the counter. He took the dollar and presented to him a key which also came from under the bar counter.

"It's number four, upstairs."

"Thank you. Can I also get a drink at this time?"

"Course you can. What will it be?"

"Regular beer." Ray requested.

A pop of the bottle cork and a bang of change on the counter, Ray chugged the drink down like it was endless as if it were water.

"Can I ask you something barman? This town, is it away from it all?" Ray asked.

"I'd have thought you knew that when you arrived here mister, Bonebag is always away from trouble in this country. That's why I gave you the speech. Bonebag just gets crap from both ends. While we say we can avoid the cry of war, we still seem to find a way to attract the dogs of war. Second, our town makes a pretty big step in markets or word of mouth about our butchers' catches, well then it's unavoidable. Both the Union and Confederacy have been here and it don't matter which side you're on, people's behaviour can sometimes be troublesome," the barman said.

"I understand that. But there isn't much trouble that goes on here, right? Other than the occasional drunken ass who enters your establishment."

The barman chuckled.

"That's usually the case here. Mayor Nichols wanted Bonebag to be its own thing. Unconnected. We still get business even though we're tough on our values. Guess that's what gets us the reputation we have. Tough on anyone that walks in," he continued.

"You don't say. So are the locals here tough-natured like your elected man?" Ray asked.

"Oh, most of them have their say on matters, but people here are genuinely good-hearted. If you're looking to stay, you got good company here Mr-?"

"McCarthy."

"Pleasure, Mr McCarthy. Keith Boston." The two shared a friendly acquainted handshake.

"Noted." Ray finished with a last tilt of the bottle of beer. He was relaxed now and knocked the counter for another. Boston got to it and cracked open another one for his paying customer.

"So, care to tell me why you left the war zone?" Keith asked.
"Not at the moment. I don't know if I'm officially done with it yet. Just done my duties and they shipped me out. What about you?"

"I would be fighting the fight, but the drinks come first. So do the profits," Keith said, putting the change away into the register. Shutting the metal drawer up Keith's eyes trailed down underneath, he came across one of his possessions near some glasses that were next to the finely polished copper kegs he had ready for large gatherings. Thinking to himself, does he know what this means, or shall I tell him? He wondered. Question is would he get the wrong impression if he presented it.

"Have a look at this and see if you know what this is," Keith said. And now brought to the bar side was a Henry rifle banging down on the wood in front of Ray. It was gorgeous, impeccable silver finish all throughout the body, the barrel as well as the stock. Upon closer inspection Ray could see the gold, real gold for that matter being woven through a beautiful string of rose thorn engravings.

"She's gorgeous," Ray said astonished.

"A rare prize I had the fortune of acquiring when stumbling across an old shack one time in the woods. Notice anything in particular about it?" Keith said with a glint in his eye.

Ray's eyes examined every part of the weapon as he held it and moved it around with his hands. Only when he looked down the iron sight did he notice something, bringing his eyes back after looking down the barrel of the beast, he saw the engraving on the stock barrel end. An insignia. The outline of a wolf's skull with an arrow in between its teeth, the tip facing west.

"The Wolf Gods?" Ray said, knowing the emblem and its history.

"Oh, yes," Keith confirmed.

"I thought they were just a legend?"

"So did I. Kids would draw their symbol on walls but everyone took it as a dime novel story. But then their treasures started being found, scattered everywhere throughout the midwest. Heard stories of people finding gold or bullets used by 'em. That rifle is the best bit of evidence to them, but still, no one knows who they are," Keith said.

"So what does it mean, this rifle? The way its built saying that they had connections?" Ray wondered.

"Why don't you look down the sight , Keith said. Ray brought the gun up again, looking down, still didn't notice anything. And then, there it was, brushed over, yet the outline was barely noticeable when drawn up to the light. Numbers with a couple of letters at the front.

The messages starting off with U and then S before the numbers rolled on.

"Military made? Guys my end never had these unless they were rich." Ray said.

"Or lucky to steal one off a dead man. Maybe of jealousy. Jealousy in the ranks maybe?" Keith pondered before he put the finely crafted weapon back underneath the bar counter, resting on two hinges.

"What, you thinking these guys were part of my men?" Ray wondered, giving Keith the raise of a eyebrow, questioning him.

"No-one fights a war for pride. Just business, gain and survival. Here's to the war, Mr McCarthy. Brings out the worst in people," Keith said holding a bottle out full of foamy beer which dribbled slightly off the side.

"Not me Keith. Promise you that." Ray said. The two clanked their bottles together and chugged back the liquor.

II.

"Bonebag. I believe I did pass by that area one time during one of my rallies. Saw the people, not the town. Very respectful. How long were you there for?"

"Five weeks. Nothing much happened apart from, of course, the discovery of what the vial could do."

Daybreak. Day three, week one in Bonebag. Ray's clothes are on the floor, creased and not washed from the last time he'd had them on. Sporting a white shirt this time around, the deserter officer lifted his head from his pillows to face the sun's rays which were blinding as they peered over the horizon. Squinting through the bright sky, he extended his arms stretching out as his spine began clicking. Like a regular, he dragged his feet across the floor to head for the bar area, where Mr Boston was ready to serve his coffee, hot and black as the night.

"Good sleep, Ray?" He queried.

"Excellent sleep. That's what I get for good behaviour, as the boss told me."

"I can see working with Mr Grove has got you earning decently. Saw the man yesterday, said you listen well and just do the tasks at hand. Keep the man working, I said, he keeps my lodging business at the saloon going," he joked.

"Well, what can I say, he pays well, and you provide good coffee that lingers in my already nasty mouth." Ray sipped again at the scratched tin mug, smoked coffee beans that were strained just right about ten minutes ago.
"With your skills with the hammer, I'm surprised you haven't built yourself a place."

"If I did that I'd be alone with my thoughts. Christ I don't wanna talk to myself at the moment. Besides, I doubt if the mayor would allow me with all that paperwork to fill in. I only just came here not long ago"

"But you're getting in with the people here nicely aren't you. I'm sure they'll repay you somehow, everyone here does a favour for somebody and you sir, are no exception. And hell, I think it would do you good getting treated after what you've left behind," said the barman. Ray had a small smile light up his face. It was true, this did feel like a low dose of heaven at this point in time.

"Listen here. If you help me in a second with those barrels over there, I'll let you have your next coffee, free of charge."

"You truly believe in your words, don't you?" Ray said as the two chuckled. Ray sipped back the last bit of his coffee before heading outside with the barman.

"Sorry, could I get the name of your boss again?" asked Roosevelt.

"Grove. Billy Grove. Owned a small woodwork team," Ray answered.

The last of the five heavy barrels now sat around the back just under the staircase. The two gentlemen both breathing heavily after the strenuous lifting. A small intake of air which was cold in Ray's throat was quickly let back out as his hands sat comfortably on his hips. He shouted out to the back of the saloon, "last ones in!" as the barman was on the toilet. Ray heard the muffled thank you and soon walked back up the stairs to get changed. With a quick rinse from his sink water, cleaning the visible crust from his eyes, slipping on an outfit from a day prior that wasn't smelling of booze, he proceeded into town. Examining his head, he noticed his hat was a tad bit crushed and worse for wear. Making a note of this, he walked back down to head outside into the day ahead. Stepping off the wooden porch, the town was just waking up themselves. A few of the townspeople who owned stores were the first to greet the day like Ray in the early hours. As Ray got to the general store opposite the butchers, the owner was just about to unlock the door as Ray asked the question:

"Do you do hat repairs here?"

While the store offered a small number of clothes for sale, they didn't have anything to fix them. The store owner pointed towards a small store further down the main road. Martha's was the store name. It was a female orientated store selling the newest of corsets and the dresses that colour coordinated with them. He said they would be able to sort out that hat. With a raised eyebrow, Ray used his hat to hide his face as he entered with an embarrassed look. The store was much cleaner than all the others. New wallpaper with a floral pattern covering the wooden walls, the clothes neatly organized as you entered with the dresses starting off, then the hats near the counter and a small section of the store to rest with a footstool to try on shoes. As he looked around, he looked more towards the table as there were thread needles and baskets to purchase. He rung the bell which sat atop a fabric tea cosy at the counter. No answer. Another try at the bell and still no response.

With nobody around Ray simply made his way out, unsure if the store owner had left for a couple minutes or forgot the store was unlocked. He shut the door behind him with the bell jingling inside the store. As he walked down the porch stairs though, a voice to his right was calling out "Sir! Sir!" It was as he thought, the woman who owned the store. She was petite with an hourglass figure with her auburn hair combed around one side so effortlessly that it rested comfortably on her shoulder. She had faint freckles on her cheekbones that complimented her blue-as-the-sky eyes. She straightened her posture before speaking.

"Was there something you wanted in the store?" she asked him with her rough, speaking voice.

"Uh, I just wondered if-,"

"Were you interested in any of the dresses for a significant other or family member?"

"No, I came for-"

"Shoelaces? Jacket buttons? Hat repair?"

"Yes. The third option," Ray said as he lifted the hat off his head once more, showing his awkwardness towards the business at hand.

"Oh, don't be shy. Clothes are clothes. I can make that hat suiting your head again in a jiffy" the woman said as she took the hat straight out of Ray's hands that were clung onto it in the manner in which a dog would beg for something if well trained. With significant strides, she opened back the shop door with the bell ringing again. Ray dumbfounded glanced back to see two workers chuckling to themselves after catching them out of the corner of his eye. Now was the time to go in to save more embarrassment, he thought. The petite woman was far behind the counter with the quilt box Ray had seen above her earlier.

"Did your horse sit on this? Because I know your ass wouldn't have been able to," she asked.

"Excuse me?"

"Don't worry I'm not one to judge a man by his ability to ride his steed. Although for me it's a requirement," she laughed. Ray still took back by her behaviour politely asked

"Mam, may I ask what your name is?" to which she replied back proudly, "Martha. Martha Newark."

"I must say mam, your place is certainly the fanciest of the shops here."

"Why, thank you. I thought it needed to be really. I gotta spruce up Bonebag somehow, so I thought to fix it up, the people is a start. Most of them, like the gentlemen outside giggling away like a bunch of schoolgirls, their overalls were made by me." She boasted, finger pointing to her chest.

"Well, don't get too comfortable with me. I'm only here for temporary purposes." Ray informed her.

"Which would be?"

"Money. Food. The other necessary things that keep a person alive in these times"

"Wars weaken mister, I think you have it good being here. No-body knows how long this war is gonna drag on for and quite frankly I wanna be away from it. Hopefully the government can straighten this out."

"Trust me, I think they can. So, you lived in Bonebag long?"

"Three years. I came back when my mama passed on. That's why I have the roof over my head now. She was a Martha too, hence the name. I wouldn't know how to run this place if the next door people didn't help me out. Their daughter who's the same age as you, even works here from time to time."

With the last snip of her scissors, the final thread in the hat was stitched in, keeping the hat straight. Martha dropped the cap onto the counter with the thread box which rested on her knee while she worked and talked.

"Right, that'll only be twenty-five cents, sir. Oh me, I didn't even ask for your name."

"Ray McCarthy." Ray handed over the money to Martha and exchanged pleasantries as he left with the ring of the bell. Back into the cold fresh morning air, Ray saw the stags pulling carts of chopped timber. Work had started for the day, so Ray followed them as they continued down the muddy road. Guiding them down, was a large bald man holding a cigar the size of his thumb in between his teeth. Squinting up as the sun lit up his perfectly shaven head, the large man wore a white button-up shirt which just barely got around the hairy stomach which hung over his jeans. Walking barefoot in the mud was a unique way of getting into that working spirit, Ray thought as he garnered a look onto him. Wagons were making their way to a wooden barn that housed timber from the woods down south of the town. Chopped down and harvested by any of the townspeople looking to earn a quick buck in their spare time.

The smokey grey barn had white painted lettering on its side which read: Billy's. An opened house barn which would recruit anyone, even for an hour. The actual Billy, Billy Grove, was short in stature and always wore an unbuttoned waistcoat that would sit comfortably over his cotton shirt. His face seemed to have not lifted a smile in years, the old man's expression had not changed with some calling it frozen in time from the last thing that disappointed him the most in his life, but really was a case of facial paralysis. Still, with his doors open to anyone wanting some dough in their pocket, he was the quickest person to see to craft a smile on. Scraping at his bushy sideburns, he caught sight of Ray moving down to him with the wagon of wood blocks, raising his hand to him with a lift-up of his red-skinned chin in greeting.

"Keeping your mules in check, Mr Grove?" Ray joked.

"Eh, a farmer must keep his farm moving through Mr McCarthy. Come for another day out?" Billy said, his voice croaky and weak from the number of cigarettes in a day that would weaken his system.

"You bet. Keeps my landlord happy."

"Right well, come into the barn I'll show you what you and these two brothers who've come in, are doing today."

The old man pressed his hand onto Ray's back, walking him to the barn. Other workers around the sides of the barn were either chopping at the wood, breaking off twigs or merely enjoying a cigarette around a fire made up of unused carvings and bark. Smoke mixed with the smell of wooden lumber was all your nose could get a whiff of around here, but the three lumberjacks, big in the physical department, were used to it. All three brandishing the strong will to hack down with their axes all the while wearing similar checkered shirts just with a different colour to tell them apart. Inside the empty barn were the two brothers, both of which were familiar to Ray as they were the two men he had caught a glimpse of this morning giggling to themselves as they watched Ray walk into the shop. Ray stood with his feet apart, lining his eyes up with them with a neutral expression.

"Right, you three let me tell you what you'll be doing," said Billy as he circled them together. The two men both shared a bright-eyed look with each other again as Mr Grove began to explain their work.

"Basically what I want you fellas to do, take the stagecoach round back with the signs to the barn and distribute them across the road down to Creek Bay. Show off the work tools if they ask but just gain some more attraction to the site. The horses are all set, you lot just do the rest. And don't be too long, no showboating because I need that coach for later."

The three all nodded in understanding.

"At least with us, we won't be worrying about our clothes," one of the two men said as they both made their way out of the barn first, butting their arms together.

"Clothes maketh the man, gentlemen. It's obvious from the way you two wide-eyed me on my way in, that they'll know who to come to," Ray highlighted as he started to move as well. Mr Grove just shook his head. The three of them saw the stagecoach attached to two horses with one of them hoping up first to take the reigns while the other took up the passenger seat leaving Ray to sit alone in the coach with the equipment and signs.

"Just make sure you put 'em right on the roads," one of the men yelled back to him. A crack of the reins and the horses began to walk forward before advancing on into a gallop. The first part to Creek Bay was the turning down the hill by the crooked tree which rested near the brow of the mountain. A tranquil spot to use when picking up riders' attention. The two men stopped the coach and knocked back at the coach to let Ray know to start nailing.

"Just over there on the tree," one-pointed. Ray took the hammer in his right hand, sign resting against his side pressed up to his armpit with the two nails sitting in his mouth like a toothpick. He walked over to the decrepit old tree which had been sat upon that patch of the hill for decades, felt a shame to put another nail hole in its already carved bark, which housed numerous names, some paired together in a heart-shaped ring. Ray, looking up at its tall trunk before pinching the nail said "No hard feelings," as if the old tree was listening to him. With a whack of his hammer, the solid flat head pushed the nail through the sign corner before hammering it again to seal the deal. The pin needed one more good hit to be tight inside the tree's skin. The sign was then raised up to level with his left hand before Ray kept it still with his foot pressed against it awkwardly, with his knee bent. He was now at an awkward angle to hammer in the last nail into the opposite corner and sure enough with a right curve of his wrists, the flat head connected with the pins. Slightly at an angle but it'll do, he thought. Both nails now were pushed into the point where you would have to pry the sign off with a good pull from the top if your fingers were slim enough. As Ray picked up the hammer, he turned to look back to the coach with the two workmen who had belittled him since this morning, only to find the tracks of it going down the hillside path. They left him on the edge of the hill with the tree.

Ray sighed. Walking onto the path, he caught sight of them, looking like a small woodlouse crawling across the floor in his field of vision. They were just pulling up down into town, probably to get all the attention for themselves. Creek Bay was much larger than Bonebag, not in terms of scale but just with how much more traffic would flow through it. Ray soon began to walk down the path to catch up with them, not even with a look of frustration. Just disappointment. The two workmen parked the stagecoach middle of the four-way junction inside Creek Bay and begun to unload all the equipment and signs to show off to onlookers who passed on by and some who sat out in their porch areas.

"Come on, gentlemen come and sign up! Billy's will give you the good ol' honest days pay with the best hours catered to you!" shouted the one workman in blue denim overalls.

"No word of a lie, work for as long as you want with the pay that'll make you think you've been all day!" continued the second workman dressed in the shirt and waistcoat. Pockets of men looked on with small smiles at the two's enthusiastic showmanship.

"Get all the tools and supplies to work with and pick up experience while doing it!"

The two carried on enticing men for easy work as Ray was just coming into town. He could see them jumping around like monkeys, waving their arms to bring the men of Creek Bay closer so they could get their signatures. As Ray came closer to the stagecoach, the man in blue overalls budged the waist-coated man's arm to draw his attention to him. They both grinned in delight as he walked closer with them disappointed look on his face that looked like it was going to change any minute into anger. The two nodded together and continued on, rehearsed in their heads they spouted in unison.

"So come work at Billy's any time, any day and soon you could be fixing your fancy britches just like ol' gay Ray!"

The two cackled to themselves patting each other on the back as the onlookers turned to see Ray who had now stopped dead in his tracks. His miserable expression made just one or two people chuckle, but others didn't know who he was and we're quite confused. Ray kept his whole body relaxed as his arm drew his six-shooter from his holster, shooting right at the horses' feet, sending them into a panic. The crowd covered their heads in fear, and with a frantic sprint, the horses pulled the stagecoach forward hurtling the two workmen to land on their backs onto the dusty ground with the signs falling on top of them. They were both winded by it, coughing even more as sprinkles of dirt rushed upwards into their mouths. The men and women of the town looked at the coach, then the two men and then to Ray. Putting the gun back into his holster, Ray walked to the crowd and placed himself firmly on top of the two workmen with his feet staying nicely flat on the signs. He took out a piece of paper from his shirt pocket and held a pen into his other hand and exclaimed: "So who wants to join Billy's?"

The coach made its way back up to the grey barn at Bonebag. Ray was now the one steering the horses, puffing away at a cigarette while the two jokester workmen followed closely behind carrying the tools and signs. Their faces covered in dirt, making their skin look dry and unsightly, they were still in pain from the fall, carrying all the equipment didn't help. Ray chuckled as he looked back at them. Pulling the coach up around back, Ray got off and walked up to Billy who remained seated upfront by the barn's doors watching his workforce cut up wood for the day.

"All done Billy. I can see you're gonna have a few people down there pick up on your place," Ray said.

"Oh, that's wonderful! How did the other two do with ya?" Billy asked.

"Well, contrary to what I thought, they definitely put their backs into it."

"Oh, good, good. Well, is that all I'll be seeing of you today?"

"It is indeed."

"Right well here is your pay." Billy drew out his cradle of coins from his pocket. "Hopefully see you tomorrow, Mr McCarthy."

"You too, old man."

The two separated and Ray began to walk back up into town just as the two men who accompanied him from the job came from around the barn carrying the tools and signs before dropping them down to the ground like they were a tonne of bricks, gasping for a breather. Ray went back to the saloon to return to his room. As he entered, he drew out his journal and began to take notes at the side of his bed. He took out the pay that Billy had given him for the day and jotted down the amount he had accumulated over a few days. On the page, it had a neat column, with the top line a calendar with the dates and the ammount of income underneath it. Just over one hundred dollars in total. But he needed more. Good progress for a couple of days, he thought. That was the only positive he took from it.

He needed more somehow. He looked further down the page to look at the expenses. The rent of this room, food, the occasional drink bracketed to cut back on as well as the cigarettes. In his mind, Ray could picture the scene, a house with a moderate amount of land to call his own. Away from anyone and the noise of the ever-changing landscape of the country. He closed up the book and placed it back into the drawer, along with the cents Billy gave him. He thought for a minute, thinking about the options he could take. Most of them involved hard labour which could affect him later on (which would include more expenses). Were there options that did not involvebreaking his back? He thought. Just then he raised his eyes up from the floor and thought about the shop from this morning. Different for a guy such as himself to be working in a place like that. Surely there would be work in that place.

Ray came through the store door, with the bell signalling to the employees. Instead of an awkward wait, Martha was already at the till this time.

"Back again? You were only here this morning," she said.

"I forgot to ask about something," Ray said.

"I was wondering if you needed a little bit more help here. Surely with all this stuff in here and how long it took you to even get to me this morning, would you be interested?"

Martha gave a simple answer back, "Yes. But don't think working here is gonna build up this image you got going on from what I can see."

"Trust me, the image is something I care little about right now. I just need more work when Billy hasn't got anything for me to do."

Martha smiled. And she wasted no time in the dying hours of the day to ask.

"Well, I guess the ol' grouch in the butchers ain't gonna give you anything, so don't suppose you could be a darling and help Millie out quickly, would ya? We both have been saying we need to sort out the supply room out. It's just a mess that needs cleaning up."

"That's easy. I'll make sure that thing is as organized as possible."

Martha clapped her hands together and lifted up the till's drop counter to let Ray behind and into his new workplace. "Millie! We got a new pair of hands!" she cried out. The sound of feet on creaky wooden steps was heard as she rushed up the stairs from the basement. The door opened, and Millie was out from downstairs. Ray blinked more than usual at the sight of her. She was young, with cat-like eyes that stared into your soul. Like getting lost in the moment of staring at the moon for the first time. Ray saw her features such as her very smooth dark complexion with a mountain of thick black curly hair which rested on her shoulders. He had to snap out of it because he didn't even realize she had greeted him, extending a hand

"Oh yeah, Ray. Ray McCarthy." He shook her hand delicately.

◆ ◆ ◆

"You don't have to go into detail about her, you know," Roosevelt said.

"Mr President. For me, she is important," Ray replied.

◆ ◆ ◆

Martha and Millie both walked Ray over to the storage room where for the next two hours they would be sorting out needle baskets and crates of women's garments. Millie turned her head to Ray while she twiddled her thumbs together.

"It's a lot, huh?"

"Nothing that extreme," he said.

"Right I'll let you two get on. I'll be locking up at six, so do as much as you can. Oh, and Mr McCarthy, will you be around tomorrow?" Martha asked.

"I can be. I don't think Billy needs me."

"Oh, good. I want you to man the front desk while me and Millie go delivering tomorrow. I'll need you in early."

"Fine by me," Ray said. Millie unlocked the storage door as Martha returned to the storefront. Opening the door brought Ray into a room where, if he extended his arms, he could manage to touch both sides of the wall. Boxes laid on the floor, some opened with fabric sheets and needles scattered out. Ray had to squint as he saw it, he didn't like anything un-organized. He was perfect for this sort of thing as he was the one to inspect his troops during his time on the battlefield, but at the same time, he didn't enjoy it. Millie shrugged, but with a grin on her face, she walked on in to start, and Ray didn't even realize she was barefoot. Surely not on a floor with needles he thought? But Millie got stuck into it as she first went up the tower of boxes at the back, labelled as 'Hats'.

"I'll start here if you want to start there," she said to him pointing over to the pile of undone corsets to the right of him. All of them looked as if they were worn but not cleaned.

"You must be in here quite often if you can walk over needles without flinching," Ray said.

"They don't bother me. What do you think could go next to the hat boxes?" Millie asked, her voice soft and delicate to the ear.

"I dunno. Maybe stack those two long boxes in a line."

"Yeah then we can put those little ones that have the baskets on top of one and the corsets on the other."

"Thinking alike, I like it," Millie wasted no time in moving the long boxes which had the dresses inside, pushing them across the room with her knees nearly grazing the ground as she bent down to push. Ray was weaving the strings back through the corsets, still looking over his shoulder at Millie who was a ball of energy shifting her eyes across the room and its items while her fingers twiddled as she thought of ways to stack them neatly.

Ray wanted to start with some more small talk but he couldn't muster any words to say with the woman who would soon be his co-worker. As he finished the first corset and flattened it, he began to start.

"So, how long you lived here?" he asked.

"What, as in here?" she joked, while giving off a nervous chuckle.

"No, I meant in Bonebag. Kinda scary for someone like you to be living in a border state, with all what's going on."

"Oh, I don't mind it. It's only been a year. My brother and I moved down here when things were starting to go south. Pardon the pun. Tried to find the most obscure place away from it all. Everyone here seems fine with it, so I'm fine with it."

"Brave. What about your parents?" Ray asked.

"Yeah, they're not around anymore," Millie said. "I'm sorry to hear that. But I guess they'd be proud of you either way. You do give off a very positive attitude when anyone sees you," Ray said hoping for the response he wanted.

"Oh, well thank you." Ray turned his head back to the corsets again with a victorious smirk. Millie too was also now looking over her shoulder as Ray had his back turned. Millie looked at the boxes she had stacked together and then back to Ray again. She asked him if he could come over to help, trying to hide her parted lips by moving her head away at the boxes.

"Do you think you could reach that top box? I don't like it up there now," she said, drawing Ray's attention to the one on the top shelf by the stack of baskets.

"Changed your mind?"

"Yeah. I think too fast," Millie said. Ray extended himself reaching up, pulling it down with both hands on its sides. Ray presented the box to her, Millie already had a smaller box in hand at the ready to trade with.

"I think we'll be a good team. You listen well."

"You think well." Both exchanging a smile as they exchanged boxes.

Martha had locked the store's door as the evening sky got darker. She waved good night to her two workers as she pulled the curtain in, with the inside lights' orange glow being blown out, one by one until the shop front was dark. Ray and Millie walked side by side for a short while before separating.

"Well, glad we got a man round the place now. I'll see you tomorrow," she said

"See you tomorrow, Miss Millie."

"It's Adams. Millie Adams."

"Pleasure and have a good night, Miss Adams."

"You too." She walked off in the other direction giving a small wave to Ray as she turned back. Ray was smiling to himself as he made his way up to the saloon. The outside light lit the front porch up in an orange glow, and Ray stepped in. The place was packed inside with customers, typical at this time after work. Smoke and alcohol aroma once again filled the air that would undoubtedly linger, come early hours of the morning. Probably soaked up into the floorboards below where he walked. Mr Boston and Ray exchanged a nod as they both continued with their business with Ray heading upstairs to his room while Keith was cleaning up glasses and taking orders behind the counter. Up the stairs, two couples were flirting with each other, one on the halfway mark of the stairs while others with their arms wrapped around each other pressed against the second bedroom door. Next door would be busy, but Ray didn't mind, he wouldn't be sleeping yet until gone very late in the night. He closed the door behind him, reaching for his journal to add another source of income to his log. 'Marthas' was put next to the top left column, and just underneath, he drew a small heart around a question mark. More time for thought on the matter would come later as his eyes trailed back to the drawer beside his bed. Lodged at the back of it in the corner was the parchment and inside it, the vial. Nothing out of the ordinary, but what Ray had noticed was something different about the fabric, it looked new like it hadn't been used or crushed down at all. Was it the light in here, he thought. Ray closed the book and brought the cloth out to get a better look at it under his light. Yes, it was. The material was clean. Suspicion arose in Ray, and he quickly unwrapped it, wondering if anyone had tampered with the contents inside the vial. Nothing had changed. The bottle still had its fluids inside with the cork tight inside at the top. It had dawned on him that Ray had not once inspected what the vial's fluids were that Akea gave to him, just as he passed. With what he told him it would certainly have to do with the tribes' teachings and mysterious practices.

"You are ready for it," Ray remembered. The words his friend spoke to him just before his eyes were about to close forever. Scrutinizing it placing it towards the light there were no lumps or traces of berries, no crude methods of extraction. It was crystal clear like water but with a hint of royal purple colour to it. Curiosity filled his thoughts, and with a slight hesitation, he gently removed the cork from the top of the vile and took a whiff of the liquid. Again, nothing. Clear like water. Perhaps these practices didn't take much to be initiated in the tribe, he thought. Speculation of the unknown taking over the thought process of what would be digested. Maybe it was poison, but why would it be? There seemed to be no reason to back that up.

Akea was Ray's friend through hell and back and all the journeys beforehand to this point in time, Ray couldn't remember anything that would give Akea the motive to poison him.
Course, a motivation could've been the many times Ray scared
away potential food during the Crow's hunting sessions. Or
the time Ray had lured a buffalo near Akea's teepee during
the night. In the end, Ray put the vial back into the cloth and
wrapped it around to keep it safe. He needed a drink, too much
to think about, and he needed his evening remedies to help
him sleep. But before he went to put the vial back in the drawer
along with his journal, he thought of something. A practical
question that would give him an answer in the morning.
Pinching the vial at the top with three fingers, he hovered the
covered bottle over the flame of the lamp, rotating it like a ro-
tisserie burning it slightly without it catching ablaze. A black
mark was on the cloth, nothing seemed out of the ordinary.
Inside, the liquid wasn't even bubbling neither was there a reaction just a slight rise in temperature. Ray waited until it was
cold before placing it back into the drawer with his journal. He
stepped back towards his door, puzzled with what his friend
had given him, before sinking his head down into his pillows
to sleep on it.

"So, we can establish that whatever is in this vial has miraculous healing properties inside of it?" Theodore asked.

"Must be. I never once saw Akea or the tribe use this. They always seemed to be on top of the game when it came to protecting themselves until the raid."

"Some things must be kept secret, Mr McCarthy," Roosevelt elaborated.

Ray's head still felt heavy from the beer from last night. He heaved himself out from his bed with his foot kicking an empty bottle that he had taken from downstairs. Clearing his eyes of the crust that had grown overnight, he came to the sink and rinsed his face with three splashes of cold water. He shook his head, water flung off the fringe of his hair across the wall and onto the floor. Coming over to the drawer with the vile inside, his head still dripping as he opened and he saw it, shocked to see the cloth again in that state. Standard parchment cloth colour, no burn mark.

"Oh don't do this to me, I've only just woken up," he said to himself. He rubbed both his eyes again to be sure, but it was clean both cloth and vial looked like they had not been hovering over a naked flame at all. Ray walked out with his hat and coat over his shirt and waistcoat downstairs to Keith who was setting the chairs up and asked: "Keith, you haven't been in my room while I've been out have you?"

"No. It was quite busy yesterday. I didn't have time to stop by upstairs and clean, why what's wrong?" he asked.

, it may just be me, but something of mine looks brand new almost, and it wasn't before. Doesn't matter but you're definitely sure no one's been in there? Even you?" Ray asked again pointing his finger at Boston.

"Positive, Ray. Even drunk Dick from the post office didn't brave going up the stairs last night. No one goes into that room but you," Keith said.

"Ok, right. Sorry, I'm having one of those mornings where I forget stuff," Ray said, looking puzzled.

"Odd you didn't even stop down here for a drink last night did ye?"

"Oh, if I did that then I wouldn't have remembered where I live, with your whiskey," Ray joked as he skipped to the front door, Keith giving him a playful slap on his arm as walked out heading towards Martha's as the rain started the day off. Trudging through the mud, he could see Martha peering through the window to see if he was on his way before rushing over to the door to open it for him. Ray kicked as much mud as possible off his boots before entering removing his hat and coat to hang up behind the counter.

"You bring work and the weather with you today, Mr McCarthy," Martha said.

"I swear I'm no bad omen."

"Well, it's good anyway having you on to man the counter while Millie and I will be out today. Have you done this sort of thing before?"

"No, but it shouldn't be too hard anyway. I can count money."

"Well, I think the best thing to do is make yourself acquainted with the prices of everything first. Everything is different but most of the things in say...the hats section, are about the same price."

"Easy. You need me to do anything else while you're gone?"

"You are just the keeper of the store today Mr McCarthy, treat it as it was your own."

As Martha finished buttoning her coat, Millie came through the front door to say that the coach was ready. She was also in a long raincoat that was almost covering her feet she was that petite, with a hood that kept her thick hair hidden.

"We may be gone most of the day, but I'm sure you can find ways to entertain yourself," Millie said.

"I'm sure I'll be fine."

Martha grabbed her suitcase from the corner by the door, and the two soon got on to the stagecoach with two horses reined together, both drenched from spending the early hours of the morning in the heavy rain. Martha cracked the reins, and the horses started to move, pulling the creaky wooden coach. Millie smiled and waved again to Ray as he watched from the front porch. Ray came back inside the shop and shut the door behind him, turning the sign from 'closed' to 'open'. He surveyed the space he had with the whole shop. Empty. Just him and a full place holding clothes. Ray opened the counter hatch, stepping behind the counter but this time to sit on the stool by the wall. Taking deep breaths in through his nose, he wondered how to pass the time. Maybe there was something in the back of the shop to do, if a customer came, his ears would surely hear the front bell go off if that occurred. He saw that the cash register was on top of the counter, he hid it just by where his stool was as he wandered back through to the other rooms. He saw the small storage room that he and Millie had tidied up slightly and across from therewas a kitchen area. Upstairs would be a no-go area as this was Martha's room. What's down in the basement, he wondered. This was where Millie had come from to see him the other day. There was no door, and he soon stepped down inside. It was dark going down the stairs but an orange glow from a candle whose wax stand was nearly gone, lit up the room. There wasn't much in here, the room was built using stone and was quite cold upon stepping in. The only contents of this room were a bed and a bookshelf housing seven books. Millie couldn't be living here he thought to himself as he checked to see if there was anything else.

"So where did you go last night then?" he said out loud to himself. There was even a travel case underneath the single bed, but he dared not open it, in case it was indeed Millie's or even Martha's. Perhaps the former owners had an idea for another bedroom but it was never completed and forgotten about. Ray had done enough searching and returned back upstairs to think further as to what Millie could've been doing down there in the daylight. He pulled his stool towards him, sitting down and began to let his mind wander some more.

Four hours had gone by, and it was now an hour past the midday mark. Only two customers had entered in that time, one man purchasing a dress for his wife while guessing the measurements and a woman coming in trying on several hats before settling with the one straw made with a green ribbon around it. Fifty cents made. Ray was in the kitchen area where he had finished wiping away the grease from his chicken legs that he had grabbed from the saloon at lunchtime. He had sat down for so long on that stool he felt that he had not moved a muscle since getting out of bed this morning. Ray continued to stretch and rotate his limbs in motion to keep the blood pumping, first with his feet then his arms and shoulders before his head began to turn in a circle too. He stood outside again, resting himself on the side of the door frame to get some clean air in his lungs. He felt the cold flow of air fill up inside him as the rain had eased off since this morning with it now only being a slight drizzle. The whole town was covered over in a grey clouded sky all day nearly with no sign of it letting up. The pathway was as muddy as it could be with your boot seeming like it could stick in the mud and come right off your foot. Ray looked to the workhouse barn was seeing Martha and Millie returning on the stagecoach again, their horses trudging through the mud. The coach rocked side to side as the wheels tried to stabilize along the uneven ground path with the two women swaying with it and almost looking like one of them would land face-first into the mud. Ray pulled the door closed behind him and walked down to them to help out.

"I hope you bought something for me to do when I'm in the store," he shouted down to them.

"Does the dog need a ball to play with?" Millie joked back stretching her head out to the side, but in doing so, the coach rocked violently, and Millie fell off the coach seat sideways with a hard slap, sound into the mud. Martha stopped the coach and Ray jogged down to her, both checking to see if she was ok.

"I'm good. I'm good" Millie said, lifting herself off the ground as the other two got to her side helping her to stand. She was covered in mud from the top of her hood to the bottom of her coat.

"Horses don't like dogs," Ray said with a chuckle. Millie held on to his hand as he got her back up to her feet. Martha decided to hop back up to the coach seats grabbing the reins to lead the horses back behind the store on foot.

"You get cleaned up Millie. Mr McCarthy, help the silly girl inside, I'll be in shortly," Martha said, standing alongside the horses as they continued up the road.

"Thank you for that little rescue, Ray."

"It was the least I could do. I was very bored today."

"Managed ok on your own?"

"Yeah, nothing much except two customers coming in and buying stuff."

"Oh nice, two more than yesterday's zero. Martha will be happy."

The two came inside the shop feeling the warmth of the place as Millie stepped in, leaving muddy footprints on the wooden floor. She pulled her hood down, exposing her long bushy hair as she took off her coat, hanging it up on the cupboard door beside the counter. Underneath, her shirt and skirt were wet with her neckerchief almost falling off her neck, it became so loose from the rain. She pushed out her hair more, before facing Ray to give off a playful sigh.

"I'm just gonna go change downstairs."

"So that place is yours," he asked with no hesitation. Millie looked again at him and with a pause then a frown.

"You didn't open anything up down there, did you?"

"Ok, I was bored, but not that bored," he reassured her.

"Oh well, that's different then. Don't worry, I don't live there. It's just there's something in there that's very personal, and I thought this place would be ideal for it."

Ray was thinking again. He saw nothing that would mainly be personal to someone. Could it be in the luggage bag he had seen under the single bed? But that question sat in the different possibility section of his mind when Millie said she was going down there to change so perhaps it was a change of clothes in case of instances like today.

"Well, that's good, cause I saw nothing there."

"That's good. Means I hid it well," she said with a toying smile that made Ray's eyebrow raise. Millie opened up the counter and made her way downstairs into the basement room. Ray walked around, wondering to himself what he could've missed until the back door of the store opened, and Martha came inside, pounding her feet on the floor to clear off the mud.

"Good and bad that journey was," she said as she made her way to the counter.

"Where did you go exactly?" Ray asked.

"Only up to Ingram. Those folks will take anything you sell. Anyway, how did you do today?"

"Two items sold. One dress and one hat, though I think that dress that sold might get returned in a couple days from the way the guy was guessing half the time."

"Well, you got my hopes up when you said two. Never mind, hopefully the idiot will come back in and buy something else. You checked out the place while I was gone?" Martha asked.

"Yeah, I had a look but didn't touch anything. Millie has already made her case about the room downstairs. That's not where she lives, does it?" he asked again, hoping to get a different response.

"Don't be ridiculous. She lives up on the hill with her brother Thomas. Nice guy but a little dim," Martha confirmed.

"Nah, that room downstairs was meant to be another storage room in case I got way too much inventory, but that rarely happens. That old bed and bookshelf were just left here when I bought it, and I didn't want 'em up in my room, so I shoved them down there. Millie keeps spare clothes down there, and I taught her how to read and write in there when we had a few spare minutes. A very keen girl, always looking to better herself. Anyways, I need you two to unload what we had leftover from the coach and maybe scrub up in here, why don't ya?"

"Yes ma'am" Ray said. Millie came back upstairs in a similar coloured shirt but with the sleeves rolled up, and some trousers on that reached down to her shins.

"Ready for work again," she said as the two both went outside to unload the stagecoach contents.

"All I've seen you do is move stuff around, it's gonna be weird watching you scrub floors," Millie joked as Ray smiled back and didn't mention at all what he had learned from Martha.

The workday was done, and all three parted ways for the evening. Ray would be working again at Billy's while both Martha and Millie worked on the shop. Ray waved good night to the two with a more cheery expression towards Millie, knowing that she was not living in a small den underneath a clothes shop. But still, he wondered why she kept so quiet over having learnt English there, nevertheless he ditched the idea of going in there again without permission. Instead of heading back to his saloon room, Ray walked on, turning left past the final store opposite the bar, to trail up to the woods. The pathway to the woods was long and narrow with the tree branches looking like they lean in closer and closer with every step Ray made. Rocks were at the top of the path as the line of trees ended, flat edges on its surface meant it could be as a rest spot for how long a person travelled up the trail or the way opposite that would bring you to Bonebag. Ray was now on a hillside that took him above overlooking the town, seeing its shops and people in the distance that they were almost like ants. He perched himself comfortably on the rock, looking out to the dying light of the day. The sunset was beautiful, that shade of orange that isn't too harsh on the eye or too dull that it can't illuminate the land seen below. Ray took it all in for a moment before his hand went into his coat pocket, bringing out the vial in the oddly repaired cloth that he had tried to burn. With a better scource of light, he lifted the vial again to it to see if there were any contents inside that he could've missed. Still, nothing to be seen. Time to put the practice in for the theory he thought. He unscrewed the cork and took another sniff of it. Exactly how it smelt the first time.

"God, I hope this ain't poison," He said to himself as he pursed his lips and took a small sip from the bottle, its liquid cool down his throat as the sensation ran down his neck. Tasted like it smelt, nothing, transparent like water. It didn't make sense to him. How was it , if the only place it had been was inside of his jacket pocket, which in turn rested against his relatively warm chest. Again, he thought back to the tribe and Akea, thinking if this was another part of their arsenal that could be used in dire situations. Was it merely an emergency source of fluids in case of a long journey? If so, this didn't seem like it was enough. He sipped it again this time, clearing everything from its glass shell. Ray sat there on the rock and let ten minutes go by with him watching the sun slide further down the horizon. Nothing. It was settled, the vial liquid wasn't poison nor did he feel the slightest bit different than when he set out. No fatigue or strain in his body, it was just water he concluded. A sigh of relief came over him, the dreaded thought of dying up here alone or even in the saloon had it been poison faded away. Ray took another look at the vial thinking about whether or not to discard it or not. But he didn't. For the sake of his best friend's memory, he wouldn't let it go. He placed it back into the cloth, wrapping it up and putting it back into his coat pocket. Now a new investigation was underway, someone must've switched the fabric over for some reason. Was it Mr Boston pulling a prank? Ray knew for a fact he had the master key to go into anyone's room sat in his apron pouch. He then thought about the possessions that he had and became worried. He placed his hands onto knees and pressed himself up to his feet, only to catch a glimpse of his hand that made him sit straight back down onto the stone. The veins on his hands were much darker than before, bulging and throbbing quicker than before. He started to breathe much faster and his eyes soon became heavier to keep open. His head tilted all the way back until his body went backwards off the stone and he then began to tumble and roll down the steep hill which led to the woods. Completely unconscious, his body was like a rag doll with his arms and legs throwing themselves across his front and back as his head smacked a couple of rocks that had been cemented into the grass. Violently, he still continued to roll until he was near the flat ground with his body being stopped by a tree stump that he collided with, back first. Ray lay there, still unconscious. Face covered in cuts and grazes with blood slowly pouring out onto his face covering it in a crimson mask. As he lay there, the last bit of light from the sunset soon disappeared behind the walls of trees and by the stump, for the whole night, he bled out.

As he awoke, it was almost midday. He had been unconscious for all of last night and this morning. A solid seventeen hours! Patchy clouds with the blue sky being the first thing his eyes laid onto. Moving his head first, Ray felt his bones creak almost sounding like they would crack if he got up even more. He then stretched out his fingers as they had been closed up for the time he was unconscious. This felt worse than getting out of bed in the morning. Slowly but surely he pushed himself off the floor sitting now upwards with his back pressed against the tree stump. He took in long breaths to clear his airways before slowly opening his eyes, fluttering his eyelids as the daylight blinded him for a moment. Ray looked up and observed the hillside he remembered sitting at the top of before blacking out, trying to make sense as to what had happened beforehand. He then remembered, as his eyes widened quickly searching his coat pocket in a quick panic to check on the vial. He felt it, not even broken from the impact of his descent down the hill. In doing so, his hands then felt around his arms, body and face. He was without a scar and the blood that had almost covered his face upon landing near the stump had gone. Ray got to his feet, brushing off the dirt and grass before rotating his head to see if there was anyone around. He wasn't in the heart of the woods, but he made sure there wasn't anything about. Ray looked up to the sky before starting to run back up the hill to head back down to Bonebag. When walking back, Ray couldn't help but keep feeling himself for anything that looked like damage, but he was still unscathed. Better yet, his posture was improved. He could breath better. When examining his face, he had a feel inside his mouth, his chipped tooth from the war had been repaired. It made him pause in his tracks, as he stopped he grabbed his knife which hung on the left side of his belt. Ray opened his hand, putting the theory to the test, he slashed his open palm with the knife, cutting it neatly in a straight line as he gritted his teeth with the wound opening and the blood exiting. The blood dripped down onto the ground below him as he rotated it, he felt the sharp pain for a few seconds before it vanished and that's when the wound closed itself up. The skin drying to form a hard crust over the perfect cut in that deep red colour before it peeling off to reveal a clean hand, like the steel blade had not even touched it. The blood had dried up with the red stains in the cracks of his skin slowly becoming less visible like he had his hands in water. His blade was now clean and without a moments, he put the knife back in its holster on the belt and he began to run back to his apartment room at the saloon. No one was in as he entered, darting up the stairs he wasted no time in opening the door before slamming it shut with his back resting on it. Sharply taking in breath after breath, he came over to his sink and mirror to see in better detail the vial's effects. His skin didn't look worn, smooth and hydrated but his natural coloured brown eyes now turned pale. Pale like a wolf's yet with no pupil.

Grabbing the knife again, this time with no precision brushed the blade against his cheek, slicing near his cheekbone. It healed like his hand at the hillside. Going even further with it, he went for the hairs of his left eyebrow, pulling back the skin as he scraped across the brow like it was his five o'clock shadow. His hairs falling into the sink, soon after hitting the white porcelain sink they curled up before disintegrating into dust. Ray saw them grow back slowly as the cycle of hair growth was rapidly sped up before his very eyes. Skin growing back over wounds, hair growing back at a alarming rate and body parts regenerating this was nothing he'd seen in his life. He took out the vial from his coat again staring at it confused and frightened.

◆ ◆ ◆

"It was like God had given you a gift. Something that legends and stories were made of," said Roosevelt.

"I was scared. I didn't know what to do. Should I say anything or keep it secret. Hell, no-one would have a clue how to help me, even if I did tell everyone." Ray wondered.

"What could they do, Mr McCarthy? You have the miraculous ability to never sustain an injury. The most useless thing they would've done would be to send you to a doctor. Besides, something like this, it's no wonder the tribe kept this secret. What did you do after the discovery?" Roosevelt asked.

"Go deeper. I started to ask myself if this thing lasted or was it just a miracle elixir that could fix any ailment at the time. It would be the thing those con artist salesmen dream of. Then I thought back to Akea and the tribe. This was precious to them. Only a certain few would've had these in their possession. Why didn't Akea just drink it before the attack? That's when it hit me, at the time the tribe had three separate outposts across the midwest. One had fallen, so I had to find the others for answers." Ray carried on his story. But as he did someone else's account started.

Through the sight of his binoculars, he could see bodies of his men and the ruined remains of the campsite where the tribe settled.

"And he said that to you in confidence, did he?"

"Yes, sir. Every word."

Lowering the binoculars, the Colonel squinted his eyes with a scowling expression turning to the young cadet, the one Ray had left in the aftermath of the bloodshed. The high ranking official was in his sixties, with a pale white bushy moustache covering his entire top and bottom lip.

"I know of this man's name and occupation to this territory, but I do not know the face. I will send a scouting party to search for him, and you will be accompanying them."

"Yes, sir. What are you going to do with him if we find him?"

"I will do unto him as I have done to many deserters and delinquents. Question, sentence, execute. Bring him back here when you find him. This will be his courtroom, and I will be the judge."

III.

Daybreak. Crisp morning with blue skies. Ray had the mission in his head and where he would be heading. Last night he alerted both Billy and Martha that he would be gone for, perhaps a week on "Personal issues". Billy didn't seem to mind though while Martha was a little bit annoyed that after only working one full day, her new employee would be out. Millie said the sweet goodbye Ray loved to hear. Maybe someday he thought to himself. He loaded onto his horse the right amount of food and water along with a change of clothes and his sleeping mat. The rucksack on the horse's side held his pistols and ammo should things become heated. He tried to remain as civil as possible, but it was always good to pack for any circumstances. Once everything was adjusted, gripped tight and all accounted for, Ray set off for a long journey to find out the meaning of the contents of the vial and what it meant for him.

"Where was the first meeting held?" Roosevelt asked.

"North West. In Missouri. I overheard Akea talk about how the tribe tried to branch off but other tribesmen competed for land as fear of war spread up. Whispers I heard all around the people. But there was one guy I knew, if he was to know anything about what I had wrong with me, it would be him." Ray went on.

"And this person was?"

"Akea's brother. The chief." Ray said.

It was the second day of travel and Ray had found the tribal land inhabited by the tribe. It was exactly like the first ground, nearly an exact replica before burning to the ground by all three hands in the conflict. Ray surveyed the land and saw everyone going about their daily chores. It was nearing night, and everyone would soon be off to their quarters to sleep. Ray rode down to the camp on horseback, slowing down and remaining as calm as possible, so it did not alarm them. Men, women and children, all watched Ray enter, locking their eyes onto him with emotionless expressions. Some continued as usual while their eyes still followed him in. He was nearing the main camp fire and stopped his horse, to speak with the tribe.

"I come only as a visitor looking for answers. I wish to speak to Chief Maluk, brother to Akea. It is of urgency, it concerns the tribe and a specific treasure that was given to me as protection. A treasure which possesses powers which I do not understand." He spoke in their language. The people of the tribe turned their heads to each other in discussion, while one man donning a feathered necklace with pitch-black hair braids wielding a spear, raised the hatch of the teepee to speak to someone. It was the Chief. Tapping the spear on the ground before shouting out the motion to make everyone rise to their feet, Chief Maluk appeared, stepping outside the teepee. The orange glare from the fire highlighted a fierce look from the big man who wore makeshift sheepskin trousers with feathered armbands and a black band around his partially bald head. The wrinkles on his skin made him look older than what he was as it looked like his expression hadn't changed as he aged. The tribesmen bowed their heads as he spoke to Ray, still in their native language.

"The white man who my little brother let live. What treasure do you speak of if that is your purpose here?"
Ray took the vial from his coat pocket and extended his arm, bringing the vial as close as he could to the chief. Maluk's eyes began to open up as much as his wrinkled eyelids would allow,

and his thick fingers gripped the vial tight to look closer at it. He smiled first when he knew what it was, but then his smile dropped, turning into a scowl as he looked back at Ray.

"You drunk it all, didn't you?" the chief asked, looking like he could explode at any moment. All eyes were on Ray again, and the chief's guards came closer towards him.

"This is meant for the most worthy of people to our cause. Bound and prepared by the most skilled shamans and you drunk from it. I should kill you for what you have done!" Maluk raised his voice, and the spearheads raised their weapons to Ray's head. His horse became nervous stamping it's feet in un-certainty, before the chief rose his hands to stop the spears from reaching closer. He spoke again, softly and said

"And yet, my brother, he spoke highly of you. Matters concern-ing the elixir is for the highest of the tribe. You are part of that group now. Leave us!" He spoke to his people, raising his hand as they dispersed from the scene and the spearheads backed away and retreated around the chief's teepee, guarding it. The leader stepped back inside, beckoning Ray to join him as the one guard held the roll-up hatch inside open for him to enter. Ray dismounted and slowly approached the chief's quarters.

"No scrounging in those bags," he told across to the spearheads, with his finger pointed as straight as a ruler.

Entering the teepee, Ray saw inscriptions and diagrams that were crudely smeared onto the teepee's musky skin through many different sizes of fingers. They were challenging to make out with the only thing Ray could fully recognize being the drawing of a man who stood next to blobs of paint that were larger in scale. The largest must have been painted by Maluk himself Ray thought as he checked to see if his fingers matched and they did. Nearing the tip of the tent, eyes narrowed, looking at whoever sits in the presence of the chief like a demonic shadow.

"Sit" Maluk said extending his hand towards the coyote skin laid out flat. Ray sat, crossing his legs and begun to listen to what the chief was about to give to him. Answers.

"You only know what my brother has taught you. About the tribe, about me. He has taught you the basics of a warrior, but now in these circumstances, I must be the one to teach you far greater things. You look clean. Cleaner than anyone of any race. Immaculate. This is the power that the vile has bestowed on you."

"But how did you make this?" Ray asked.

"Like I said, it was through persistence of fine craftsmen that made this. Not I. Nor anyone here in this sacred ground. I only know...what it's capable of-"

"Then, please tell me!" Ray quickly spat out impatiently. He apologized shortly after. The chief chuckled with his lips shut before reaching for his bull hornpipe. Taking a long breath, he exhaled slowly to clear his mind before speaking again. The smoke was thick, dirty thick. The kind of smoke where you couldn't see and your sense of smell would be overwhelmed.

"In a moment, I want you to smoke from this. It will relax you. You should not be worried, young one. What has been given to you will make you stand the test of time like the holy spirits who created this drink of ages. As you see, look up and see the drawings. Our tribe has long known of someone to step out into this brave new world and sacrifice himself against those who dare shake the solid ground that our people walk across. No one believed it could be an outsider like yourself. The last time my brother and I connected, he spoke of you and the bond you and Akea shared for many years. You betrayed your own race to save us in many instances across the land that you like to call America. Little did you know that the spirits of Jugda still reside and watch over."

"You believe this is me?" Ray asked.

"Indeed. And it is my duty now to see you off to better yourself.

Now, please smoke." Maluk handed the hefty bullhorn over to Ray which he held in his hands before turning the pointed tip towards his lips and inhaling its contents. Ray began to cough; it was that strong. Nothing like tobacco. It tasted weird, a mix of leaves with dry old berries and otherworldly substances that he had yet to try.

"What is Jugda? Is this where this stuff comes from?" he asked.

"Jugda is this land, and it was unlike any other land. Vast teaming with life that you have not yet laid eyes on. The life was beautiful and life that was created from demons. Otherworldly beings that may even hold power in their bodies that you now possess," said Maluk. Growing more and more into the realm of fantasy, Ray cast a doubting look onto the chief.

"If you say that these...things on the walls exist then where are they? America is growing by the day even in war times and not one single thing you have told me, has been seen by anyone but yourself?" Ray questioned. Maluk leaned in slowly with a grin on his face and said, "take another smoke from the horn". Ray's eyes looked down again to the horn that sat in his lap wondering as to what would happen if he did. But he was a smoker he thought, he could handle this as he raised it up to his mouth again, he inhaled and exhaled the bullhorn with its contents burning a dark mist from the other end. The second take of the bullhorn was made with moreconfidence from Ray and inhaled for much longer to prove his smoker lungs were ready for it. But he wasn't.

"Now young one, let your new eyes see the land before the colonizers. See the history before your time," the chief said. Ray's head became heavy, his eyes stretching open until blinking became a struggle, as everything in the world around him started to blur.

"Let it wash over you. The smoke will take away your doubts, and you will soon take notice of your newfound power," the chief said to Ray as he heard his words beginning to sound stretched with an echoing sound. He soon heard the chief chuckling to himself as he stood up to start chanting above Ray, keeping his thick hand placed on top of his head. The chant soon became louder and louder to the point Ray felt it could damage his eardrums, and then it stopped. Ray's eyes widened again, and then he felt normal, as he could blink again. That powerful rush which made his body feel weaker than any day he felt sick, quickly faded away. Chief Maluk crouched down to meet him eye to eye and said: "How do you feel?"

"Different," Ray answered.

"Taken it like a true God. Now look again, white man. The paintings. How do you see them now, hmm?"

Ray's eyes wandered back up to the most significant painting of them all in the teepee, the one which looked like the shadow of the chief was now glowing and looked far more detailed to him.

"Only the truest of the gods' warriors can see the true horror of Jugda. Your America, is much more than you think," Maluk said. "Now. Touch it."

Ray came closer to the wall behind where Maluk had sat as he moved away. He took a look at the chief once more to see him nodding his head in anticipation, till Ray brought his finger to the painting and eventually touched it, dead centre. Nothing seemed to happen on the point where he had felt the picture until he looked up at the eyes of the creature. Those harrowing eyes now looked more real than ever, black with white blood pulsing through it with a ring of uneven torn flesh for eyelids blinked for a second before the creature brought its head forward, out from the painted outline within the teepee walls with a coarse ripping sound. The creatures head made Ray fall to the floor in shock as he saw the creature looking at any moment to tear its whole body out from the coloured outline. Its head was as big as the chief's entire body from head to toe, and as the head came closer, Ray could see more of its features. Whatever this thing was, it had undoubtedly crawled out of hell, from what Ray gathered. Its head was that of the skull of a bull with the snout and jaw broken with the muscle just keeping it hanging loose instead of falling on the floor. Its teeth were too long and curved awkwardly if its jaw had been like it should be with its eyes that Ray had seen first sunken deep into the skull's sockets. A single horn from its left side curled out with a vine of thorns wrapping around it which continued down the creature's neck like a noose. What skin left on the beast was around its necks and shoulders, black, unkempt for many years with the skin underneath grossly infected. It was truly hideous and just when he saw everything, Ray caught a glimpse of what it would be like inside the creature's mouth as it let out a squealing roar. For a second, Ray could see more teeth inside the creature's throat, layers upon layers of teeth that looked normal for a bull but moved in a pulsing motion as the beast's neck muscles moved inside, while at the very back you could see the tongue hiding away. Ray still motionless on the ground, cried out in panic before Chief Maluk waved his arm through the creatures head, highlighting that it was just an illusion as rippled into dust before retaining its shape.

"This is only one of many. Monsters exist, and now you can see them. Your body can heal, your eyes now see, and now your mind will soon know more answers than questions."

"What in God's name was that?!"

"Something, our Gods want gone from this world," the chief said. He sat himself back down and continued to explain as the dust from the illusion faded down to the floor.

"What you saw was a Wendigo. A mix of man and animal; this thing lives up north in the winter hills slaughtering innocent people who tread up in search of rescue. You will soon have to face this creature, for your journey is long and full of obstacles-"

"No, no, no, that was just wacky tobacco, surely you can't be serious?" Ray asked. The chief was.

"No, you're looking at the wrong guy here I-I can't be this thing that you're building me up to be," Ray said confused and still shaken by the apparition.

"I cannot tell you. For it would lead your mind away. I am simply setting you a course. To cheat death is something that would've taken years, centuries even to craft from the minds of many and for a good reason. These creatures are a thing of the hellish past that many tribes have come across. If nothing is done then your America may not survive," the chief warned.

"So, I'm like some kind of weapon to these people?"

"Yes, you are. But I see you as so much more. Your courage and determination from what I hear was one of the many reasons my brother sought to give you the vial in the first place. Our numbers are dwindling, and your people are in a war. This is the right time to set you out to help both our people. For the greater cause of preserving our people to see through to the future where I hope our two can see eye to eye. Wouldn't you want that?" the chief asked. Ray paused to think about it. He thought back to the times he shared with Akea and everything they went to. Then he thought of Millie. She is in a situation similar to that of the natives. Vilified even when up hearing the laws America wanted to present itself to the world. How would she see the future if this evil still continued? He sighed and with a much more accepting voice said,

"Where would I need to start?"

"Not far from here. The mountains. There is a cave inside of them from which the people gather. All sorts of rituals going on in there. Someone in there of higher status was in collusion about the creation of the vial. But he was not rewarded and be-trayed with his head for death. He brought his followers there to protect them. Find him, and you will know where the others are."

Ray nodded and stood up from where he sat, as did Maluk.

"Do not feel frightened. For you, there is no turning back. Take this opportunity to become something great. Remember, knowing more answers outnumbers the number of questions." The chief patted Ray on his shoulder before seeing him out from the teepee. The spearheads brought Ray's horse back to him, handing him the reins. The two walked side by side going past the massive fireplace from the campsite, but the chief spoke one more time to him.

"Ray. No one is to know about this."
He nodded again before taking himself up the hill before mounting the horse to ride back to Bonebag.

"This must be awkward for you, I'd imagine," Roosevelt said.

"You think?"

There was an awkward silence in the room. Ray still looking at the president with anger in his eyes while Teddy continued to twiddle his thumbs. Roosevelt tried to speak to end the silence, but Ray spoke up first.

"You've made me go against my promise. The threat is still out there, Mr President. I'm only telling you how I got here. I should be carrying on with my mission right now."

"I know. I wanted to get this out of you because I want to see this story continue. Mr McCarthy, you may think that we are merely taking this gift of yours away from you, away from your peers but in actuality, we are endorsing it on a bigger scale. I will get to that later, but as of right now, I'd like you to carry on."

Ray came into Martha's at the usual time. Early morning start, back again working behind the counter. Martha and Millie were both working alongside him this time. No deliveries. The day went well with the odd customers now and then every two hours, the stocking and rearranging the store displays with the new items picked up from before and the quiet lunch break. Millie and Ray worked alongside each other most of the day, exchanging pleasantries and attractive looks towards one another only to be broken up upon Martha calling one of them for help. It was at the final hour, near closing time, Ray decided to pluck up the courage to say something to her. But it wasn't what she'd expect at all. They were both at the counter, Millie counting up the day's total at the cash register while Ray was wiping down the countertop. Ray spoke first with a calm and quiet tone.

"That wasn't too bad today, was it?"

"Not at all. You're getting the hang of this, working with two ladies."

"Don't see the difference. We work too well," Ray said as the two playfully smiled at each other again.

"I like you, Millie," Ray said in a spontaneous second. His cheeks burned red, Millie for a second thought she wasn't breathing correctly before mumbling,

"I like you too." The two both smiled again, but their grins were much broader and happier than before.

"I wish I had more time to show you how much I do" Ray continued.

"What do you mean?"

"I...I have to leave. It's urgent. The other day when I took off, I found out something bad about the family. They need me back home," he lied.

"Oh, it's OK, if it's family matters you go. I can wait for you," she reassured him.

"But I don't know how long I'll be."

"Shush. I can wait. That's something else I'm good at," Millie said, coming over to his side to place her delicate hand on his shoulder. Behind them, a door slammed shut as Martha came back inside, making Millie quickly take her hand back to her side as the boss of the shop came in.

"Everything alright, you two?"

"We're fine. Just needed to see if I got the change right," Millie said, scrambling to string together a convincing response.

"She's getting better at it Martha," Ray said helping out in the situation.

Martha smiled as she came to turn the sign on the shop door.

"Hope you two aren't counting anything extra there without me knowing. I know when things have been taken," she warned the two. They both nodded, putting on their good employee impressions. Millie put the change back in the cash register as Ray got hold of his and Millie's coat from the hanger. They both said good night to Martha, before stepping out of the shop to continue their conversation.

"Wait here for a minute," Ray said before darting in the direction of the saloon with Millie waiting patiently on the porch area of the shop. She caught sight of Ray in the upstairs window of the bar, seeing him jostling around trying to find something. Before long, he was jogging back out from the saloon towards her, smiling. He had money, lots of it. What he brought from deserting in the war, and what he earned with the two jobs in Bonebag. Millie was confused but excited at the same time.

"This is all I've got. Keep it with you, use it for yourself until I come back," Ray pleaded to her as he nursed it into her hands.

"Ray! This is too much. How long are you going for?!"

"I don't know, and I don't care. You need this more at the moment."

"I-I really don't. I wouldn't know what to use it fo-" Millie froze as Ray leaned in close with his head almost making the connection with his lips and hers, but he stopped as their noses touched. Her eyes were more prominent than ever as her mouth hung open slightly showing just the top of her teeth as she anticipated the soft touch of his lips on hers. Ray's eyes locked onto hers as her hands slowly moved up his forearms.

"That was something I would've given you, but not now. I want to do it when you use that money to buy a house of your own. Away in a nice part of the country with wide open fields where we can enjoy each other."

Millie couldn't contain her smile from what she was hearing. She hadn't heard of bigger promise than this.

"Ray, if I do, what about my brother?"

"Think about it later. I have to go," Ray said

"Don't you dare break your promise then," Millie said with a cute giggle.

Ray lowered her hands back down from his arms to grasp tightly the money he had given her before turning away to head back into the saloon. Millie stood frozen in the middle of the town road looking back at the money and again to Ray, who just before entering the bar, looked at her one more time. He stepped inside, with Millie turning to head home with a large sum of money taped together, pushing it up under her hood, hidden in her thick hair. Inside Ray began to pack, taking everything with him, with the last item to put away: the bottle. He carried everything with him down the stairs of the saloon, jostling himself to keep steady as he walked down each step. Mr Boston saw him come downstairs and asked him:

"Where you off to at this time, Mr McCarthy? It's drinking fun times."

"Out, Keith. Family business up north has come back to me. Might be gone for a while," Ray carrying on his made-up excuse.
"Well be careful on your travels, Mr McCarthy, we are still in war times ya know."

"I know, I know. Here, it's rent," Ray put the change down on the counter as he brought it out from his coat pocket, some change spilling onto the floor.

"Hey, hey, slow down, I'm sure what's come up must be important but you gotta be level headed when riding out at these hours. Here, take that with you in case you miss the taste from here." Keith brought a bottle of the whiskey his saloon was known for. It was intense and burned the throat, just how Ray liked it.

"Thank you, Mr Boston. I'll see you again, somewhen."

The two parted ways with nodding smiles before Ray came to the side of his horse to load up. As he pulled his horse off the hitching post he rode down past the town past Billy's barn before trailing the roads to begin his search for the creators of the vile.

IV.

Ray's journey started off in good weather, the sun out with not a cloud in the sky, and the woodland kept the shade over him. Coming up to the border of Missouri, the woodland was flourishing. Its a lush mix of green leaves, and thick brown bark along with its stretching rivers were pleasure to the eye. It reminded Ray of his childhood. Wandering the woods for hours, letting your imagination growing larger till even a simple stick could be something extraordinary. Ray would explore the woods for hours so he could escape the family house and its chores. Ray would sometimes even forget he lived in a small wooden shack outside of town on the brow of a hill he was out for so long, only to be trailed back by the sound of his father calling out his full name followed by a gunshot. It was in woods like these that his father trained him to hunt and how to survive. His father was a skilled trapper and dealt within the trade, earning his way before the turn of the century. The young ten-year-old Ray would grow accustomed to hearing his father's stories telling him of brave explorers and outlaws as well as his own perilous journeys through the American wilderness. He used to beg and beg his father to take him along, but his father would always say no, but that didn't mean he would leave without teaching him something new before setting out again. Like the time young Ray first fired a gun. Ray remembered it well, hearing that metal trigger click back for the first time as his unsteady hands tried their best to stay still, holding the gun between his hands. His father would keep his hands on the handle as he showed him when to fire, always on the right breath, with your shoulders relaxed and then...bang! Ray fired a shot into the air to see if anything would call out in the woods. Mostly birds chirped and flew off as he looked up through the tree branches. The occasional squirrel would leap from branch to branch as he and his horse walked through the thick forest. Now there was a peaceful ambience throughout the walk, just the sound of the wind moving through the trees as the branches brushed each other. Walking through them, he came to a small crossing through a shallow stream where he let his horse take a drink before continuing. It was crystal clear, and the sun's rays made it sparkle back into his eyes. Ray took the time to wash his face over with three splashes from the water he had cupped in his hands, by the tree on his left, looking out to the family of deer walking past in the middle of the bright green field. Four of them to count, it seemed to Ray that they had come running out from the woods by something that

had startled them as their heads turned around in all directions to see if it whatever it was had still followed them. It had.
Suddenly the family of deer began to sprint again as three coy-
otes still at full pace charged towards them with both groups
running into the west side of the woodland not to be seen
again. Now Ray came out from hiding with his horse this time
dismounting and leading him by the reins. Out in the field, it
was bigger than expected. The wind still blowing cool air to
both Ray and his steed as they continued north where the
ground was even. Reaching the end of the woods on the other
side, the two were soon standing on a cliffside overlooking the
many more acres and acres of land to travel in search of a cave.
It was only early into the afternoon, but Ray knew he would
have to set up camp around a quiet area, away from any threats
like the ones he saw chasing down the family of deer. It could
surely be something much more threatening than simple coyote roaming around the area. But for now, he took in where he
was standing for a full hour. Once rested, the two continued
down from the cliffside, diving into the woods to look for anything that could lead them to their destination. The woodland
was untouched by anything human-related it was like looking
for a needle in a haystack. Still, this part of the area was quiet,
to say the least with Ray only spotting beavers at a river that
seemed too deep to cross. It was now starting to get dark, and

in the woods, it got darker much quicker than expected. Ray saw no reason to carry on at this point and decided to set up camp. He had chosen a spot by two large oak trees that were the closest together with a large pile of branches near them, perfect for a fire. Ray got the fire burning and soon took off the luggage that his horse had carried for a whole day, stroking him where the bags hung on the animals' shoulders. The horse soon was hitched on a makeshift post between the two oak trees. Ray unpacked what he needed, with the first item being the bottled whiskey that Mr Boston had given him. He wasted no time in taking a quick sip from it. Its taste burning his throat, making it feel drier than what it already was. He was soon thinking of what to have to eat. Whatever he brought with him, he would have to ration it, and most of it was canned food. He could've caught something today, but he wanted to cover as much ground first. He decided for tonight it would be the beans. Simple and easy to cook under fire which was already burning well. Taking his small pocket knife from his coat pocket, he unfastened the lid ripping it off and discarding it with a good throw. With a small piece of rope from the roll that was inside one of his rucksacks, he tightened it around the can and a strong branch and soon had it hung over the fire. Five minutes he let it cook before bringing the branch back towards him, the contents of the tin were steaming and ready to eat.

Not forgetting his companion, he gave his steed a carrot letting him eat first as the tin was left to cool slightly. Ray tucked into his beans shortly after, watching the firelight up the area around him. Looking out again through the branches, he caught sight of the stars as they slowly began to shine brighter as the sky soon turned completely black. As peaceful as it was, the sleep would not be the same. That night as soon as Ray closed his eyes after being sat comfortably by the large oak tree, visions soon clouded his sleep. Screams of demonic creatures or people, he couldn't tell, was all he could hear. He woke up twice during the night as it kept on getting louder and louder with each minute he was asleep. The second time around was when the screams of something came with terrifying shadowy figures which would be right in his face, pushing him in different directions until the sensation of falling woke him again. Ray's heart was pumping, and he took heavy breaths to calm down. His horse opened its eyes too to gaze at his master who was visibly shaken. Ray reached over to the horse to stroke him, whispering that everything was fine in its ear. The fire's light was slowly fading at this point, and Ray had to get some sleep, this time laying his head down onto his rucksack for comfort. It proved to work as he soon awoke to the early light of the morning with the fire now just a pile broken branches and ash. He stretched out his arms before moving his head around, the awkward position from which he slept on the rucksack made his neck feel stiff on one side. Ray brought himself up to stand and fill his lungs up with the crisp woodland air. The horse's eyes opened with the rustling of the grass and twigs. Kicking over his empty can of beans onto the ash pile, he loaded his rucksack back up with what he had brought out in the night and encouraged his horse to stand. Once everything was loaded up, the two continued on through the woods to the mountains. This morning, however, something would occur that would be a step in the right direction for Ray as he would soon encounter someone who would give him the right way towards his destination. It came after a sudden shriek followed by a fall off his horse, the second they left the campsite. Clamp! The bear trap went shut right on the horse's leg, buckling him down to the ground with Ray landing on his back. Getting back up to his feet, Ray immediately cradled his horse by the head as it began to kick violently with its feet with the one that was in the jaws of the traps steel teeth seeming like it wouldn't come off. Ray slowly went to his horse's leg, keeping his arms out as protection in case the horse should suddenly flick upwards, landing him square in the face. The horse was still in a panic but keeping his movements slow he got his hands around the bear trap and begun to pull them open. The traps steel frame creaked as the teeth came off the horse's leg which had sunk in, deep into its skin, until with one strong pull the trap was open up wide again and his horse's leg slid out. The horse was still writhing in pain, unable to get his balance to stand up straight as the pain in its leg was too excruciating to put weight on. Ray nursed his horse in his arms again, giving it as much comfort as he could, as he no idea what to do. The shrieking neighs coming from the horse were not a pleasant sound to hear over and over with no options on what can be done to treat the horse, until his eyes flickered up with an idea. Ray accepted the idea even though he was a softy for when it came to animals. The gun in his holster was drawn, and he stood up to face the horse as he aimed at the horses head. He could see the animals big wet eyes stare right at him as the horse jerked around more as the pain was becoming more excruciating by the minute. But then, the faint snap of a twig behind him. Ray turned his head towards the trees to see someone emerge from the gap betwen the two towering trees they had camped by. A kid. No more than seven years old. He wrapped his arms around him as he had nothing on except a pair of shorts which were just crudely cut denim. The child had blonde hair with a bowl cut style and looked like he hadn't bathed in weeks, but the thing that made it weirder for Ray was why he was out here all alone and what were the painted markings around his neck.

"Are you lost? What you doing out here, kid?" Ray asked.

"Pops said the fires told him you'd be coming. I got told to wait out here and bring you to him.'

"Cute. Was it you who did this?" pointing towards the bear trap, the boy nodded with a slight grin, pleased with his work.

"Well, in future, if you want someone's attention just simply say hello. That's how most folks do it," Ray said, raising his voice.

"Pops didn't want you bringing in anything to our home. Said it might anger something in the fire," the child said as he avoided eye contact.

"Well at the moment the only one who's angry is me so if you could-" a gunshot echoed throughout the woods sending the birds up from the trees in a frenzy. A rifle shot had gone right through the horses head, putting an end to its suffering. Ray, sinking down to his knees, was in shock for a few seconds before rearing his head back to see another person beside a tree. He was older, bald, in his fifties and skinny as a pencil. The man also had painted markings across his neck, only for the pattern to trail down his torso and back, looking like a neck scarf. While his head was bald, he sported a ginger beard that had been knotted and he too was wearing crudely cut denim trousers. He lowered the rifle, which was still smoking from the barrel as he walked to Ray's side.

"The gift the gods have given you is precious, but it is a curse. You will soon have to learn that not all things can live as long as its power," the man said with a grizzly voice.

"Come. On your feet. The boy and I will take you to the mountains. Keep up with us, we will carry your bags. Boy! With me!" He snapped his fingers, and the young kid picked up one of the rucksacks to join the pair as the older man carried the largest on his back. He handed the rifle to Ray, giving him the order to watch for predators and Ray begrudgingly obliged. With the morning sun creeping higher the three began to move with Ray as the man at the back with a rifle in hand. Eager to learn more about the two as time would undoubtedly drag, now on foot instead of horseback, Ray asked:

"Are you two related?"

"Not by blood. But that doesn't mean that we are. Everyone in the mountains is part of the family. The gods are happy our differences bring us together closer. Perhaps Father will bless you soon as well."

"I have no intention of doing anything until I understand everything that's to do with this vile, Mr..."

"Call me, Eade."

"OK, Eade-"

"And I'm Ty," the young boy said, chiming in.

"Pleasure. Who is this Father?"

"He is like the title suggests. He tells us how to live how the gods intend each and every day. He had told pockets of our people that you would be soon arriving and that we must search for you."

"Is there like a spiritual connection between everyone? How is it everyone knows where I am?"

"That I do not know. But I'm sure the Father does. He has the connection from which he sees and speaks to the gods. Through the flames that have burned eternal light, he will most likely show you given your predicament" Eade said.

Ray was still dumbfounded, but he carried on with them any-way. The land filled with trees seemed to be never-ending, with Ray thinking he had walked this path already, but the man and child still pressed onwards with his belongings, so he didn't have much to complain about. The three began walking through muddy water from the ground that was covered in a layer of water from the stream up north. Ray was grateful he had boots on unlike his two leads who seemed accustomed to it. Soon enough, the three made it to the stream that was flow-ing down the woods at a fast rate. It was unlikely the three would be able to walk through it without being swept away, to which the bearded Eade stated they need to continue up east to reach a narrow point to cross. The consistency of the ground was near to the point where it would be un-walkable, that is until Ray began walking on boards nailed together, creating a walking path. It began reaching upwards towards the trees, and Ray soon saw there was a system of tree houses where the pathway took them with the boards being held, now by tied rope hung from the thick branches. They creaked, but it was sturdy to walk on. The circular tree houses wove them-selves together and with the forest being so vast, it looked like these seemed to go on forever, an endless circut of make-shift housesRay wondered just how many people lived up here. Soon the three made it to the crossing to the other side of the ferocious stream. Looking down onto it, Ray could see more of the woodland in the distance as the trees parted, giving him a broader canvas of the entire land. He could see the trees range in height and colour as he travelled across the rickety bridge. The three followed the pathway which took them back down to the ground and continued on through the woods. They had been walking for over three hours without stopping and while Ray began to feel the need to take a break, the young Ty and grown Eade pressed forward without breaking a sweat. Ray considered that out here to survive in their conditions, it would require a healthy amount of stamina to keep going even in the search for food. However, the thought of rest was over as Eade signalled to him the discovery of the mountain's gate, which was no more than sharpened tree branches. Seemingly blending with its surroundings, Ray didn't even notice it as an entranceway into anything had Eade not pointed it out.

"That's not the only thing that can tell you of something nearby," he said. Ray didn't quite understand until his eyes looked around and saw tens maybe even hundreds of heads peering out from the sides of the trees. Hundreds of eyes stared at Ray, looking as if they would soon break away from their posts to swarm around him like a colony of ants. Luckily, they all seemed to be in a statue-like state with the only thing moving, their eyes, before returning to face their tree.

"Any particular reason everyone is like this?"

"It is praying hour," Eade whispered.

Ray was still creeped out by the many pale eyes from all ages looking at him as they carried on through to the mountains opening. Soon walking past tree stumps, the walkway into the dark passageway inside the mountains was visible. The sun hit the three after stepping out from the woods before stepping into the darkness of the mountain. Eade lead the way with his hand gripping Ty's before reaching out for Ray's who followed suit. The white light behind them was the only thing lighting their path before Eade lead them to a sharp right turn, covering all three's sight in complete blackness.

"We are nearing the Father. You will soon hear him" Eade said with his voice echoing slightly.

Ray didn't think of it as anything good. Miraculously, Eade lead him and young Ty effortlessly without tripping or bumping into the sides of the very narrow pathway. Soon enough as the bearded one said, Ray could quickly hear the voice of another in the distance. The Father. The shaman. His voice was deep and eerie as it got louder with every step chatting in an obscure language that Ray could not understand. He now knew his name and what he sounded like, but he would soon see why the people of the mountains saw him as the leader of the colony. As the three turned again, this time to their left, the pathway in front Eade was a dim shade of orange from the fires Eade had spoken about. How big were these flames?

Ray thought the path was quite a stretch. They could now see the formation of the rock walls around them, as they reached the end before the turn the chanting from the Father was loud enough to be heard and understood correctly by his followers. He was a simple turn away. Stepping into the main hall of the cave, the orange glow flickering on the rock walls around them. The logs of the fire were tree trunk sized, and the flames were so tall they nearly touched the top of the cave. As Ray stepped out to the side of his guide, he could see it all burning bright with followers sitting beside it on a rock ledge which was part of the rock formation. Ray kept walking to his side to see the face of the Father, which was hidden by the giant flames burning so much that Ray felt he needed to take his coat off. He soon saw him, arms stretched out with his palms opened up, the Father continued to chant but more disturbingly with his eyes rolled back. The Father possessed a muscular body with long black hair that nearly stretched down to his knees, and unlike his followers, he was draped in the skin of animals woven together in a nightmarish collage of heads, feet and bones.

"If I could paint a picture of hell," Ray said to himself, but in doing so, the Father stopped chanting as his head snapped back to look at Ray with the pale whites of his eyes.

"Blasphemy!" he screamed, and his eyes rolled back, and the black pupils were where they should be. The Father walked from the high rock formation, like a woman in a stage play being introduced down some stairs, he was the centre of attention.

"I want you to try and say that again. The gods speak through me. Now they are listening too, outsider!" he shouted in a deep demonic-like voice that echoed throughout the cave.

"Father shaman, this one the gods told us about. I found him in the woods down south," Spoke up Eade with Ty gripping both hands onto his arm. The Father listened and with a tilt of head observed Ray and what he had with him.
"These are his belongings, Father shaman" Eade continued. The boney hands rummaged through until he felt the vial.

"I see it now, as I predicted. An anomaly. Someone of obscurity that he can't fathom everything that will be presented to him. A man in denial but has no choice but to accept the role that has been bestowed upon him. And he is still foolish." The Father with a good swing, backhanded Ray sending him to the floor. The followers sitting, now stood to watch the show, cheering for their ruler.

"This is who the gods have chosen! So we must make him a God by any means!"

Ray gritted his teeth as he got back up to his feet, getting up to the shaman's face to stare him down. The Father smiled.

"That is what they want. That right there," pointing his finger, "Anger, in the face of a threat. Warriors stare. I have your attention now, and now you will listen," said the Father as he walked around Ray, making his voice travel ear to ear.

"I was part of the creation of the vial. But not for the intentions the others want you to fulfil. I see you as a beacon of light like our fire, burning every second of every day. The key to happiness for people everywhere across this land and maybe, beyond that. I'm sure you know what you'll be up against?" he asked.

"Mostly as the others and probably what you'll call demons of the night. Creatures."

"You only know of a few. A handful of beasts that walk this land unseen by the regular man. But you can now see them. There is more to this land than just those shown to you. State influence will continue to grow and expand, it is the way of things, but I and like others will say, the native influence is dying. They saw you and others they had told know you exist. If these beasts continue to thrive off decimating the ones who kept them in line for centuries, then this land will be overrun with monsters."

"Chief Maluk, of the Crow tribe, he spoke to me about these others you speak of. What were their intentions exactly?" Ray asked. The Father turned his attention to the fire, turning his back on Ray, but as he did, the flames changed colour. Now black and white, the Father had rolled his eyes back into his skull waving his right hand across the fire, like ripples in water, it moved with the movement of his hands.

"To them, you are the weapon they craved to be," he answered. He waved his other hand across the fire now, twisting the blackened flames until with a circular movement of his wrist created a spiralling tornado of fire. In a sudden thrust, arms thrust outwards from his body, the whirlwind of fire split in two and flew onto the cave walls sticking to it like paint out of a bucket. It dried and blended into the rock walls in an instant only for then to change into the colour white and morph into characters of people, acting out a scene from the father's memory.

"They came to me for an ingredient. The two of them knew my tribe possessed it, perfecting it with everything we ate. Like a spice, a plant called the Yeto. Bloomed like a daisy only to grow as tall as the trees you saw outside. Its leaves were the spice when ground down. It was special, and they knew it. I took it upon myself to give the seed to the one I saw fit, they explained the plan to create something that could only, at the right circumstances, be achieved only once. It was proven to be right, but they wanted more than just a seed. They wanted me to change for them."

"Change?"

"In what I believe in. In how I treat my brothers and sisters. I couldn't and wouldn't. They saw it as a weakness and took our home from us. That is why we are here now. Hidden away, but the gods still protect us. The Yeto plant is gone now, but the fire rages on to guide us all, to guide you." Snapping his fingers the animated black marks on the stone grew hot again until they shot up, joining one another to then shoot down into the pit to burn up before reaching up to the top of the cave again.

"Touch the flame," the Father said to Ray extending his hand out to lead. Ray was reluctant, still unaccustomed to everything going on but always wanting to see further down the rabbit hole. Looking around at the other followers and to Eade and Ty who were all eager to see him learn, he took a deep breath and stepped toward with the shaman who pressed his hand onto Ray's back. The heat was unbearable, at a distance between him and the fire, Ray knew he would begin to start sweating, looking as uncomfortable as possible. The Father broke the tension with his hand, now grabbing the smaller Ray's wrist, lifting it upwards to show to his followers before inching it closer the fire. Closer and closer, Ray could feel his fingertips burning, he clenched his fist to stop the burning sensation, but it wouldn't stop as soon as his knuckles felt the sting and then with a good tug his palm took the heat. Ray screamed in pain as the shaman kept his eyes fixated on his hand, maintaining a firm grip should Ray feel the need to break loose. The pain was then lost, the elixir's effects took over with Ray's veins glowing a shade of dull purple. The shaman smiled with glee as Ray, now with his strength back, looked up to see what was happening. His hand was at the centre of the roaring fire, now healed of any burning sensation with his skin repairing itself. The Father rolled his eyes back, still with a gleeful smile before beginning a rhythmic chant. His words were spoken softly before rising in volume, reaching a crescendo, the Father yanked Ray's hand right from the fire till it was above his head and the two stepped backwards. The flame was connected to Ray now, attached to his hand like a snake, pierced down like teeth into your arm not letting go. The Father howled with playful laughter as Ray, and the fathers' followers looked on in terror as to what would happen next. It came when the entire fire seemed to drain into Ray's hand as the force of the heat was clamped down by Ray's hand turning into a fist, blackened and smoking. Amazed. Shocked. Ray didn't know what to think or believe in at this point. The father pried his hand open with burnt skin cracking as the fingers opened up, revealing his palm, which had a plethora of burnt markings around a perfectly woven spiral. Trying to feel them, the Father watched as the marking, and the spiral kept on sinking into Ray's skin and saw that it soon began to look like the lines in his hands like it had been there for years. Again, he chuckled in delight as he proclaimed

"The deal is done! Sealed by the gods themselves!"

His followers cheered, and the cave was filled with applause. Ray looked on in confusion before the Father rushed back to him, with his hands this time, grabbing the sides of his face and then lifting Ray from his feet.

"What do you see?" the Father asked. Ray stuttered to answer, but it wasn't enough for the Father who then threw him back to the ground.

"The gods stand tall with us. We must know about your future. You now have them guiding your every move. Tell us the truth! Are their plans like how I have been told!" he screamed. Ray now felt like he was in danger, the feeling that he could be crushed by this madman at any moment when suddenly Ray's hand started to glow again, with his eyes now rolling back inside his skull. In a moment's notice thick smoke burst through Ray's chest, forming a giant arm that stretched over to grab the Father by the throat, lifting him from the floor. Ray's white, pale eyes now flew like his hand and his jaw begun to hang loose, opening his mouth that spewed out more smoke up to the cave's stone ceiling. It sprouted a head. The head of an elder native whose headdress was stitched onto his skin, and his eyes were glowing pale white like two moons in the night sky. The apparition bellowed down to the Father, speaking in the chant-like rhythm the Father had conveyed to his following before the two spoke in their language.

"Shaman! We oversee the future of this man, you have done your part. As of right now, you will no longer serve us nor will you influence the actions of this man, Ray McCarthy!" The apparition's grip was so tight had it not been from the blinding light that shot out from his eyes you could make out the Father's face was turning a shade blue. With as much power as he had, the shaman tried his best to pull away from the hazy smoke, freeing him of the pressure enough to let him speak.

"My lords...I was...part... of its creation. I can tell him its secrets," he mustered.

"Bazka lives! He knows of it because of your incompetence! You knew who they were, and in doing so, we knew who they were. You had the opportunity to get rid of them, but what did you do? Like a child, you came to us begging for the answers when it stared you right in the face. As we have decided, you will not take part in his journey! We will decide from now on what needs to be done. But since you have been a worthy follower of our word, we are feeling generous." In finishing the smoke-made arm released its massive grip from the shaman's neck, and he fell to the floor landing on his knees as he gazed up to the head of the gods' smokey form.

"The mountains are yours to control, shaman. Spread the word of this man, he is the only one who can stop Bazka and his maniacal way of thinking. He will be the one to end the monsters reign on the land. Heed our words, do not oppose us." And the apparition's head sunk back into the opening from Ray, and the arm retracted back inside his chest. Faint smoke scattered around the cave, as Ray's eyes began to dim before he rolled his eyes back to normal. As he was released from the otherworldly being, he hunched over breathing rapidly as though he had lost all the air from his lungs. Ray raised his head to see what had happened, only to see the shaman trying to stand with one knee bent holding his body upward after the whole ordeal. Ray had no idea what had happened, and the shaman was almost refusing to look him in the eye any more. The Father, resting on his knees, had his back hunched over with his head looking down at the ground.

"Did I? Was something inside of-"

"They will tell you in good time. But as of right now, you can leave this place and never return," said the shaman in defeat, having felt his place in this whole situation crumble away. He felt unimportant, like it was all for nothing.

"If I did anything to-"

"Just. Leave," he snarled flaring his nostrils up as he gritted his teeth with the spit from inside his mouth trying to escape through the gaps of his teeth. Ray was shocked at the sudden turn in emotions being showed by the imposing Father who was now sunken in defeat. As he got up, Eade and Ty walked to his side to show him the way out. Ray looked over his shoulder to see the Father, for what would be the final time, before venturing back into the darkness of the cave's tunnels, kneeling on the ground, staring into the floor with blackened firewood by his side with his followers looking over at him. He thought he heard him sobbing, a giant of a man reduced to tears by something that he had done that was out of his control.

"So, you vowed by his word to never see this 'father' again?" Roosevelt asked.

"I gave him my word. I learnt what had happened in there later on."

"By Eade?"

"No. The Chief." Ray said.

◆ ◆ ◆

A day had passed since Ray had stepped into the caves of Missouri. He had returned to Chief Maluk. His head was full of questions that needed answering once again in the chief's tent where the visions of monsters had first appeared to him.

"You forgot to tell me that this guy was deranged."

"Well I thought the mere sight of him would give you an impression" he chuckled.

"A very lasting impression. The Father seemed hell-bent on breaking me unless I followed his every command until something happened."

"What did he do?"

"I think it was something I did, but I can't remember. He was on the ground with his head hanging."

"And you can't remember what you said?"

"Yes." Maluk smiled. He got up from his seated position to reach again the bull hornpipe that he still had and offered it to Ray. He wasn't this fazed by the contents of the pipe this time around, as he thought it would surely mean seeing visions again.

"I think this will clear everything," Maluk said.

With no hesitation this time, Ray puffed at the tip of the bull horn, blowing its thick, dense smoke up to the teepee's tip. The effects this time were with him at a seconds notice; the rush of energy, followed by the numbness of his body before slumping back onto the mat he sat on only to sit back up with a grunt that you would make after you woke from your bed. Rubbing his eyes, the vision he awoke to was a bit more subtle this time. No monster painting coming alive or the sounds of demons screaming but instead, three other people of native origin appeared in the room, sitting with their legs crossed looking at Ray. To Ray, they looked the same, all three wore the same style of clothing with the only thing to distinguish the three was a different marking on their foreheads. The three wore matching headdresses with feather neck garments and straw lined ankle bracelets. Chief Maluk sat back down with that cheeky grin on his face as Ray came too, still rubbing his eyes a bit.

"So who would like to go first? Ray?"

"Um, maybe some introduction would be nice."

"Well, at least we know who you are. Ray McCarthy," spoke the native leader to his left.

"We are the gods of Jugda. Your American gods if you prefer." said the leader on the left side of Maluk.

"Good to know," Ray said.

"We apologize for the confusion back in the caves up west. We saw it would be wise for you to not be involved with the shaman father."

"How so and was that the reason why he wanted me to leave?"

"We had to speak on your behalf."

"Maybe ask me first before doing that."

"Ray, the leaders here were only protecting you," explained Maluk.

"He had done his part, and he would've been detrimental to

your quest had he continue to follow you."

"He is very clingy," said the leader to Ray's right.

"But nothing will come of him. He simply did what was done for you to connect with us, just as you are doing right now."

Ray's eyes hopped from one leader to the next before settling on Maluk.

"Chief, I dunno what you put in that horn, but how are you seeing the same people I am right now?"

"I passed their trials many moons ago, Ray. It is common for me to communicate with them with or without the bull horn."

"What did you say to the Father?"
All four heads shared a look with each other before the leader on Ray's right spoke up.
"Like we said, he had done his part and we cut him loose. The reason we did was that, as loyal as he was, we needed to be prepared in case he used you in secret like the other creators seek to do so."

"These remaining two used him purely for gain, and if you had to hear him for many years, you know his sort of behaviour after that would be quite, questionable," continued the middle leader.

"But they are merely pawns to Bazka. Taking them out would lead him to fend for himself in the land filled with the monsters that he cannot control."

"Bazka? I'm after this guy now? I thought I was going up against monsters?!" Ray piped up.

"And you are, but taking out the people who brought these creatures into the light would be a step in the right direction," said the leader on the left.

Ray now trying not to get frustrated at the mission presented to him calmed himself with a motion of his hands and sat peacefully again before continuing to speak.

"OK, I'll bite. Explain to me about these two guys who made this Bazka fella," he said while bringing out the vile to cradle in his hands.

"Their names are Waywood and Goida. One hides in the north while the other is far west. We saw these two as the main proprietors to create the vial after the Shaman told us of their wisdom. In a single move, we alerted the other tribes to our cause, and they swore to protect it. The vial was taken and hidden from them for years. The tribes waited and watched for the right man. One special creation, keeping the balance of the land without our involvement. But we underestimated the choices of one Akea who saw his vision, that being you, as the one to bring balance," said the leader sat by Maluk.

"Waywood was a pupil of the Jugda tribe which ran up the colder climate grounds. He betrayed his leader to rule his tribe with an iron fist and by the sharp edge of his axe. He killed anyone, from his tribe members to your other white men for sport. He is ruthless and wanted the vial for himself. To be the ultimate killing machine," the leader to Ray's right continued.

"Goida was one to hide. His people are scarce as he saw them as fit creations that should not reproduce as they were too perfect, but even he couldn't mind the elixirs power to keep him alive as the purest of the land. We saw them, and we tried to tell the Shaman what to do, but he panicked. He was blinded," said the leader the left.

"And what about Bazka?"

"Bazka is the one who fell from our sacred ground. Manipulative and a liar. We are three, but he was the fourth. We expelled him and locked him away, deep in the hell that he wanted to create. Goida and Waywood found him and his vision of the land matched their interests. They're doing his bidding, releasing the creatures into the land, creating chaos while he hides in the shadows and his word spreads."

"And they will hide with him. Clenching at his legs like good little children." continued the elder on Ray's right.

"I would've told you all of this Ray, you know I would've. But the elders here told me that you needed a taste of what you're up against and they thought the Shaman would be the ideal start" Maluk explained.

Ray took a moment to process everything told from the three elders and chief Maluk. A mix of monsters from a realm unbeknownst to anyone in the southern and northern states, mad dogs who did evil deeds. And to top it off a being who was previously an elder like the three in front of him, hell-bent on making America the picture described to him as a child in a church: Hell. I guess the four of them would've said to anyone who drunk the vial, that was the start of things. It would only get much weirder from here.

"Bazka. These creatures. Can they...hurt me?" Ray asked.

All three natives looked at each other, nodding in agreement before the elder to Maluk's right spoke first, his first sentence sighing out with a hint of hesitation.

"They can. Killing you is just a lot more difficult for them. Your body can take much more punishment, but you will still feel pain."

"The only thing that still remains the same as you, is your will power. Your inner spirit which the others here cannot touch. This is what drives all men. You now know the risks, and you now know who you are. I pray to Akea that his decision that day, will not be in vain. Ray, save our people. Save this land. Please."

The horses trotted side by side as the band of searchers with Colonel Biden centre stage of the pack in front of his three searchers. Their road was flat, and the sun was out with the clouds patchy across the midday sky. Biden raised his hand up with his palm flat, signalling his band to stop. Reaching into his bag which rested to the side of him from over his shoulder he pulled out his binoculars, he cast his sights forward to observe what, from this distance looked like an ant but was really someone else on horseback moving along down the same road.

His horse rode slowly like the pack, and the person riding the horse was young, in his mid-teens. Biden's men squinted to see if they could make out the same thing as the Colonel could, but the Colonel brought his binoculars down from his eyes and placed them back into his bag. His arm raised again, but this time with his two fingers signalling to move forward and encounter the man fifty feet from them. They still moved slowly like their designated target, once within arms distance from each other they simply walked by only for the Colonel to turn around and stay his horse firmly in place. His band of searchers then picked up speed slightly faster than their target that was still at walking speed as they cameup to the man before turning around in a circle before the young man pulled at his reigns to stop his horse. He asked a question of what the three men were up to and gave a simple answer to the question. The three men froze, and the searcher in front of the young man nodded to make the young man face Biden behind him.

"Good day, young man." said Colonel Biden. "I would like to ask you a few questions. You're not in trouble, do not worry," he lied. The man in his twenties saw military uniforms and immediately thought that he had done something wrong, he was relived for a few moments before the Colonel asked: "If you would I simply wish to ask where you are travelling from?"

"Uh, Bonebag sir. Up north from here."

"And how long is that from here exactly?"

"Not far, uh' bout an hours ride, if your horse is galloping. I started from this morning, slow ride."
Biden's false smile resided across his face; it seemed welcoming to the untrained eye.

"Lovely to know. Hear that men, not far now. Now the second question, are there any new people to that town at all?"

"W-what do you mean?"

"Anyone new. Someone who's not regular from where you're from."

"Can't say, sir. A few new people come into work at a place that hires people on the go, so a lot of people come through."

"And this place is?"

"It's the lumber mill. Just right the west side of the town. Big grey barn, can't miss it. The old guy there runs it."

"That'll be of great use. Thank you for your time." Biden's hand raised and snapped his fingers, making his search party clear away from the young man. They rejoined the Colonel and continued down the road. The young teen spoke up once more.

"Is the town in trouble, sir? Is the war coming through this way?"
Biden turned his head around with the group still trotting forward. "No, no. But someone may bring it."

Ray stood, as did the other elders, all of whom, like Ray were tall enough that their heads could touch the top of the teepee, but they were apparitions who could simply go through it. They were delighted that Ray chose the path they had set for him and Maluk as well.

"Please Ray, if you will," Maluk said, extending his hand to stand in the centre of the teepee. He stepped forward, and the elders placed their ghostly hands on top of Ray's head, their hands going through one another as they brought their arms down. In unison, they closed their eyes and began to hum, all in the same grave tone that came from the back of the throat. Ray's eyes went to Maluk for an explanation, and he happily obliged.

"They are blessing you." Short and sweet. Even though the elders were just apparitions and he could easily walk through any of them; he could feel the energy radiating from their hands. He now knew what they were, the power they possessed whereas before he may have nailed his thoughts to it being nothing but the heat from inside the teepee with it being so close to the outside fireplace. One by one, the elders took their hands back down to their sides with the deep humming tone, slowly getting quieter as one took his hand away. Then another. And then the last.

"We are proud that it will be you to save this land. We hope you do well. We will be watching," the middle elder said. An in a moment's notice, the three faces of the elders were blown away by the air kept inside Maluk's lungs. He coughed a little and then sat back down onto the animal skin rug.

"I take it that's your way of getting out of arguments when things get heated," Ray joked and Maluk laughed.

"Trust me, they never squabble. But at least the first task of initiation has been completed. You are going to be the first white man to step into the world of Jugda."

"I'll stick with America." The smile just grew even more on Maluk's rubbery face.

"Well, time is of the essence. And it is time for you to prepare for the beings that await you. For that, you will need this." Maluk reached down behind him to what was hidden under the turned up bit of the animal rug. Another small bag holding contents of what appeared to be seed, judging from the shape of the bag.

"I don't know nor do I care how you slay the beasts, but I do know how you will keep them inside the hell from which they came." Maluk opened the bag to reveal what looked like burnt remains from a tree, the pieces were hard and sharp should you have to crush them.

"The crust from the opening. Like a cut that has been bleeding it's blackned exterior can seal fates for good. If a beast is slain, sprinkle this on them. Anywhere, it does not matter, but it can be used to keep their souls from ever returning."
Ray looked to see the broken black pieces inside the small bag.

"Like seasoning a chicken," Ray said.

"It is called blood bark. The key by which to lock them away.

Use it sparingly." Maluk handed the bag to Ray after tightening the rope which kept it sealed.

"Will I need this for these two goons they told me about?" Ray asked.

"Etirely down to you. Those two are slaves to Bazka and he too will know of the consequences when going against the natural order."

"Is it possible to let anyone know about this?"

"Again. Entirely down to you."

It was Millie's turn on the till now. Her mind was on other things, drifting off with wondering questions. It was now a week since she last saw Ray and the burning desire to do something with his savings was increasingly tempting. A token of his love to her, without even saying that three-word sentence. Martha was heard behind her cursing at the man she was speaking to at the back door. It was a heated back-and-forth before a slam of the door was heard.

"Stupid con artist!" she yelled as her heeled boots stomped on the wooden floor. Millie was unfazed by the drama behind her, keeping her composure as she was now about to serve a customer, she heard the ring from the door. Outside, she recognized the face, it was her brother, who was out of breath.

"Millie you gotta come with me now!" Thomas said in a frantic voice..

"What's happened?"

"Union men, rounding people up out of their homes. I don't know what they want, but it looks serious. I saw from up where the house is, they're dragging people by the collar." Panic now came over Millie's face as she and Martha overheard the situation and went to the till to listen. Before Millie could even come out from the counter, the sound of broken windows and people in distress was heard from across the shop. Looking out from the window, they could see people being pushed together by men in military uniform. Millie's brother was itching to pull his gun out of his holster as he exclaimed: "I bet those damn crackers down south are here." The sound of a rifle shot was fired into the air and silence reigned as voice soon called out.

"People of Bonebag! Do not panic, we simply wish to ask some questions. There is a threat which has presided over the town.

We simply wish to snuff it out. So if you could all come out from under your beds, hold your tongues and speak when spoken too!" bellowed Biden. Stepping out first, was the Sheriff, wearing a small white bowler hat with a brown waistcoat and matching slacks. He was in his mid-fifties and did not have a stern face of intimidation unlike Biden but was relaxed about the situation.

"Now what seems to be the trouble here, sir?" he asked.

"Apologies Sheriff but we have been drawn here to simply ask some questions pertaining to a mission of ours."

"Well there's asking questions, and then there's pushing the people around here like trash. A bit unnecessary, don't ya think?" Biden was now trying to keep his fake smile up as his frustration began to grow.

"Don't you worry Sheriff, as a Colonel of the mighty union this is just procedures-"

"Don't talk to me like your superior. Just because you wear that uniform doesn't mean you can instruct people to round together like cattle. I'd like to ask you the question of what's going on?" he ordered. Biden shrugged. Suddenly, in a heartbeat, Biden whipped his gun from his holster putting the curious lawman down to the ground with a severe thud. The townspeople were in shock that their sheriff of twenty years was struck down by a high ranking official of in their eyes, the good guys.

"What's going on is there are stray cattle. And I'm sure one of you has seen the little guy? You will all step into the Sheriff's office to give statements to me, this is of great importance we find this man. He could bring the war here." Fear kept the locals in line for their lives.

"You heard him, everyone in line at the Sheriff's now!" barked one of the men in the group and the locals all moved slowly toward the front door of the police department. Martha wasted no time in joining the line, but Millie remained at the counter.

"Millie don't be stupid come on." said her brother. Millie with her hands clamped together came too and walked out from the counter, feeling as nervous as ever. What if it's Ray they're after she thought. Was that the reason he gave her the money? As a bargaining gift to give to them? Millie and her brother joined Martha at the back of the line. She went back to her thoughts as she waited for the dreaded interview. The line moved slowly toward the door one person at a time, with everyone in either disarray at had what transpired a few moments ago with the sheriff and others in nervous wrecks still crying at the thought that it could happen to them. Millie peered her head over Martha's shoulder to get a closer look inside, see if she could catch sight of anything going on. She saw only the Colonel and his ideally kept moustache still with that deceiving grin on his face making it seem that this was all normal to him. She saw him tilt his head and the person stepping out from the side door of the sheriffs' department was a woman in a regular striped dress. With her out the line moved forward again. Millie brought her head back as one of the Colonel's men stared at her after closing the door. She saw the woman walking back in the direction of the line and tried to get her attention.

"Psst. What did they ask you about?"

"Millie! Keep your head in line," Martha snapped while keeping her voice down.

"Please, just tell me what did they ask you?"

The woman hesitated and looked back at the guard, seeing that his attention was drawn back to the door to open it again. She quickly rushed to Millie's side to whisper in her ear:

"They're looking for someone. Some guy called McCarthy. I didn't know him but-"

"Back in line, miss!" c out the guard at the door. The blonde-haired girl shuffled back in behind Millie, who was confused.

"They wouldn't take that for an answer."

"What do you mean?"

"They said they want to ask me again. I think they're doing this with everyone."

"Why would they ask you again?"

"He said he was going to hear it again but with a different approach, miss" as the girl finished a scream was heard, a male one.

"That's Mr Bentley. It's torture miss," she panicked.

"This can't be just something with the war. They'd never be this violent with regular folk."

More cries of pain came from inside and not long after Mr Bently was thrown from the side door onto the dirt. But he did nothing to get back up, everyone's heads shifted in his direction, and Millie rushed over to him with the guard repeating the sentence he said the blonde girl. She rolled him over to find that his head was caved in, the forehead of his skull was bent back so much, and his eyes were bloodshot. Blood trickled down his nose as it looked like the worst of all things, he was a very brittle man.

"He's dead," Millie whimpered out, stunned that the branch of military looking to protect her was doing such a thing. Two boots planted on the board by the door. Colonel Biden was there in front of her, hands on his hips.

"This one is very sentimental. I think you'll be next ,miss." He smiled, as another guard was behind him with his rifle in hand. She had no other option but to step inside past the Colonel's large frame and the door was closed. One of the guards pulled out a stool, under from the desk while the Colonel sat in the Sheriff's chair on the other side, playing around with deceased man's possessions.

"Now then. The last name, please miss."

"Why did you do that to Mr Bentley?"
Biden looked up from his paper, annoyed.

"Miss, it is time to start answering my questions, not answering yours."

"This is not just a simple question and answering session, this is barbaric. What's this all about?"

"A man. Who came into this town, quite recently. McCarthy. He's dangerous and a traitor miss. Do you know him?" Biden asked. Millie tried her best poker face possible to back up her words, but Biden was too good at reading people. He read her instantly and knew she was lying, and he was sure going to get it out of her in the end, question by question.

"Don't know the name. What does he look like?"

"Medium height, regular build, partial stubble, quite dirty in the face. About in his thirties," Biden described, more and more and that familiar image came back to Millie. While Biden painted the picture, she remembered the voice that told her not to worry and wait for him till he gets back. So comforting yet shrouded in secrecy. Millie pressured more questions out of Biden to get to the bottom of who he was.

"Lots of guys look like that, sir. What exactly has he done?"
"You didn't answer my question, miss."

"Answer mine!" Biden had got her now. Leaning back in the chair, he put his pencil down and began to widen the picture for her.

"Mr Ray William Mccarthy. Former commanding officer of one of my regiments. He served the union well until he lead a group of boys destined for great things for them, found in a pit, dead. He fed them to the savages. And then, knowing that he had no way of hiding it, he ran, far away hoping to find the simplest of towns to hide. Now that my dear, is desertion. Did he even tell you about this?"

"Well, that's terrible but, like I said many guys come here looking like that and we don't think nothing of em. Men come and go in this town, working for the old man at the wood barn-"

"Thank you for that, miss, I'll hear from you again in a minute, Stevens would get the owner of the wood mill barn please." Millie was then brought back up to stand by a hand grasping under her arm.

"Put her in the cell. Oh and miss, don't try to hide your relation to Mr McCarthy after I'm done with the next person. He is clearly nested here, and I'm here to cut this tree of deception down."

Millie was then restrained and thrown back where the two jail cells were. Millie tried to think, what could she next that would prolong her secrets. But at the same time, Millie didn't know if she could bring herself to with what she had just heard. If it was true, then what's the point in hiding she thought.

Ray had travelled back from the chief's ground onto the road that would take him back to Bonebag. Along the road again, he noticed it was quieter than usual. You saw plenty few who would be on horseback making their way into and out of the town, it was a hot spot for work and trade. On his way back through he glimpsed again at the way he had come and wondered if he should've begun the journey west to find the men the elders had warned him about. But his heart was on Millie, he had to tell her what had happened. Even if she didn't believe him at least, it would be a load off his chest if he did. He pictured her standing there, in the same spot as he last saw her. With a smile on her face, hands twiddling together, waiting in anticipation to relieve that kiss that he wanted to give her but didn't think the time was right for it. He rode on.

Billy was now sat on the small stool pulled out from the table. Shaking slightly he tried to relax as he had never been in this type of situation before, and when he spoke, his words were rushed, stumbling a bit, trying to escape this situation as soon as possible.

"Look, the barn is mine, I had no payment given to me by anyone bad, I swear."

"Relax old-timer, this has nothing to do with your workplace. It simply pertains to one of your workers."

"You're joking, aren't ya? I have hundreds of different men come in every month, sir. I ain't gonna remember everyone who comes in."

"I'm sure you will with this one Mr..."

"Grove. Billy Grove, sir."
Biden jotted down the name with his pencil and paper.

"And you've been the owner of this wood mill barn now for how long?"

"Twenty three years," The pencil scribbled down again.

"Now Mr Grove, I know as a man nearing your age, that it can be hard to remember every single person who comes into your line of work. People from all across the country far and wide, close to home anyone. You're a very charitable man. Willing to give anyone work. But I'm sure there had to be some favourites that you could remember."

"I guess so, but that doesn't mean I took part in anything that would be outside the restrictions of the law."

"I'm not saying you have Mr Grove, I'm saying someone you know has. A more recent employee. You know Mr McCarthy?"

Billy squinted. He knew the name, and he refused to narrow it right down to Ray.

"A few."

Biden took a deep breath in through his nose, trying to hide his frustration. The old man is not going to be simple, he thought.

"Could you possibly narrow that down?"

"I've known three McCarthys in my time, sir. Remember I have been in the business for two decades."

"I'd like the most recent one, please."

Now Billy had to think. Does he reveal who Ray is or does he lie?

Billy saw what had happened to Mr Bently a few moments to go and was worried if that would soon be him, either way, whichever answer he gave. Billy couldn't lie to save his life. Swallowing hard, he spoke out with a hint of grief.

"Yeah, I know. It's Ray, isn't it."

"Yes. Would you mind looking at this description to see if it matches?"

Biden slid the paper over to Billy who now felt so heavy chested that he thought it was going to be a struggle to even move. He got the article to read the description. It matched who Billy knew. But as he read down the report, Billy grazed through the paragraph which spoke of his crimes. Billy was stunned, rubbing his eyes in confusion before planting the paper on the table.

"God damn it! He's not a bad boy, honestly."

"That's all I need. Stevens put the old boy next to Miss Quiet over there." Billy was hoisted up and chucked into theother cell with the steel bars, both holding back the two captives. Millie and Billy shared a look of disbelief as to what is happening before Billy hung his head in his hands.

"Right Stevens we've met the description, now we lay the trap and wait for the rat to catch the bait. Inspect the barn and then rally everyone inside. Make sure the whole town is in there, everyone except those two." With the plan set, the two walked back outside to round up everyone who was still in line.

"Ladies and gentlemen, thank you for your cooperation. We now have two suspects waiting in custody now. On behalf of my team, I apologize for what seemed to be a hostile meeting, but with the two suspects in captivity we need to bait out the man in question, we request if you would all move down over to Mr Grove's barn down at the end of the town."

"What will we do when we get there?" asked a random man from the crowd.

"Nothing. Minimal effort. Just simply remain inside, and Steven's and the rest will instruct you what to do should anything change."

"Aye, where's my sister?" Millie's brother spoke out from at the back of the crowd.

Biden knew it would waste time and ignored the question.

"Right, let us not waste time, off you all go!"

"But where's Millie! What have you guys done with her?!" Thomas shouted out louder until one of the guards with a hard swing pistol-whipped him on his back to keep him quiet and in line. Thomas grunted in pain and nearly fell to the floor but was kept up on his feet from the supporting hands of Martha, who was to his left.

"Honey, try to relax, they may do something worse to you if you're not careful," the two continued with the crowd down the road with the menacing guard right by their side. Biden watched as Stevens returned to him.

"All my men have the barn cornered off, sir. I've given them strict instructions not to address anyone unless I say so."

"Excellent Stevens. I'll need you by my side. The two inside have good relations with Mr McCarthy. They will be the first to go when he arrives."

Inside the cells, Billy's hands were placed firmly behind his head while Millie rested her back on the brick wall next to the bench.

"Did you know?" Billy asked.

"Not a thing," Millie answered.

"Stupid boy's gonna get us all killed. Or we're gonna starve to death in these walls, who knows what that Colonel will do."

"We gotta hope, Mr Grove. Hope that Ray comes quietly and gets all this over with."

"How do you know him?"

"Through work."

Billy chuckled. "Same."

"But I'm kinda more than just a work friend, Mr Grove." Billy lifted his head from his hands. Curious, he asked,

"Partners?" There was a short silence, but Billy knew it was true.

"He's using us. Had to go through the townsfolk to find someone he knows. Did he tell you anything at all?" Millie kept the silence lingering, leaving Billy without an answer, slumping back to the wall.

"He just gave me money and said he'll be back. Wanted us to head out into the country, have a home away from it all. Just me and him."

"A bit much with the money I give him."

"He had more. I didn't question it then. But I have to now." Millie and Billy's attention was soon drawn back outside the jailhouse as another gunshot was heard from down the road. They could both hear the distant sound of the townspeople in horror but couldn't see what was happening down at the barn. Millie's brother was riding in pain as a bullet had shattered his shin. The bone caving as Martha tended to his aid as the townspeople feared for their lives.

"All of you back against the wall!" ordered one of the guards. The townspeople nearly packed up most of the space in the barn but just slightly managed to back away from the guard with both Martha and Millie's brother who both by the guards' feet.
He gave them a small smirk of delight before slamming the barn doors behind them. Locking them tight, the three guards took positions at the door. Millie's brother was riding in pain as Martha begged for a handkerchief to cover the wound. One

stepped toward with a clean one placing it flat onto his leg while Martha used her hairband to keep it tightly on. Everyone kept close to one another inside the barn, arms around shoulders and some laying their heads on them. Some were in tears while others were speechless as the horror of being the next Mr Bentley, started to sink in. One man with a black beard tried to peer through the holes and cracks of the sides to get a glimpse to see if anything else was happening. Nothing, just open field. The guards' feet could be seen when looking under the door, and they were certainly not going to budge anytime soon.

"What if we all pulled this piece here, we could all take turns in slipping out," said the man with the beard.

"Don't be foolish. They'd only gun you down. And besides, how can you pull wood apart quietly?" a woman remarked. He still continued to ponder while everyone rested in silence. Martha kept the pressure on Millie's brother's leg with him now gritting his teeth together trying his hardest not to scream as every small movement he made with his leg, felt like it was being shot at again.

"You gotta straighten it son. That way you can relax back" she assured him. Now with a closed mouth, he nodded frantically in agreement.

"Just do it quickly," he said. Martha then took one hand just underneath his knee cap and the other on his thigh and pushed down, forcing the leg to straighten. Thomas bit on his clenched fist hard as he could now lie down and relieve himself of any tension. Some woman at the back of the barn looked away in fright that something else would break. He thanked her before reaching out to grab her hand. "My names Thomas by the way."

"Martha. Now someone get me some hay to put behind this boys head. The man's suffered enough." The two nearest to the haystack got as much as their arms could carry and placed it behind Thomas's head. Back inside the cell, Millie and Billy still remained quiet. Unclear as to what would happen to them within the next hour if they even made it that long. Both them and the people of Bonebag were being used as hostages while the Colonel had no idea of Ray's whereabouts. No one knew where he was, and they would certainly meet their end if the Colonel thought otherwise.

"Do you think it's true?" said Billy.

"Is what true?"

"That Ray did what they say?"

"Maybe. Ray may have done. I don't know much about him before he came here. He could even be a different person posing as a guy called Ray. I wanna believe the opposite to that really Mr Grove." Millie answered.

"Well, if it is, we can't just take the Colonel's word on this. We have to hear it from the horse's mouth. He is... a good boy. He wouldn't keep things from us."

"So what do you call all this then Mr Grove?"

Billy turned away from Millie's frustrated gaze as her eyes started to widen. And again, the room went quiet.

"It was quiet when I entered past the sign. It's never quiet." Ray said.

"In your head, what did you think had happened?"

"Possible outlaws. Every town has its fair share of criminals who like a game of dress-up."

"Not law enforcement?" Roosevelt wondered. "Did it strike you that they had caught up to you?"

"Goes to show how much my words can do on people. No one takes it seriously."

"Apart from one," Roosevelt said.

Walking under the Bonebag welcome sign this time was unnerving. The now eerie silence almost made it feel like Ray was walking into a graveyard. A ghost town even. A place he knew now ransacked, everyone was gone, now just a memory. The horse trod slowly up to the first turning in which you could see the barn. His eyes widened when the familiar uniforms stood armed in front of its doors. He stopped in his tracks. Unsure what to say at that point, they were all loaded and ready to fire when given the order. Instead, their eyes locked onto him first. The one guard to the far-right stepped out from the perfect line formation to whistle out. The guard on the left then walked towards him. Ray's hand was beginning to twitch as he wanted to reach for his sidearm but couldn't as it would end in a three on one situation; even more, if he continued to guess on how many there are up in the town. He just had to take what was coming next on the chin.

"Leave your horse here. Come with me," the guard said. Ray followed the order and slid off his horse, raising his finger to order it to stay. The guard went behind him with the barrel of his rifle placed firmly into Ray's spine. The other guard who had whistled out soon joined his side behind Ray while the middle guard remained in place, still like a statue in front of the barn door. Ray's eyes looked everywhere to see if he could catch anyone looking out from the windows. Nothing. Not even a slight sound was heard from inside Mr Boston's saloon. He feared the worst for everyone, especially Millie. A happy thought in his head earlier soon became a feeling of dread as instead of seeing Millie standing in the same place where he last saw her, it was Colonel Biden. He stood with his arms behind his back, free from restraints, unlike Ray. The two guards then stopped him with one hand holding Ray's shoulders, before stepping back. Biden looked up and down at Ray inspecting him.

"Take his guns," Biden ordered, and the two guards stripped Ray of his pistol and rifle.

"I thought you did special hunts for enemies from the south, Colonel."

"From what I've heard of you, it gives me an implication to suspect that you are one. Why else would you lead a unit of youth to their deaths?"

"So the young man told ya. I thought you took your orders from the superiors," Ray said with a playful smile.

"Going off script is something I do quite often, Mr McCarthy. I've dealt with people far worse than you. But leading a group of young men to their deaths in this time? Did the south put you up to this? Is that why your absence led to the confederates victory of the red river campaign? Explain yourself, sir!" Biden's voice grew in anger.

"Putting me in the wrong story won't give you closure Colonel-"

"I am the judge, jury and executioner sir, and by my hand, your absence and ability to lead that squadron into death proves you as something other than a unionist. A traitor more like. Now you will give me the answer to why your absence was made, or your accomplices will face the consequences! Stevens!"

Stevens made his way inside the jail to unlock the doors or both Billy and Millie's cells and raised his two pistols at their heads. The two slowly walked out with him behind. Millie was the first to step out, and her eyes immediately met with Ray's. She started to run to him but was stopped dead in her tracks from the Colonel's pistol, blasting the ground in front of her before Stevens gun soon pressed against the back of her head. He moved both Millie and Billy to the side of Biden before he continued.

"Don't think I know, Mr McCarthy. Your activities outside of the military obviously come rooted outside the law of the land. And what a pretty little face to keep it hidden with. Impressionable little lady with hopes of using it without wondering as to how it got there in the first place? Luckily, she is a smart one, didn't even bother to hide it well. Where did you acquire this money?" Biden asked ripping the money out from underneath Millies breast inside her corset.

"It's my savings-"

"Liar! No one in the military could acquire a large sum of personal savings in that service span, regardless of who you are! Now, Mr McCarthy, I'm losing my patience. You will tell me the sins you have done or so help me, I will gun down both of them!" Biden lifted his heavy colt gun to Millie's head, and Ray screamed in defiance. Millie started to cry with fear as the Coronals thumb pulled down the safety lock.

"Alright! I'll tell you what you want to hear." Ray begged. Biden still with his hand tightly grasping the gun, relaxed and awaited his answer.

"Your testimony. In full, Mr McCarthy, if you please." Ray relaxed his shoulders before giving Millie an encouraging look to say everything is going to be alright, even though the tears streaked down her cheeks.

"See the reason for all of this...is I've sworn my soul to the natives whose gods have blessed me with the sacred task of keeping the land clear from the hellish beings that roamed this land way before us. And in doing so, I must be the knight that must put them down or anybody that comes between the natives and me. That money I have, Colonel, is from my years in the army and so be it, if you want me to be the unholy traitor that you have painted in your head for this war then do it. Cause at least I know I have done the real duty to protect all of us who walk this earth! And if you stop me now, welcome doomsday. You won't have no knight to save you from the horrors that lie waiting to strike." The street was silent. Everyone had confusion on their faces, even Millie who gave him a tilted head in response. Biden smiled.

"Fantasy certainly isn't your strong suit, Mr McCarthy."

And without any hesitation Biden lifted his arm holding the gun and fired directly at Ray's throat, jolting him backwards with his eyes rolled back, and his head hit the ground. Millie screamed in terror while Billy looked on in disbelief as to what he just heard and saw.

"Guilty for the books. Sentence: Death" Biden stated while placing his gun into its holster. "Stevens deal with the body. And as for you two, I'm sure we'll make a good deal about whose story gets in the history books. Won't we?" grinned the Colonel who pushed his chest out in overconfidence.

But the cocky nature of the Colonel was short lived, from as soon as he finished speaking, Ray rose up with a huge gasp of air which whistled weirdly through the shrinking hole in his throat. The guards and Stevens jumped back in shock at the sight of a man presumed dead, rising. Millie, Billy and Biden all shared the same expression with their jaws looking like they could be touching the floor. Biden tried to get his words out but kept stuttering in shock. Eventually he found the word he was looking for was "Impossible!" As Ray got to his feet and was eye-to-eye with Biden, the hole in his throat had healed entirely, and the bullet spat out right there on the ground where he had landed.

"That's tricky not to chuckle over," Ray said with a hint of glee. Biden couldn't take any more at seeing the strange sight and fired again this time using the available five bullets that still sat inside his gun barrel. With the power in the gun, it knocked Ray back down to the ground with force with each bullet piercing his chest. The guards had now rushed over with Stevens to Biden's side as he said in a panic:

"Take the girl and the old man over there!" With that order, Biden rushed back inside the police station while the three guards and Stevens ran inside the saloon. Biden slammed the door shut and barricaded it with chairs and the Sheriff's desk before relocating at the back of the station next to the two jail cells. Stevens brought Millie and Billy up the stairs towards the rooms. Steven's ordered his men to retrieve the keys for upstairs, and the men rushed over to the bar counter, knocking over glasses and furniture until the youngest found them. Billy was left in a room on his own while Steven's preyed upon Millies fear even more by staying in the last place with her: Ray's room.

Ray lay outside, regaining his breath as he slowly rose up once again. Each hole in his chest oozed thick red blood while the wounds slowly stitched themselves back together coating it-self in dry blackened blood and skin. Two bullets came squeez-ing out of Ray's chest as the flesh of his body mended itself. A small cut was nothing compared to the adrenaline he was feel-ing right now, his hands were shaking, and he wondered if he could get up quickly the first time, but his legs felt like they were going to buckle as soon as he got his balance. He came to, and after a moment of getting his footing right, he was up, now he had to fight the drunken sensation in his head, as if he suddenly gained an extra five pounds. He rotated his head, and the sensation wore off quickly. Everyone who was in his line of sight was gone, but the cry for help was still in range. As he looked up to the saloon on his left Ray, saw Millie at the win-dow before being thrown back by Steven's. As she was hurled back onto the floor in the bedroom, the second in command broke the window with the butt of his sidearm before rotating it back to point the barrel at Ray. He didn't show any hesitation, and the bullet was fired but Ray ducked in the nick of time and soon rushed himself away from the line of fire before landing just onto the porch area as his foot clipped the top step. On the floor, he brought his head up quickly to see the two other guards by the windows with their rifles drawn ready to shoot through the window. Still, Ray rolled to his left and started to crawl by the porches side, hiding as he made his way around the building to find the side door which he remembered from nights when he returned more drunk than what he felt a moment ago. The door was locked as expected, and Ray reached under the wooden step to find the spare key lodged under the groove. Ray was hesitant at first, placing his ear to the door to see if the two were near, a slight misstep made the floorboards creak, and Ray drew back his head to rest against the wall as the sound came quite close to the door. The two men and Stevens weren't going anywhere at this point. Millie had tried her best to manoeuvre and escape Stevens clutches, but Stevens outmatched her, and he also had a gun. Millie had her hands tied to the coat hanger on the door, the bedsheet wrapped tight around her wrists. Her voice cut off by a pillowcase which had been ripped off, woven around her mouth. Ray from the outside was starting to get his breath back and his mind becanme more focused. He thought about the key and wondered if it could open the third door, which was behind the bar area where Mr Boston worked. He didn't give out keys willy nilly, but was it possible this key was a master key? Ray crouched down and crept around the saloon, making sure he wasn't spotted where the windows were, and he watched his feet just in case the slightest sound could get the guards attention. The guards started to get even more anxious inside, with their rifle ends they smashed the windows and thought the furniture round in frustration as their seemingly undead target was no-where in sight. They cursed in such anger that soon it drew the attention of Stevens to come out from the room with Millie as his prisoner. Ray had come round to the third door and in dis-appointment, saw that the door had even more locks than the second and the key would not unlock even the main lock. He needed a way to get back in, he could hear all three of them shouting inside, calling out his names with imaginative in-sults stitched together to lure him back inside. Then the win-dow above him opened, it was Billy. The two mouthed out a plan to get the guards' attention and Ray soon ran back, crouching again, to the second door. Billy grabbed the decora-tive vase from the end of his room and dropped it down from the window to the floor with a mighty shattering noise, draw-ing the two guards attention to the outside. They both scram-bled to the nearest window to peek outside while Ray unlocked the door. Stevens, however, was still on the upstairs balcony and saw Ray enter, raising his gun again after a small intake of air rushed in from seeing him and fired at Ray but only con-necting with the door. The two guards looked back in fright from the noise and Steven's got a return shot from Ray which grazed his shoulder, which made him stumble back to the wall as he held his wound. The two guards wasted no time and fol-lowed up with retaliation shots from their rifles, one then two and followed with the rest in their clips. Ray was being hit, only in the arms twice and once in the chest but he held on, drawing the strength he could muster to keep on his feet with the pain coming at him but soon fading away. With another rush of adrenaline, he lifted a table from its pedistal leg, turning the flat surface in the direction of the two guards and thrust toward pinning them to wall. The two men's rifles pressed into their chests, metal and wood uncomfortably pushing into them as they tried to free themselves to put down their target. They managed to slide their hands to the round edge of the table and pushed back, Ray falling down as the table spiralled on its single leg before landing on its side. The two men scrambled to get their guns off the floor but Ray wasted little time and threw the first punch, connecting it to the tallest man's jaw sending him down. Ray went for the second man was brought to the floor again from a stiff and quick takedown from the man's stretched out arm connecting with his neck. His hands soon reached for his neck looking to squeeze the life out of Ray but his opponent soon got hold of them and the two soon began to try and out-power the other. Ray got the upper hand by kneeing the second guard in the ribs as he was only kneeling to the side of him, leaving him exposed to any retaliation from the legs. The guard soon fell to the floor clutching his side after Ray dished out three strikes and then soon the first guard came back for him with a flurry of strikes aimed for Ray's head. They were strong but uncoordinated and Ray weaved his head away to his advantage from the guard as he was still rocked from the first punch and was desperate to kill him. Ray took a swing back at him after two unfocused punches came his way, clocking him again on his jaw and another swift jab to the nose, the guard stumbled back and Ray, eager to keep him down, crunched his leg up to his chest and booted the tall guard's knee, sending him down to the floor, Ray brought his foot behind him and soon knocked out the guard with a swift kick to his jaw again with the full blow coming from the tip of his boot. Blood shot from his nose as he slumped to the floor but before Ray could even breathe the smaller of the two leapt onto Ray's back and held him in a chokehold. He wrapped his legs and arms around Ray tightly as Ray shook and swung his body furiously to shake him off while his fingers tried to pry off the guard's grip. It wasn't successful, the only thing to do now for Ray was to throw himself towards the walls, back first, to weaken the guard. He ran up to the wall and then a second time before Ray's legs started to buckle, the grip of the chokehold, getting tighter and tighter, was soon beginning to take Ray's breath away. In a one last ditch to get him off, Ray hurled his body over the bar counter and the two crashed to the floor behind it with glasses smashing around them. Shards of glass were everywhere and that is when desperation kicked in for the guard, as he grabbed the biggest chunk of glass which came from a wine glass and sliced it through the air hoping to catch Ray in the face but it was unsuccessful. Ray jerked back a step further, and again, as the guard still with the intent of letting the glass come right across his neck didn't show any signs of stopping. Ray had to fight fire with fire and reached for the empty beer bottle beside him, cracking it across the counter the sharp edges now pointing towards the guard and the two were standing in fencing positions waiting for someone to strike first. Ray threw a fake swing, and the guard took the bait bringing his shard of broken bottle downwards, hoping it would slice Ray's kneecap, but it was far off, and Ray poked the glass at the guard's shoulder making him back off. The guard let out grunt of pain and came back swinging some more, more furious slashes came but were again unsuccessful; connectingwith air instead of flesh. As the last slash came, the guard struck his hand on the counter and Ray soon took his boot up to chest level and kicked back the guard to the floor. He tried to scramble away, but Ray hoping to keep him down, picked up the guards leg by the ankle and with his leg in a bent position, brought his leg back down hard to the floor with his knee taking the full shock on the way down. The guard clutched his knee in pain but in no time Ray was by his side and without hesitation, kicked the guard straight in the face knocking him out cold as more glasses fell from the cabinet. It was now silent for a moment, no noise from downstairs or upstairs. Ray looked around and slowly crept around the bar, trying to see if anyone had made it outside through the windows. His attention was then brought upstairs with the rooms. Still in a quiet motion he came up the stairs to find Stevens who was the last of Biden's men inside the saloon. Unsure with the quiet ambiance, Stevens came from the last door on the right and Ray dropped behind the stair rail, as quickly as he could. Stevens peered over the balcony to see the remains of a bloody fight, broken glass, smashed furniture but unable to see bodies. He called to the two men to no avail. As he checked, Ray had crawled slowly up the rest of the stairs making sure his body would not be seen over the railings. He heard Stevens come his way and like a spider ready to pounce on a fly caught in his trap sprung up in Stevens face with his hands gripping the rifle and the two began to fight for possesion of the firearm. The two gritted their teeth and flared their nostrils at one another with their eyes staring into each other, both focused on coming out on top. Back and forth they pushed one another, Ray now with his back pressed against the balcony and it soon began to arch more as Stevens raised the rifle's body, inching it closer to Ray's neck. Ray could see it coming closer, and the edge of the balcony where he would fall and in a quick spurt moved the rifle to his side, pulling Stevens to him while delivering a cracking headbutt to the second-in- command. With Stevens stunned, Ray heaved Stevens over his shoulders and back bodied him over the balcony onto one of the tables below, the wood breaking with splinters flying across the bar floor.

The trouble was over, and Ray headed into the room from which he had seen Stevens exit, and saw a gagged Millie tied to the door hanger. Untying her and ripping off the pillowcase, the two embraced each other, before Millie dished out a fat slap across Ray's face.

"Is that a thank you?" Ray said.

"It's not until you've told me everything."

"Nice to know, come on," Ray said in a rush as he left the room with Millie following downstairs. The two came to the second room where Billy had been placed, but the door would not budge, it was locked.

"Stay back Billy, I'm gonna try and kick it!" Ray said from the other side of the wooden frame. Billy backed away when he heard it. Ray gave the door a quick kick at first, nothing, he tried harder with a run-up, nothing, these doors were sturdy.

"Tall guys got the key, Ray. The son of a bitch must have it in his pocket!" Billy shouted.

"Of course," Ray said, slumping his shoulders, bringing his focus back on to Stevens who was still limp and lifeless on the floor below. Millie waited on the upstairs balcony while Ray went down the stairs with a sprint, coming to the side of Stevens he checked to see if he was still out, he was. The key from his inside coat pocket was found and Ray again with a sprint, ran back up the stairs to Millie's side at the locked bedroom door. The key turned then clicked, and it was pushed open and both sets of eyes from outside of the room caught sight of Billy, but there was something wrong, Billy was clutching his chest, his hand over his heart. Billy acted as if nothing was wrong, to hide his pain, but Ray was soon by his side to help him walk and with Millie on his other side, the three made their way out of the saloon. Ray and Millie sat Billy on the step just as they got outside, Millie sat by his side clutching his hand in support and wiping the sweat off of Billy's forehead. Ray, who was standing, turned his head towards the Sheriff's department and drew an angered expression as he made his way over to face the Colonel. He hid away in the corner, twiddling away at the left side of his bushy white moustache before the door began to be kicked in. The furniture blocking the door shifted slightly as Ray kicked harder and harder and Biden began to fear more for his life. Soon the furniture moved over just enough for Ray to slither in through the door and his footsteps could be heard on the wood floor. Ray came face to face with Biden with the bars of the cell keeping the two apart from each other.

"Your men hurt my girl and my boss. Holding an entire town hostage is not the way to go about things Colonel."

Biden, still with his eyes open wide, couldn't believe the man he shot was still walking and talking to him, as if nothing happened.

"I shot you."

"Then your business is done here isn't it? Mine's not," Ray pulled his gun from its holster and shot at the lock with the one bullet left in his six-chamber pistol. The lock broke off, and the barred door moved all the way back from the force. Biden was now more scared than ever, like a child he kicked and pushed himself to the wall as close as he could as Ray took a few steps into the cell. Ray did nothing but stare as the Colonel still uttered the same sentence to him, twice more.

"I shot you. I shot you!"

Ray couldn't hold back a smile now. The power and adrenaline were getting to him, and he couldn't waste a moment of this.

"Oh, you did. But that just doesn't work for me anymore." Ray had let the Colonel's cries of terror get to him, and in the last moments of their encounter, Ray burned an image into the old man's mind that he'd never forget. Ray gripping his knife in a quick motion cut off the middle finger of his left hand, the blood shooting out and the finger landing on the floor pointing in the direction of Biden. With not a care in the world, Ray picked up and held his finger in between two others and slit the tip deep underneath the cut off finger. With the stroke of a match, Ray hovered the small flame over the base of the finger which it had been severed from his hand and proceeded, with a deep breath, to smoke his own finger in front of the Colonel, puffing away at his flesh like it was the sweetest cigarette he had ever had. The mix of healthy muscle with the contaminated blood, made Ray puff out dark purple clouds of smoke and the air in the cell began to smell like a outdoor hog roast but poorly done. Ray raised his eyebrows comically, giving off an impression that the taste of it was a pleasure to his senses but really a facade at how terrible it was. The smoke lingered, and the Colonel was breathing so fast he took it all in through his nose. It was foul, Biden couldn't take anymore and soon fainted at the sight of it all his shoulders slumped down the ground while his head was pushed up uncomfortably.

Ray could now drop the charade and began to cough and splutter from what he had just done. It spooked him even more as he soon discovered what his body could do now. The slit at the end of his finger rapidly healed, the base of the finger held in place, and strands of skin knitted together and with a click of the bone it was fixed. A moment of wiggling the finger back to normal and Ray closed the cell door again before returning to Millie and Billy. Billy had been sweating more and more as his eyes continued to squint. His breathing was shallow, and Millie and Ray had no idea what had happened to him to make him be like this. Millie had found no blood or bullet holes on him anywhere, but Ray knew it was something much more straightforward to figure out, Billy's heart was going. Ray came close to his side, clenching his hand firmly in his and kept on calling the old man's name before Billy's head lifted from his shoulder and he faced Ray. Billy tried to speak, but it was hard to make out, it was much slower and croakier than ever.

"Kid...Wh-what...did you...do?"

"Nothing Billy, I promise. You stay with me now you hear," Ray replied.

"Cut the crap...what-what did...you do?"

Ray found it hard, to tell the truth, he was with both his lover and his friend/boss who were both itching to know what he had done and why he had lied about. Billy had given him a job and befriended him he couldn't bear to see the old man suffer in silence. Finally, he spoke.

"I'm a deserter. I lead a group of boys to their deaths and I fled here. I was just going to pass you two by like it was nothing but...you took me in for who I am-"

"You sure about that?" Millie interrupted. Ray hung his head for a second and then continued with his head up again.

"I may not have been so open as I am now, but, I did it only to protect you both. To protect this town. That's what I thought anyway." Millie shed a slight smile about his honesty. Billy started to try and talk again, but it would sadly be his last sentence.
"You're...a good man, Ray...but...how...are you...not...dea-" Billy let out his last breath, and his eyes were now relaxed closing shut as his head fell back onto his shoulder. Millie laid her

head on his shoulder with tears down her face. Ray still holding tight to Billy's hand released his grip as the old man's hand started to slip through his fingers. He hugged the old man tight in his arms as a single tear rolled down his cheek.

"I'm sorry to hear how your employer passed. From his bio, it said he was buried that day. I assume you had the service that night?" Roosevelt asked.

"We did. Billy was buried under the barn house. Everyone was there for him."

The service for Billy Grove was held outside the barn house with Billy being lowered into the ground beneath it as the pastor said the Lord's prayer. The town still in shock after what had happened that morning was emotional for the next few days with Mr Bentley's funeral being held the day after. That night after the service, Ray took Millie to his old room in Mr Boston's saloon to tell her everything. She, like anyone else, would think it was just a joke, another reason for her to question Ray's credibility but as Ray carried on Millie saw the seriousness in his eyes. Millie had seen him rise again from a bullet when displaying what his body could do Millie soon began to believe him.

"So where did the Indians say you have to go to find these guys?" she asked.

"West. In parts unknown. I just gotta find them before they bring worse things around here."

"So that means you gotta leave me again." Millie said quietly like she didn't want him to hear it. Ray looked back at her when she mumbled those last words and didn't want to give her the obvious answer, but he did.

"I have to. Like the first time, maybe it's for the best. I don't want you getting caught up in this like today. What happened to Billy was my-"

"Don't you dare say it was your fault. It was those men, those so-called upstanding protectors of the union that did all this. The towns in mourning. We just gotta move on, like you have to do."

"But I don't want to forget you."

"With what you've told me it seems best if you do."

Ray hated hearing those words, but he knew she was right. It could take him months to get this mission from the elders done. He had to be focused, but mostly Millie wanted him to be strong.

"You're right," Ray said. Upon finishing that sentence, Ray found the courage and gave Millie the softest of kisses on the lips. It was brief yet sweet. Millie knew the sentiment, but before she could say anything, Ray had got up from the bedside and walked downstairs. She didn't follow him, it would only conflict him more, he had let out his emotions with that one gentle kiss that's all that was needed. Now Millie had to live up to her own advice while Ray took the long journey ahead of him. Millie could hear the jostling of the horse reins, the rucksack put over the horses back and then the first steps of the horse as it trotted away from the saloon. Ray had left Bonebag again this time he was gone for way longer than before. All Millie did was hold back the tears as she sat slouched shoulders forward watching Ray ride off into the distance until all she saw was the horse's shoe prints in the dirt road.

"How long was it before you saw her again?" Roosevelt asked.

"I didn't." Ray answered.

◆ ◆ ◆

Millie came back outside as the lanterns were beginning to be lit for the night. She looked down the road to see a quarter of the townspeople still chatting amongst themselves from the reception of Billy Groves funeral down at the barn. Millie could see her brother, bandaged from earlier but always in high spirits as he saw her approaching.

"How are you feeling big brother?"

"Doing fine. They did good service for Mr Groves. What about you?"

"I'm alright," she lied.

"What do you think they'll do with that guy with the moustache?" Thomas asked.

"Don't know. But I hope I get to help out."

Roosevelt leaned back in his chair. He breathed in and out loudly through his nose before he sat back forward with his hands together.

"Do you know what became of Colonel Biden?" he asked. Ray was vacant, it never crossed his mind.

"No idea, sir. For all, I know the people at Bonebag tore him limb from limb for what he did. Maybe he died in the prison cell I don't know."

"But surely you went back there and asked about him once the mission was done?"

"They didn't want to bring him up, or me for that matter. They may have taken him out back like the old dog he was and then..." Ray left it to the President's imagination.

He didn't change his expression with the thought as the President looked out to the window to see the night had settled in. Time flying fast with these stories.

"I think we'll continue this talk tomorrow Mr McCarthy, good that you remember well, more than what I can with a pen and paper. If you go out the door you came in, I took the liberty of making up one of the spare rooms. Do hope you enjoy it."

"Thank you, Mr President."

"Please, call me Teddy," Roosevelt said, extending his hand. Ray looked down at the extended hand of the President but did not return the favour.

"With all due respect, Mr President, I'll shake your hand when I finish the whole story."

"I understand. Good night, Mr McCarthy."

"Call me, Ray."

V.

The next morning was a relaxing wake-up call for Ray. He woke up to clean white walls around him with a more-than sturdy roof over his head, not worrying about any cost. The sheets were straightened up nice by the maids, and the window had been opened. Ray squinted, his eyes still could just make out the shape of the maid, leaving something on his bedside counter; it was breakfast for him. He could smell the bacon, cooked for six minutes with two pieces of toast on the side with eggs on the other side. Coffee was put next to it on the coaster. The maid said for him to enjoy, he was still coming too, and the blurred shape of the maid became a bit clearer, but he couldn't make out the face. By the time he expressed his gratitude, the door had closed, and he was on his own again.

"You butter me up too much like this bread, Mr President," Ray said to himself.

An hour later, Ray was up and walked out of his room in the White House. The hallways were quiet again just like yesterday when he stepped foot into the front door. Ray was unsure, should he walk back the President's room or wait until he was collected by a member of staff, so he stood with his back against the wall looking up at the ceiling. It was tranquil, Ray thought if he called out for someone, it would echo throughout all the hallways in the house. Soon though in the distance, he heard footsteps coming closer to him. It wasn't Roosevelt, he was dressed accordingly like the President but it was not him. Mearly another member of his faculty.

"Morning Mr McCarthy. Sleep well?"

"Very, ugh, please do say thank you for breakfast."

"I will do so, sir. Ready to continue?" the man asked.

"I am."

"Walk this way with me." The man said, lifting his arm in the direction they would be heading. It was away from the President's desk. The guide explained the reason.

"Mr McCarthy, I'm afraid the President had to be called away today, something to do with the railroads, he told me. But in the meantime, he asked me to bring you downstairs. There is someone else who will continue the pardoning process with you."

"And who exactly is that?"

"Best not say until we get there sir."
Ray understood the job of the President, and when sudden events occur, it can lead the man out from the desk, but he had just become accustomed to the President's ability to listen in full. He would have to repeat the trust process again he thought and this made him slump his shoulders back. The two men soon came to a bookshelf, a small bookshelf standing in the middle of the hallway.

"Are we waiting for the said person?"

"No. Just security," the guide said.
Men with guns, an excellent start to the morning. The guards this time were in suits, ironed pressed without a single crease, both came with a gun in hand. They stood together and looked Ray up and down before one of them asked if he had any weapons on him.

"No need Mr Edwards, Mr McCarthy's holster and weapons were taken as he became acquainted with his sleeping quarters last night. President's orders."

The guards straightened up again, and the guide then pulled one of the books from the shelf stood next to the four men. The bookshelf then clicked, once from the bottom, the middle and then the top. It then moved to its left, books now becoming hidden behind a patch of the wall which lead to a staircase lit by small lights that didn't have the decorative glass shades that presided over most of the lighting in the house. It was crude, and the wires were taped to the wall, leading down the staircase.

"You first," said Ray. The guide took the first step, and Ray then followed, then the guards but only one came down the stairs, the other was the one who pushed a button and guarded the bookshelf door which slid back into place as if nothing had happened. Down the staircase, the headspace soon made the menlean forward to avoid grazing their heads on the exposed brick. It seemed to go on for a long time round and round once, then twice, then three times until that number was tripled. Soon the guide stopped, and Ray nearly pushed him it was so abrupt. They stopped at a familiar setting, another bookshelf with the similar book being pulled just slightly until the sides of the shelf began to click again, and it slid to one side. When it opened, Ray felt rage building up inside him as the first thing he saw as the bookshelf moved to one side, was that of a man sitting behind a desk. The man was old, but his face struck a chord. The same eyes, the worried look on his face even though he was calm and the familiar uniform which was pressed neatly sitting at the desk. It was the young man that Ray had told to lie to Colonel Biden, forty years older. As soon as the image of the man clicked in his brain, Ray pushed past the guide and tensed himself, ready to flip the table, but the security guard latched his arms around him holding him back. The man looked terrified as he saw Ray coming towards him as he leapt out of his chair, backing away from the table as Ray struggled to break free from the security guards grip.

"Mr McCarthy! Please refrain from hurting the individual across the table-"

"That snivelling little shit is the reason that people got hurt!" The man looked back to the guide for answers, as he was unable to speak.

"Do not worry, Mr Dunn, do not worry. Mr McCarthy, as you remember is here to reconcile with you."
Ray stopped struggling in the security guard's arms.

"You want me to break bread with this guy?!" Ray angered by such a proposal.

"Mr McCarthy, the President, has made it quite clear to me that today you would continue your talks of the past, but he also said for me to patch up loose ends."

Ray looked confused yet still angered. What was the purpose of this? What would this help to accomplish? Ray was now free from the tight security guards grip and slowly stepped toward to the table in the middle of the room, placing his hands down on the chair head to lean forward casting his eyes onto Mr Dunn's. He was anxious to step forward, but the guide assured him that everything would be fine with a simple gesture of his hands. Mr Dunn stepped forward, more slowly than Ray and sat down in the chair, closing his legs and hands together, making himself very isolated from everyone else. The guide stood to the side of the table, his arms crossed behind his back, placing an envelope in the middle of the table where two men occupied either side.

"Gentlemen, the President, Theodore Roosevelt, has instructed me that the two of you, after a verbal exchange, to sign this when you are done." The guide slid the paper out of the envelope and placed it back down on the table with the text being presented first to Mr Dunn and then Mr McCarthy.

"Both signatures are required. This document will be confidential as soon as the pen ink meets the paper. I hope you two have read it through accordingly?"

'Confidentiality agreement. Full information disclosure.'

"Haven't we just?" Ray said with his attention still on Mr Dunn with him keeping his head down to avoid eye contact.

"Can we just sign this and I can go?" Dunn whimpered out.

"Not until you open your mouth and tell me what you did all those years ago."

"What else could've I done?! Stayed silent and eventually be brought to the court myself for the deaths? Did you not think that I would've had what you had done to you had I not spoken?"

"I guess you would have. You were obedient but not a snake." Ray said.

"You look like you'd be happier, either way, Mr McCarthy," the guide said becoming part of the conversation.

"Anyone who had been involved in hurting my friends I swore to find a way of getting back at them. I lost friends that day you selfish asshole! Yeah, I'm angry with you, and I just want you gone after this." Ray had said enough, swiping the paper over to his side he quickly signed one of the lines and pushed the paper to Mr Dunn, with the pen nearly rolling off the table.

"Just answer me this though. Rumour went round you were dead. And yet you turn up hear looking like you haven't aged since the day I last saw you near that hell hole I fought in. How are you still alive?"

"Like we said, Mr Dunn. Confidential."

As Mr Dunn looked back at the paper, he caught the last line before the signature line. It read 'participants both accept the detailing of events inscribed here and are willing to keep each other's persons protected from any harm to each other.'

Mr Dunn felt that something could be done should he say anything. He knew something was up, but he was sitting under the most important place in the country and knew the consequences should he go against anything written down today. He simply sighed and jotted his signature down.

"Thank you, gentlemen. The President will be pleased to know that this transpired. Mr McCarthy, you will leave first and return to your quarters until the President returns. Mr Dunn, you will be escorted out once the doors have reopened." The two men both looked at each other one last time, both giving each other a look of disdain.

Ray pushed back and got up from his seat, leaving with the security guard behind him while the guide stood with Mr Dunn. The bookshelf slid open again, and Ray went up the stairs back to his given room. Ray McCarthy never thought he'd meet that man who had ratted him out for what he had done on the battlefield them years ago, and it was now signed in writing that he wouldn't see him again. The guide made sure that Mr Dunn was escorted away, but it was never specified to him, how he would leave.

VI.

Six hours passed since the meeting, and Ray was still itching to speak his mind to Roosevelt. Telling your side of the story was one thing, and Ray knew he had been honest about everything he talked about, but for a moment down in the secret room, Ray couldn't handle a second outlook on the story. His word was being used by the administration right down to the smallest detail. Would this mean that there could be more voices to be heard? Ray was unsure of what lay ahead in the future when his story came to an end. All he could do at the moment was sit on the edge of his bed and think through different questions and scenarios. It was later near the evening hours in which he heard voices outside his room. A party of men collectively asking questions to a single man, it was President Roosevelt. Ray rose from his chair ready to stand and talk with the President until he heard the man's voice raise in volume outside from his bedroom door, silencing the different men surrounding him. Ray was just about to open the door when it happened and instead put his ear to the door, listening in wouldn't be a problem though as Roosevelt stood right by his door with his voice level still loud and defiant.

"Look, as much as you all collectively voice your concerns on the matter, I will not break! That man seems to think that an overwhelming number of people's voices are going to be un-heard under my rule but that will not be tolerated. I will not change my mind on the matter gentlemen, and I will continue to oversee the events with Mr Morgan in no time. Now a good evening to you all, I'll be in my quarters if anyone needs me with more pressing matters."

"Sir, what about Mr McCarthy?" piped up one man from the back of the group. Theodore turned his head back to cast his eyes, protected by his small pince-ze glasses sat on the bridge of his nose on the bedroom door.

"Leave Mr McCarthy to continue his pardoning process tomor-row. He has already put up with a lot today."

With Roosevelt heard, Ray went back to his desk chair and the group of men who followed the President slowly disbanded. Ray reclined back thinking of what the outcome of his future would be if he continued this process. It looked encouraging at first, the thought of not being hunted down, moving from state to state to avoid anyone looking for an incredible bounty to claim from his head. But all the encouraging words of free-dom seemed far fetched now as the talks seemed to be more personally applied to scripts and signature waivers. Maybe this was leading him into something else, more work in Ray's mind. Ray decided to drift off for the night, laying his head back down onto the bed pillows to rest and leaving his memory to trail back to other times that may be asked about.

The day went accordingly: Eight O'clock rise with breakfast. Nine o'clock till one thirty pm, pardoning procedures. Hour break, then return to the President for the rest of pardoning procedures till Six O'clock. Ray didn't really keep to schedules this much since his time in the military. It was like work for a holiday that might not even be given to him. The President sat at his desk, as usual, writing away with a cup of tea by his left hand, he had already been up two hours before Ray's body even thought about it. The most powerful man in the country never looked tired or stressed, and he had only been in this position for a few months. Ray entered, with questions and memories in his mind. He pulled the chair back to sit and gave the President with a stern look.

"How and why did you get him yesterday?"
Theodore wasted no time with an answer.

"Everything has to be submitted in writing Mr McCarthy. Everything. My administration will waste very little time in seeing that everything is as exactly how you put it to me."

"Why didn't you tell me?"

"To see how you would react. You stuck by what you told me two days ago even in the presence of someone who ultimately brought you displeasure was right in front of you yesterday. With the two of you both submitting your signatures, I can fully advise the government officials in my administration that everything you have told me so far is true. And as the waiver said, the two of you will go your seperate ways for good. Mr Dunn will be of no more concern to you," the President promised.

"You got any more people in line for me then?"

"Not at this moment in time but if you wish to carry on from where you left off, it wouldn't be off the table," Roosevelt reassured him.
Ray trailed back to the first few minutes after leaving Millie in Bonebag for the second time.

"I rode all night, didn't stop. I carried on west of there."

The early morning sun was just beginning to rise as Ray's horse slowed to a stop. He and his steed were once again in wilderness and away from conventional roads. As the horse rested, laying on the ground, Ray jumped off and leaned himself against the side of the steed. Reaching into his rucksack, he found a can of beans, ripping the already pre-cut lid off and chugged them back like it was a beer. Some beans spilt over the corners of his mouth while he ate, any that fell off on him he offered to the horse. The two lied there perking themselves up for the ride to continue for about ten minutes, Ray finishing the beans in three. They carried on through the woods of Mississippi until they entered Kansas, still along the southern side of the state and it was vast but with green and not desert.

Coming onto a track which showed both the paths of north and south, Ray stopped the horse in the middle of the road looking back at these two paths and straight ahead of him continuing west. It only struck him just then that he had no lead to find these two targets set by the elders other than a simple direction. One west, one south. Ray frustrated dismounted and rested his hands on his hips. He mumbled to himself about what he had gotten himself into before kicking the dirt beneath him. The ground was dry, and the dust lifted up with his boot. He turned his head again looking around in all directions, suddenly, his eyes went back to the point in the ground where he had kicked as dirt somehow hit his back. He slowly turned the dip in the field and brought his head closer to it with his hand lifted just in front of his face in case of something unexpected. Ray saw something rustle underneath and in a second the dirt flew up to his face with his hand covering his eyes, something was coughing and spitting from rising from the ground, and as Ray brought his hand down from his eyes, he could see clearly, a face in the ground. It was Chief Maluk. His usual red face had dirt coated all over, even over his eyelids which dried in his wrinkles.

"Ray! I knew I hadn't lost it!" he chuckled.

"How the hell are you in the ground?"

"Nice trick. It helps my people communicate over long distances. I felt that you were confused so allow me to explain."

"You didn't really do that before I left."

"I thought you would return to my ground. But I can tell, you have felt lost these past few days and I am deeply sorry."

"It's fine. My mind is everywhere at the moment, but that doesn't mean I won't stop with what you've sent me to do."

"You are strong Ray, and you will grow even stronger from this. The vial will make you live forever as long as your spirit remains strong. Experience can better you, and so will this." As Ray felt relaxed from the Chief's kind words, his large hand grabbed Ray by the scruff of his neck and dragged his body through the ground to emerge in the Chief's teepee again. Ray did not feel the impact of the land nor the dirt which piled all around him as he passed through places. He was stunned, as he took in his surroundings.

"You may need to take slower breaths. This is similar to how someone dies for a minute and then returns to normal," the Chief explained as Ray's breathing was fast, lifting his chest up and down.

"That was-that was unbelievable. I don't...feel like myself," he stammered.

"You won't. Not on the first go at least. You will soon feel nothing once you have done it a couple of times. This a simple but effective method of travelling from one place to another, this is how the elders communicate to those long and far away, the earth is vast, and we can use it to our advantage."

"So if ever I need you or anyone, I just stick my head in the ground like an armadillo?"

"Precisely. But only the earth," the Chief confirmed.

"Any more things I should know about?"

"There is but, I think you need more time out so-" as the Chief neared the end of his sentence he opened his hand and pushed Ray backwards sending him back through the ground which he could see whizzing past him with all the bugs and roots of the wildlife moving in time. Ray regained his body with a sharp intake of breath as his body which was still teetering forward, but with the sudden rush, he was thrown back again on the ground, his head rocking back as he landed. He sat back up and just could see the chiefs face poke through still but at an angle were his square chin was only moving.

"Remember Ray, these techniques are found through those who are willing to see further. They will come to you the more you believe. And remember, keep west." As Maluk finished, his face sunk back down through the ground and the earth returned to the way it was before. Ray brought himself back up but was taken back again as he soon realized where he was; a different place to the one he had left. His horse stood in the exact location he had been before he was pulled away from Chief Maluk and the road looked like a carbon copy of the one he had been on before. The day had not changed nor had the weather he had simply moved a lot further away from Kentucky than he possibly thought he could. He didn't know exactly where he was, but it was most definitely somewhere far west of the country. As he looked, he saw the environment around him, desert and lots of open ground with mountains in the background. The ground was more sandy and rocky with tiny little patches of grass which tried to penetrate through the dry surface. If Ray carried on west like the Chief said it would lead him around the mountains. Just as he turned around, he could see his horse was a little distressed, lifting its hooves and beginning to trot backwards slightly. Ray comforted the horse with his hand on either side of the horse's nose, keeping his vision locked onto him, but he turned his head in the direction the horse had looked originally. At first he saw nothing but then he noticed something. Something quite big. The sun made Ray squint, and therefore he couldn't see the thing properly as it was simply a silhouette, stood with its back arched. Whatever it was, it let out a sad sounding grunting noise which was loud and then quietly faded. It let out another, sharper bird-like screech, as if it was in pain. The things head was hanging low, dangling down its arched back as though its-neck was broken as it swung slowly side to side, knocking the bones on its back. It continued to cry out, and Ray became more reluctant to move in closer to get a better view, but this was the problem, the creature was west of him. No other way around the creature without getting spotted in the empty setting where they stood. Making the decision while biting his lip, Ray got back onto his horse, ready to think his way around the creature. It would have to be fast and decisive should he want to make it to the other side in one piece. He focused some more, thought about it again as the creature let out another sharp call and then making the decision, Ray kicked the horse's side to begin a slow build-up to a sprint. The horse then picked up the pace and was soon in a racing sprint to head around the creature. Whatever it was, got closer and closer until its neck ascended upwards lugging its head over its shoulders. Ray could see the creature better, and as its head was being lifted slowly, he could see the thing's scales fall from its neck like leaves off an oak tree. Ray could hear the creaking of the creature moving, it was slow, and at any moment, the creature could swing his hands across the ground and crush Ray and his horse into dust. Its legs were like stumps with its body rolling over each other with multiple folds and scaly flab, it didn't look like it could catch up to them if it tried. The creature got closer, and the true size of the beast was frightening, taller than any building Ray had ever stepped and bigger than the tallest tree he had ever gazed up at, the ground rumbled, and the stumps for legs on the creature turned in Ray's direction. The head, unlike the body, was thin and showed the outline of the creature's skull, it had huge pale white eyes with a single black dot for a pupil, but they were so sunken in that there was an ugly looking bright red ring around them both. The nose began to flare, and its crooked and mangled teeth stuck out awkwardly from its bottom jaw, they were long enough to even go through its nostrils slightly. The small little black dot had Ray paralysed and took position for an attack on its oncoming pray. Ray knew the beast was looking to lunge at him and kicked the horse into overdrive, making him sprint as fast as he could. The creature saw the opportunity and positioned itself to strike, cocking its head back and whipped it. Round its shoulders and threw his head across the ground instead, using its long arms to steady itself. Ray saw the creature's head circling around, grinding its chin across the dessert ground and in a moment's noticed halted his horse with a hard and sudden pull of the reins. The horse pushed his hooves down hard until the desert ground pushed over its feet and creatures head just brushed across them, only a few inches away from contacting them. After a gust of wind and sand came their way from the force of the creature, Ray kicked the horse's side again, and the two were soon sprinting through the archway of the creatures wide spread legs. It roared furiously as it didn't capture its dinner and the huge head of the creature tilted awkwardly to find its prey running away behind him. Angered, the creature turned itself around to face in the direction of Ray and his horse, its feet stomping down with a massive thud that rocked the ground. Ray could see the gap upfront, an entranceway into the mountains, which would take him towards his destination. It looked long, narrow and dark. No use looking towards the light anymore, he thought as he again with a kick of his heel made the horse sprint faster with the steed letting out another distinct call. The beast behind Rays back began to move forward slowly as his behemoth legs scraped up the ground beneath its toes. The power in its size was so massive, Ray could feel the dirt hit the back of his neck, even though it was nearly a mile away, the creature loomed over Ray and his horse, looking as if five steps would be all it had to take before his jaws could edge closer to eating its little snack. It was now on its third step, and Ray looked back to see if he could outrun the demonic beast which stood nearly fifty foot tall, although at any moment, the creature looked ready to extend its almost broken neck forward and bite, but Ray was almost there. He could see the darkness inside the tall opening in the mountain and was rushing towards it. The creature brought its foot down with another big thud on the ground again as it screeched with its jaw brought down, so its massive crooked teeth were on full display. The horse ran with all the speed it could muster, and soon Ray and the horse were now inside the opening with the only light to see, coming from behind them. The creature swung its head forward with its neck stretching, dragging its body along as its jaw scraped again along the ground towards the mountainside gap. Its head hit the narrow gap hard as it cracked and rumbled behind Ray who now had no light guiding him or the horse, but the two kept on straight, still sprinting through the mountain's dark inside until they could see absolutely nothing. The sound of the horse's hooves sped down till it brought the two to a stop. Darkness was everywhere, and its silence was deafening. The sound of the horse's hooves echoed in the natural hall inside the mountain along with tiny stones falling from its giant uneven walls. After the chase had come to a stop a minute ago, Ray was just lucky to get his breath back from the shock of nearly being a thing from another world's breakfast. The horse was also relieved to be catching its breath. As the initial shock wore off and the two became more relaxed, Ray's mind quickly began to think of what lied ahead. Although it was very claustrophobic inside the mountain, continuing forward would lead Ray forward in his search for Goida. The two soon continued on but rather slowly.

Darkness encompassed Ray and his horse for what had already been ten minutes, but the fear of being jumped by something soon or maybe being buried alive by falling debris was present. Ray noticed that the ground beneath the horse's feet had not changed at all during the time that they had walked from the opening passageway. It was still flat, no feeling of the ground moving up or down with each footstep forward. It felt bizarre like it had almost been paved by humans. The notion seemed almost certain as Ray heard a noise coming from the front of him, it was quite far ahead and sounded like a whispered word. It wasn't English from what he could make out. He thought of holding the horseback but continued anyway. Seeing a human again that wasn't an apparition or a creature was welcome now. Sure enough, he heard it again this time from his left but way up high above his head. This trail he and the horse he was walking on wasn't the only one. Soon enough orange balls of light lit up around him, highlighting the mountain gateway into something more than what it was. There were more walkways, to Ray's side and above curling and weaving through the structure of the mountain. It was a connected system of pathways that looked like it would span deeper into the heart of the mountain. Whoever was holding the flames never spoke another word again. Only the tops of their heads were shown with the deep circles from their eyes being illuminated. There appeared to be hundreds of whatever they were, and they all followed Ray through their pathways. Ray kept a cool head and appreciated the light but then what drew him to a stop again was by everything else stopping in unison. Ray turned his head side to side, slowly looking at them all, all their eyes were on him. He didn't reach for the gun as he thought he might startle them should they not be harmful and lose his light. He almost drew the gun close as one of the hidden few threw its flamed stick just in front of Ray's horse, startling him slightly. It did not land on the ground, instead, in the hand of one that had been in front of him without Ray knowing. It brought the flame down slowly to its face and while thankfully it appeared human, there was a slight difference which made Ray move in closer for a better look. It was a woman, smooth skinned looking immaculate like her skin had not been bruised by a single thing inside of here, but her face looked wrong still. The eyes were bigger, the nose smaller, and she had no lips around her mouth. Ray noticed, as she tilted her head up, it pulled open her mouth, and he didn't know if it was because of the light, but she appeared to have no teeth at all, nor even gums for that matter. The woman let out a noise from her mouth as she blinked almost sounding like a small bird chirping in the morning. Ray showed his confusion. "I'm looking for someone. Does this lead through somewhere?" he asked. She politely moved her head in the direction he was heading before looking back and making the same noise again with a blink of both her eyes. Ray simply nodded, and the woman brought herself forward to lead the way. Ray followed her and noticed that the rest of the group of people remained there, staying to the mountain walls. His head turned back around, and the light from behind soon vanished, leaving one sole ball of flame in front of him, leading the way. They carried along the flat path butcracks began to show and soon the smooth rock floor had chunks of it missing with gaps appearing. It was still strong and sturdy as the rock formation was rooted deep down into the ground below. The woman in front kept her distance before she walked a little bit faster in front, leaving Ray wondering if he'd be left in the dark again. Still, in actuality, they had reached the end of the path and a tall wall with engravings carved into the rock about a few centimetres deep towered over the two. The woman turned her head back toward Ray, letting out another little chirp of noise before raising the torch in front of her; she was asking him to take it. Ray dismounted and placed his hand on the torch above the young woman's hand who did not release her grip. She walked him over to the mountain wall, and in tilting the torch towards a centrepiece that looked like the torch, the head would fit perfectly into it like a jigsaw piece. Once angled right, the torch head slipped inside, dowsing the flame and the darkness washed over the two once again. Ray still hung onto the torch handle moving his other hand in to feel if the woman's hand was still there. When he felt it, he sighed with relief just before the circle lit up bright above them. The fire soon followed through the engravings lighting up every little piece on the wall above. The heat rose as the orange glow soon laid out the engravings, a huge canvas of fire -woven lettering and symbols with connecting patterns almost blinded Ray but the woman stared on as she was impervious to its blinding light. The fire continued, growing and it shot through all across the mountain walls lighting up the pathways and every dark crevasse. Ray could now see how many walkways and entrances there were inside of the mountain, bigger than he could have imagined and possibly more of whoever the woman creature beside him was. His jaw hung down slightly at the beautifully hidden city as he spun around, catching sight of the fire speed through the engravings. The fire was controlled chaos, never spiralling out from the engravings nor catching ablaze on anything beside it. The inside of the mountain cave was now lit, and the woman turned to show

Ray the pathway on his left with the torch, showing a smaller entranceway that Ray as though like he would bump his head upon entry if he didn't take his hat off. It would mean that his steed would have to remain here. The woman showed no other way, but the passage on her left and Ray gave a small goodbye with a rub on the horse's nose before taking his hat off to walk inside. He turned back to the woman and said "Does this lead outside?" The woman simply tilted her head again in the direction. Ray would have to trust his gut instincts hoping that this would lead him back outside and not be a walkway to his death even if he didn't quite understand how far his newly given powers would take him. A slither of the flame light trail ran through the small trail on Ray's left, the side of his body glowing a light shade of orange as did it with the pathway. Ray pressed on with his head slightly lowered, but as he carried on, he noticed that his neck and back were becoming more hunched. It soon became too much for his neck, becoming uncomfortable and Ray was crouching as he walked, feeling the pressure come to his knee caps. His back was straight again, but the cave only got smaller as he carried on forcing him to go lower until Ray was in a full crouch position. It made his movements slower, and his walk through longer but the cave still carried on getting smaller and smaller. At this point, Ray was no longer crouching but lying on the floor, crawling on his hands and knees. The crawl then later became a full-on body lying flat crawl with Ray remembering his training in the military all over again. It was a slog to get through. At this point, Ray was unsure if he was going to see the light from the outside or a dead end with something behind him following him to eventually finishing him off. He crawled for what seemed like ages looking back occasionally to see the way he'd come from but he could not. Turning his head back, the fear of nothing being there was gone a the orange glow soon began to dim away as the light from the outside burst through hitting Ray in the face. He shielded his eyes from it before putting his hand away back on to the floor to crawl quicker. Bright white light was in his sight as Ray's head was now outside, the wind hitting his face as he pulled himself through onto a rock ledge below him. The stones and dust from the tunnel flew out with him as Ray brought his feet out to land awkwardly onto the rock ledge, big enough to accommodate his whole body. Dusting his hat off, Ray could now see where he was, an open dug area in which heavy machinery remained stationary. It was a mining operation. No one seemed to be down below, the machines looked like they had been there for a couple of months. Tracks leading back inside the mountain and down below into the ground were nearly hidden away by the amount of dust blown this way after the mining party had left. The carts were empty and the tunnels were no longer lit which made Ray all the more curious. He had heard of the times bands of men who had got together in search of riches buried deep beneath the earth below. The mighty gold rush captured peoples attention far and wide across the first states, and many more people found gold in the oddest of places, going on to live wealthy lives. The dream was real and finding even just a nugget could change peoples lives for the better or worse. Whoever was here last must've found what they were looking for and gone back to the nearest bank around to get that check of approval for what they found was proven to be genuine. Ray, with his hands and feet, slid as carefully as he could down the steep hill from. Ray still wondered who those people were in there as his hand jolted awkwardly, trying to stabilize himself on the way down. The rock formation soon turned bumpy, and he had to stop himself as he could seriously break something if not careful. He got his bearings and stood up again, mapping out each step as the uneven rocks blocked his path before stepping on flat land again. The first step was a bit of leap, but it was onto a smooth rock with a flat surface where Ray's feet landed just at an angle, making his feet turn north-west. The second was slightly broken and sharp on its edges, but it was easy to get a grip on and for this closer leap Ray stretched out his finger to keep himself steady as he caught onto the rock with his back arched as he landed with both his hands and his feet. The third and fourth were the same, angled but manageable to stand up straight on. A couple more big steps and Ray was soon landing on the dusty flat ground, dusting himself off properly from crawling earlier. He saw the ground were the mining operation was and noticed the carts sat together just in the middle behind a small wooden hut, possibly where the ring leader of the operation would sit. The whole place was founded by a company, Simms Int. A small trading company that obviously was trying to make bigger riches with the correct permitting. Ray inspected the hut and found the map of the area. It wasn't professionally illustrated, crudely drawn with some exits and entranceways marked by a cross with text over in conjoined by a curved line. It was unclear where gold was found, but some routes underneath weren't even completed, perhaps gold was found, and the search groups all came together back up to the surface to be merry at their discovery. Another theory would be they ran out of railing tracks for the carts, but that was proven wrong as Ray saw when walking to the hut that there were two bails of tracks about to the height of his knees were left out in the open. Ray went to inspect but as he left his eyes were not able to see across the table of a tin dish that was used as an ashtray. A cigarette stuck out from it, and it had only recently been lit given at how fresh the tobacco was inside. Ray walked to the two carts which sat in the middle of the ground, the metal dented, the rust just underneath the wheels were starting to crawl up its sides. Inspecting the wheels further, Ray was unsure if the carts were safe to run. Both of them had bumpers locked to the rails, stopping them from being moved at all. Ray went to the hut again to see if the keys were still there and they were, hanging from the wall by the small open window. The keys all hung on to a metal circle, twenty keys were dangling from it so it would mean Ray would have to test them all on the bumpers locks. After about five keys, one eventually got stuck in the lock, and Ray jostled it around, pulling it tight from the key end as much as possible, but it wouldn't budge. He then, after a quick thought, he pulled at the metal circle to see if it would give way, his feet pushing against the bumpers as his hands pulled on the thin circle until it was broken. The keys all came off, sliding down the metal chain onto the ground were Ray picked up the ones he hadn't used and left the ones to the side while the sixth one stayed inside the bumper's lock. Fourteen options to choose from with all having the same etching pattern, but before he could try another one, Ray felt something in his head. It felt heavy as his brain scrambled to work out what was happening. It was like his hearing had been turned up so that it was sensitive to even a pin dropping on the floor, but nothing was seen around him that could be giving this feeling off. His head felt like he had a headache without the pain. Instead, all he had was a weight making his eyes strain when trying to look around. He brought his head down and slumped his shoulders, clutching the back of his head to soothe it, while it only got heavier. He wondered, could it be from the ground below? He got down to his hands and knees looking at the ground, and indeed felt heavier like now a cylinder block was now pushing him down. Ray remembered from earlier and did not hesitate as he lit off a smile of remembrance. He dropped his head down to the ground, and his head rushed through the dirt, dust and dead bugs brushing past him as his lips sunk against his teeth to keep anything from entering his mouth unexpectedly. He came out from the other side, and the weight on his head felt heavier than ever, but the visit to another side was short-lived. A man's face had appeared directly looking Ray dead in the eyes with an expression of dread. His skin was leathery with his pale blue eyes looking into Ray's. He had pitch-black hair, and his beard was neatly trimmed along with his eyebrows. The two were both shocked, Ray pulled back and like a fish on a fishing line flew out from the ground and landed on his back gasping for air. Rays hand paint brushed the dirt off of his face and scrambled back over to the keys. Whoever this person was, he was right below him, in the mines. Three more attempts with different keys and one soon clicked on the lock. The bumper could now move on the railings, and Ray lifted it with both hands underneath it chucking to his right side with a rattling bang as it landed. He pulled at the cart, and it was still able to move with the slightest of sqeaks to its wheels. Nothing was inside it apart from dirt, he pulled it away from its parked stop in front of the hut on the main track. Ray went back to the hut for the third time to inspect the map again, seeing which way the track lead to an abrupt end, it was the one to his right. The entrance inside was dark, but Ray saw that the candle inside the lamp hung outside still had enough wax to burn. Ray reached into his coat pocket to grab one of his matches, striking up a small flame between his finger and lit the candle, closing the glass door on it he held onto it as he hopped into the cart to journey down the dark tunnel. The speed wasn't too fast as the track carried on straight and Ray felt relieved to sit down for a bit. Inside the tunnel, he could see a few bits of equipment on the floor, such as pickaxes and some shovels with the occasional barrel sitting up against the rock walls. Crates sat stacked on top of one another with wood bolted above keeping the rock ceiling from crumbling. Ray leaned toward to see the first dip coming up from what he remembered on the map, the cart sped up as it went down and Ray put out his hands against the sides of the cart as he went down with his foot pressing firmly on the candle in the corner of the cart without breaking the glass. The dip down further into the dark only lasted for a few seconds before the cart was again on a flat path, but at a greater speed, Ray had poked his head up from the cart with the lantern in hand and saw the track ahead, it seemed to go on and on as the cart started slowing down. There seemed to be less equipment where he was now and soon the cart came to a creaky stop. Ray hopped out from the cart to investigate the tunnel, treading carefully, the orange glow again lighting the oval cave from where he tread carefully as he began to call out.

"Anyone down here?" he said, with his voice echoing down the dark path. Nothing came back to him, and he tried again but a bit louder.

"If anyone's down here show yourself. I'm friendly" Ray said. Again nothing returned back except his voice bouncing off the walls. Oddly the weight in his head was gone, as he realized. Perhaps he went the wrong way, he thought. It was dark, and nothing else could be heard except for his footsteps. Ray carried on without the cart walking alongside the wall to his right. The path ahead didn't seem to change, the rock walls were still bumpy and uneven as Ray kept his hand gliding along with it. He stopped for a second, the sound of a tiny rock falling came from behind him, his head swung back along with the lantern to see if anyone was there, but there wasn't. Unfazed by it, Ray went back just five steps to view the rock in the middle of the track, it had bounced off the metal railings, and Ray looked up to see if the ceiling was stable with its unfinished wooden framework keeping it from falling. Ray didn't want to take his chances with this tunnel and began to walk back to the cart. As soon as his hand reached the wall again, it cracked loudly. Suddenly a hand reached through grabbing Ray by the throat pulling his head straight into the rocks. The pain combined with the sudden return of the weight from earlier, made him feel like he wasn't going to be able to keep his head up as he fell to the floor, dropping the lantern. Before he even clutched his head the hand came back out again, this time from the floor, grabbing Ray's shirt collar instead, just missing his neck and pulled his head down through the floor, his head still whirling before it was pulled up to the same face from earlier. This time he was not so shocked. The bearded man with his pale blue eyes came up close to Ray's face and said: "Leave me!" with a growl before sending him back up through the dirt flinging him back against the cracked wall. The torment didn't stop there as again, the hand again came through the same crack gripping onto Ray's jacket collar pulling him up from his neck. The arm moved up near towards the ceiling leaving the wall to break open even more as Ray was left dangling before being forced across the tunnel, his head cracked against one of the wooden frames and Ray came crashing down into the mining cart awkwardly, with his legs up in the air, his neck bent up against the metal sides. Soon the arm came out from the ground and begun to push the cart back up the track as the ceiling started to crumble, and the wagon started to race again up the tracks as rocks came down with the wood breaking off from their nailed down points. Ray just kept his head down as the cart sped through the tunnel. The rock formation around him began to crumble, the light from the outside blinded him momentarily as the cart still on its tracks shot out from the entrance all the way back to the middle of the mining ground, where the little hut was along with the second cart. Back inside the tunnel had collapsed upon itself, rocks blocking off the track and the progress made by the former workers. Ray crawled out from the cart, wincing in pain as he landed on the ground with a thud.

"Why can't I still get a grasp of these things," Ray said to himself. Suddenly the rocks began to part as the bearded man stepped out amongst the rubble. The light hit his side, and Ray could see his face fully as he sat up. He was tall and thin, wearing a white button-up shirt done up to the top button, a brown waistcoat with matching trousers and black shoes. His sleeves were rolled up, and Ray could see that the man had markings on his arm mixed in with all the cuts that had mended themselves over the years. He smiled as he walked outside, closing his eyes and taking in a deep breath as he waved his hands around like a cook smelling his prepared dinner. Ray, up to his feet, was on the verge of pulling his gun from his holster, but he waited as the man began to speak.

"Doesn't help my reputation, ya know. Hiding in these caves like a bat," he said.

"The one who hid like a coward. You're Goida, I presume? You don't look like someone who's hiding."

"You don't look like someone who just got thrown around by my hand," said Goida, cocky with his thin smile.

"Doesn't happen like that every day" Ray answered.

"Neat trick, isn't it? All Shamans learn this one easily. I can see that you're still a novice in all of this, pretty funny, almost thought you were gonna head butt me" Goida chuckled. Ray wasn't smiling.

"Takes getting used to."

"You came looking for me or some gold? Or maybe you'd like some gold in exchange for finding me. The elders sent you, didn't they?"

"They explained to me who you are and what you're doing. They left out the part where you're a wise ass." Goida chuckled to himself again.

"It's cause they can't handle my jokes or my rebuttals for that matter. As wise as those men are, they can't imagine how they would react if the best was meant to happen to this land. They'd be helpless and so will the many who inhabit this land. America is still a baby, Mr McCarthy, someone's gotta raise it the right way."

"By killing hundreds with monsters and witchcraft?" Ray exclaimed.

"Not hundreds, sir. Millions. That's the number Bazka asked for. Torture many with death and destruction, and soon they will grovel and beg. God won't save them, neither will the elders."

"God doesn't work like that, I'm afraid."

"Oh I got a preacher now have I! This is too rich! Bazka will show you and the world what true God-like power is!" Ray paused for a moment, his hand was firmly on the trigger of his revolver. He took a breath in, like he was about to speak, but Ray instead lifted the gun out flawlessly, and the first shot landed straight into Goida's chest pushing him back slightly. The gun wound didn't phase Goida at all, as Ray expected. He laid the rest of the five bullets from the silver chamber into his chest in rapid succession. One, two, three, four, five they sped into his chest, landing in different parts and the blood started to trickle down Goida's clean white shirt and over his waist-coat. It brought him down to one knee, and his head rested onto his arm that now sat on the knee which was raised. Goida lifted up his head after a few breaths and smiled like a mad man.

"True God-like power, Mr McCarthy. You'll soon understand it," he said. Goida then sunk his whole body into the ground and vanished from Ray's sight. Anxious for another fight, Ray started to reload the revolver as quickly as he could and cocked back the safety ready to put a bullet in Goidas head. He took a step back and another, twisting his head and body round in anticipation of the man to spring out, but there was just silence. Ray waited a while before rushing back to the little wooden hut to find cover, Goida like an unhinged door swung out from the door frame and caught Ray by the throat. Goida with one hand slammed Ray again down to the ground before raising him up again and this time into the wooden side of the hut. Ray, after taking the blow, kicked against Goida's stomach and then again with more force down on his hip, releasing Ray from his tight grip. Ray threw a hard right hook clocking the bearded Shaman across his jaw before he retaliated with a shoulder charge, which pushed Ray back into the wooden walls of the hut. The two both tried to get the advantage over the other before Ray had both of Goida's hands in his control as he got him by the wrists. Holding his hands in front of him Ray delivered a head butt which struck Goida on the nose. Pushing his hands away from him Ray threw an uppercut, which sent the shaman back with his hand holding his chin. The two walked away from the hut and Ray got hold of Goida's waistcoat and with a swing threw him into the side of the mine cart which still sat on the track. Goida had had enough now, his eyes soon changed to pitch black and like a gust of strong wind, the Shaman opened his mouth wide and sent Ray flying with a thick black cloud of energy. Ray was sent crashing into the wooden hut, the ceiling falling down as he landed on the small tables where the maps were spread out. Goida had gotten to his feet, and the dark energy that shot from his mouth was now circling around him like heavy cigarette smoke, trailing around his body and spurting out from the bullet wounds in his chest which began to mend themselves. Ray crawled out from the ruined shack and saw the demonic Shaman walking toward him.

"You know, with the way you're fighting right now, it's still selling me on you being the cowardly one?" Goida said, with his voice now deep and growling as the energy surged through him. Ray moved further away from the ruined hut, and as Goida got closer and closer, Ray grabbed a nice piece of wood and swung it into Goida. The energy in him now was too strong, and the wood simply broke as it connected with his face. Ray noticed the bullet wounds in his chest, they were covered in thick black tar from the dark energy weaving around and through him. Goida clicked his neck in anticipation of his next move, but first, he spoke softly with his deepened voice, "Your blood is what I need. All of it." The energy behind the tar-like scabs soon burst open shooting a wave of the smoke like energy again at Ray, this time not shooting him into the air but instead spreading his arms out with his legs bound together like a prisoner in chains. It pushed him back to the floor before he rose and the two locked eye to eye together.

"The elders always knew that there would be ones who would defy their word. They just could never fathom it would be the

252

ones from their own inner circle. And now they put their faith in an outsider who was completely out of the equation? Again, Mr McCarthy, I'll show you what God-like powers can do. Can your God do this?"

With the end of that question, Goida's eyes rolled back, and the energy slid up covering the whites of his eyes before they were filled up with the black tar-like goo that rested on his bullet wounds. His head began to crack as he contorted his neck in sharp movements before his head came laying back as far as it could before a slit in his neck began to open and peel back the flesh to reveal rows and rows of small stud-like teeth that moved with the motion of the muscles in his transformed neck. Inside his neck sloshed around with saliva spewing from the crevices of his muscles as it started to growl. Ray didn't know what to do, his arms were held up with the energy gripping his wrists, and he couldn't kick as his ankles were held together, he tried everything to break free, but it felt and looked like Ray was Jesus nailed to the cross, where all he could do was plead to God. The energy which held him now, angled him forward bringing his arms and legs together like on a board, he was going to go in headfirst, and Ray would see how close he was getting to being somehow swallowed alive. He soon realized where his hands were now, on his hips, next to his holster with the gun still sat inside nearly on the verge of falling out. He wiggled his right hand and got a slight grip on the handle, each finger trying to angle the gun just right until his index finger sat on the trigger and he pulled it back. The shot fired went in just under Goida's stuck out chin, and the mouth in his neck squealed like a pig. Ray, not satisfied fired again as he angled the gun lower into the demonic mouth in Goida's neck with the shots breaking pockets of the teeth off in the process. After the third shot, the energy had to work, healing the wounds and Ray hit the ground again as more dark tar dripped onto the ground before filling up on the wounds like crust. With his hand, Goida simply gripped tightly of his beard and yanked his head back into place closing of the mouth housed in his neck, with a vile sounding snap. Goida growled at how his prey was still standing as Ray began thinking of his comeback plan.

"God-like powers. I listen to God's powerful words, Goida. And he tells me that I should fear no evil!" Goida in anger darted for him, and Ray let out the last two shots from his gun into the Shaman's knee which sent him down to the floor. Ray started to run to the other side of the mining ground towards the left mining entrance trying to reload his gun while keeping a good speed. Goida clutched at his knee as it started to heal up, and as he lifted his head back up, he could see how far Ray had ran, and he got even angrier. His face tensed as he rose up and his hands were pressed against both sides of his face as the energy inside began to make Goida's head sizzle until finally, with a loud scream, black energy shot out from his mouth towards Ray, sending him hurtling towards the entranceway as the rocks shook. Ray rolled on the ground as landed. With the energy released, Goida brought his attention to the mine cart behind him, his energy wrapped around the steel cart like vines around a tree and threw it across towards Ray. He scrambled and Ray again with a sharp intake of breath rolled forward out of the way as the cart hit the ground hard on its corner before bouncing off to the side. Ray knew the gun wasn't going to do much good and he needed Goida close again to do any sort of damage, he got to his feet and ran inside the different cave with no light and trailed off into the darkness of the mines. Goida stood still now with a smirk stretching across his mouth, his prey is isolated, he thought and he sunk himself down into the ground with delight. Inside the cave, Ray had his hands out in front of him, fear of falling or bumping into something inside dark halls of the mine. The greater fear was trying to scout Goida who could out burst from any point inside of where he was. Ray was now slowing down as the thoughts and ideas grew in his head until he came to a complete stop. Yes, the idea clicked in his head. He knew how Goida could be stopped, and he had to look deep from within. It seemed pointless closing his eyes in the already darkened halls of the mine, Ray did so anyway to concentrate. He saw a light flicker in his mind, a spark, then he felt it. The feeling he got when he ingested the vial's liquid not long ago. The rush of energy, it's purple aura soon began to light around him, surrounding him with power that he nested inside. Just then Ray heard a click, the click that a rock makes when it chips off another rock, it was small, and it dropped from behind him. Suddenly the wall burst from the right side, and Goida's arm had again broken through reaching for Ray's neck, but he had heard it and quickly dodged the on-coming attack. Ray drew his gun out quick-firing through the palm of his hand, and it jolted around like an injured horses leg. Goida sunk his arm back through the wall, the cracks from where he had burst through started to lengthen up the walls and to the ceiling. Ray came back to the middle of the hall glee-fully smiling as he heard again the faintest of sounds which now sounded loud in his aura. Goida came at him again, arm stretched with his hand opened to grab, but Ray didn't even move as he shot again from his gun into the palm, barely even moving this time around. There was a slight pause, that's when Ray moved further down the mine, with a full-on sprint. His aura lit up his path, and he could hear the rumbling beside him, Goida was now not even trying to hide where he was, he was angry and wanted to kill Ray with everything he had. Ray knew how to tease and soon halted his run just before Goida could spring out from the ground with both arms out in an attempt to drag him under, but it had failed, and he came out and landed face-first on the railing. Ray went in for the attack, forcing Goidas head again onto the track as he grasped his hair tight. Ray then brought him up and struck Goida with three strong strikes to the side of his head with his right hand knocking him down again. Goida hissed, and his eyes rolled back again as he shot back up. Still, in doing so, Ray shot from his gun again right through the bottom of the chin up through his head, then again and one final time until the head threw itself back and the demonic mouth ripped open from the neck exposing itself again to Ray. The bait was effective, now to go in for the kill. Ray saw the lone rock on the floor, next to where Goida had emerged from, the debris it left was a hole with dirt and rocks, Ray saw the opportunity and got hold of the biggest rock in the pile and shoved it into the demonic mouth with its teeth pressing down puncturing it. The full strength of these teeth could now be seen as Ray imagined that could've been his head as it cracked from the pressure, Ray wasted no time and with all his strength, pushed Goida down with his hands pressed against the rock into the mouth in his neck. Ray kept applying pressure as the rock began to choke Goida out, his aura slowly fading and unable to stretch out to remove Ray from him until it eventually sunk back up to Goidas head to seal up the bullet wounds. The pressure kept building until a slight crack of bone was being heard, Goida with his demonic and regular mouth squealed out in pain until he began to beg for his life.

"Ok! Ok! I give, just get off me!"

"Put this thing back in your neck then!" Ray retorted. The teeth released their grip and Ray could now lift the rock up from the muscular neck which began to shrink back, bringing Goidas head back with a deep click.

"Now, tell me where exactly Waywood is. And don't answer me with that mouth."

VII.

"These powers seem very unique. Each reacting differently to different hosts. Do you think you could be able of such things as Goida, Mr McCarthy?" Roosevelt asked.

"Wouldn't particularly like to have another mouth. People say I don't even open this one much." Ray said, making the president chuckle.

"What became of Goida? Did you get the information from him?"

"He told me where up north Waywood would be. It's in the mountains, camps everywhere. Goida operated on his own like a rat hiding in its own little system. Waywood had backup. Hundreds dedicated to him in the name of Bazka. They didn't care if they lived so long as they swore to protect him at all cost. Goida was really just a footnote, like the elders said he would be."

"You killed him?"

"No. He gave up. He knew his job was done. Delivering me was to him his final part in the grand scheme of everything. I saw what he became when he eventually gave in, that's what might happen to me when I doeventually."

"Like I said earlier, Mr McCarthy, different people, different qualities. But still, even if Goida didn't take God's word of man being made equally, then he wouldn't have suffered such a fate. I think that will be all today, Mr McCarthy, but if you wouldn't mind, I would like you to take a walk with me." The President asked, sitting up from his desk as he put the pen away, which was sat comfortably on his ear. Ray didn't feel like talking anymore, but the walk might help that he thought. The president made himself next to Rays side, and the two stepped out from Roosevelt's office. They did not speak until they were out in the central garden, a large open field with precisely cut grass while two guards, bearing arms as they followed the two at a distance.

"So by now, I think you know the full extent of what you can do with your abilities."

"That's correct," Ray said with a second of hesitation. Roosevelt stood still letting Ray continue for a step more before he realized the President had stopped.

"You have plenty of room, Mr McCarthy. I trust you won't use it against me," said Roosevelt with a smile. Ray wasn't the slightest bit comfortable doing what the President was asking of him.

"Sir, with all due respect, I really would not like to bring the aura out unless it's absolutley necessary."

"But you are safe here, Mr McCarthy. There are no threats here."

"I've not even finished my side of the story yet Mr President," Ray said with a hint of anger as he gritted his teeth with the last word of his reply. Roosevelt was taken back by this, and one of the guards behind him raised his rifle slightly in fear. But Ray remained calm, he was older and more prone to be like the angry old man he didn't appear to be. Ray snapped more at little things more than what he used to. He apologized and relaxed.

"I'm sorry, sir. I've always been one to hide this in any circumstances. You don't know what it's like feeling that you want to die one day, and then you bring yourself not to do it for the sake of others. I feel like I'm cursed sometimes. Tied down like a dead-end job with no reward at the end, except death. I don't know if I want to carry on or not." Roosevelt was moved. He walked up to Ray's side again and placed his hand on his shoulder. "I'm starting to really believe this outlaw has a heart of gold. Ray, I believe that men must do what they have to do to do what they really want to do. You carry a special gift, it may be long and sometimes unbearable, but it will soon lead you to my desk again with your name in writing, free from any trouble in the future."

"Thank you, Mr President," Ray said.

"I think we're done for the day. It's cold out actually, let's continue with a nice warm coffee in the morning." Roosevelt said, getting up from his desk.

"Agreed. You should really write down what you said," Ray said as the two walked back through the open field, overlooking at the White House.

The fresh morning coffee smell. It went through the two men's nostrils with its massive but alluring scent lifting up from a beautiful steel-cut cup, engraved with cursive patterns which were also on the saucer. Both Ray and Theodore took a sip, placed the cups down and began to record once again.

"Feel ok after last night?" Roosevelt asked.

"It's gone away with this. That's some sweet coffee we got here."

"From what I've learnt about you so far I'm taking that as a yes. Now, after what happened with Goida..."

Maluk came round to his teepee entrance to meditate as usual after the day, the fire inside had just been lit, and the light from it gave that familiar orange glow. As he entered, he froze as the sight of Ray sitting before him with his legs crossed and his arms stretched out behind him, holding him up as he relaxed by the fire. He froze with a smile, not a look of shock.

"So I take it Goida was pretty much the decoy to send me up north, was he?" Ray asked.

"That was always his purpose. Goida was selfish with his lust for eternal life; that's why he was sent away from the main plan of Bazka. Bazka knew he would turn on a whim that's why he beat it into him. Even though you truly saw with what he is, he was always weak and he knew it, which is why Goida is no longer an issue," Maluk answered as he took a seat at his regular spot.

"He still gave me the whereabouts of Waywood Chief. He will be expecting me any day now." Maluk had listened with his eyes closed and finally exhaled a deep breath.

"You feel stronger. Your aura has grown. You know what you can be capable of. You've seen it first hand."

"Does it ever feel like it could get out of control?" Ray asked. Maluk inhaled and instead of his exhale being a breath, he let out a deep hum. In doing so, an orange glow came around the Chief and tiny bright streams of light with tails disappearing as they circled around him like shooting stars. They shot out from the fire with a little wisp sound, and like flies sat on him in different parts of his body. Maluk finally ending his deep meditated hum relaxed his arms and opened his eyes, revealing nothing but the same light from the orbs which came from the fire. Ray watched in awe as he leaned forward to marvel at the beauty of the Chief's aura.

"This power was given to me fifty years ago. Mine burns bright every day and will continue to do so, so long as I keep my mind in the right state. You were focusing back with Goida, but it wasn't at full potential."

"So there's still loads more that I can do with it?"

"There is. So long as your mind never trails off to the thoughts of death and despair."

"Meaning...?"

"When you give in to those thoughts the aura leaves you. Goida knew his time left would not be long. He was living like a rat anyway, so there was not much point in fighting you for long. The elders are the only ones to know how to live beyond and bestow their wisdom. That is the only thing that I cannot explain to you. Your aura is attuned to you, understands your body, your mind, and when you let it in full, you will be linked. Both understanding what can be done in an instant. That is why I think it would be best for you to head south before heading north to face Waywood." The Chief said as he puffed out his chest and folded his arms.

"What's down south?" Ray asked.

◆ ◆ ◆

"A woman. A woman who would test me, he said."

"And the Chief knew this woman?"

"He did. But not with fondness. She was one to lure men of his tribe, leading them to their deaths. She was a manipulator, but she knew things." Ray explained.

"Why didn't the Chief teach you?" Roosevelt asked.

"He said he couldn't be harsh enough. I needed to know how cruel it can get. How the person behind the aura can shape a person through their desires. And she was wicked enough to show me that" Ray said his eyes venturing off recollecting that day.

The swampland was grossly unkempt, and the thickness of the air was unbearable to breathe. Ray could feel his sweat down his back and head as he struggled to keep cool. He was only in his cotton undershirt and trousers with his waistcoat, neckerchief and coat sitting on horseback behind him. With the air being thick, it was sometimes hard to see past the fog with its dark green and yellow coat. The mud was thick and heavy with the grass sprouting out, reaching up near the middle of a person's shin. There was no path, Ray simply had to look for the woman that the Chief had described through the many trees and alligator-infested lakes. The bugs were the most annoying. Flies were nipping the back of Ray's neck while the rest were smaller and flew in a pack towards him while half of them landed on the horse's face. Ray noticed to his left a trio of alligators, all three of them had the heads looking at him as he carried on past the lake. Passing through the trees, a lake was now visible it was dirty and teeming with fish and algae which had given it that mucky brown colour. Along it was a small pier bridge which was not in the best of shape to even be stepped on even with your big toe, just the slightest amount of pressure could make it crumble to bits. Ray looked across from where he stood, noticing a small shack with the orange glow of the candles sitting on the window. Perhaps someone could be in there. Ray and his horse went over to the smallest openings from the lake where the alligators couldn't spook the horse he rode until they were passed by thick trees covered in moss and bugs nesting in its cracks. The shack was run down, the wood was damp, and the smell was foul like forgotten eggs. The front door was left ajar ever so slightly leaving a slither to peak in as to what could be inside. Ray dismounted and walked slowly over to it and knocked respectfully in case the woman was present. "Anyone in?" he called. No answer. He brought his hand up to knock again but stopped himself, what was the point in being polite on urgent matters and in a place like this, he thought. Ray instead wrapped his fingers around the door and pushed it open, revealing a mess of a house.

Pieces of wood from the ceiling were snapped, some of the floorboards were missing with the familiar green algae latching itself to the wood. Dragonflies hovered in and out the empty window panes while flies buzzed around the forgotten food on the kitchen counter, if you could even call it that at this point. A broom, a crowbar and a small collection of chains were on the floor, and the damp swamp-like smell was more potent in here. At the back of the shack was a small single bed with a rocking chair to its left and Ray was hoping that someone would be sat in it. He walked in carefully treading in case the wood might break judging it by the unerving creaking sound as his size nine boot pressed down. At the back, where the bed stood, an old bookshelf with nothing on it and a picture frame with cracked glass was to its left on the wall. A woman's eyes met Ray's, but it was from within the picture frame, her expression was empty, and her posture looked as if someone was straightening her back for her. That could've explained the face. Ray wondered if this was the woman Maluk told him about, but it wasn't. Ray would have to find a much shorter woman with a devilish smile to her reputation. Her eyes were blue and her hair a light shade of brown. She was here, at least that's when Ray noticed the note nailed to the top half of the doorway; it left a crack in the wood when it was hammered in. Ray took it off with a clean pull the paper not ripping it as he swiped it off the nail. There was no writing on it but three sets of dots, two close together with a break and then another pair and another. There was also quickly scribbled lines below them, and that's when it clicked, the alligators. Ray had left the house and circled back up the trail he came down from, sure enough, the alligators were still there not moving a muscle but their eyes following Ray. And that's when she appeared, she stepped out from the fog between the two trees behind the alligators, and she looked more alluring then what Maluk had warned Ray about. It was apparent how her plans worked out for her, she didn't seem real, everything looked perfect. Her cheekbones, the way she walked and her hair flowing almost down to her knees with that clean shine to it didn't have a single hair out of place. Her entire body was one big trap for unexpecting men who cross her path as she wore nothing letting the paleness of her body attract her victims like the moon shining bright at night and just when it couldn't get more alluring she opened her mouth and spoke.

"Hello, my darlin'. My clues are pretty easy, aren't they?" She said in a soft drawn out southern accent. "Who might you be, if you don't mind me asking?" she continued.

"Your name first please," Ray said sternly.

"Cassie Bloodgood, sweetie. Now you." she said playfully. The name was the only thing ugly about her, Ray thought.

"Ray McCarthy. I've heard you're a woman who can get things."

She giggled in a high tone before she spoke, "Naturally. It's my talent."

"Do you also give things? I'm giving you my full attention here."

"Steady sweetheart, I ain't no hussy in a bar." She smiled. Ray didn't concentrate on his aura and let the colour shine around him to speak for him. Bloodgood fanned herself as the light grew around Ray until he retracted it, and Bloodgood clapped her hands softly with hardly any sound coming from them.

"Well, you certainly won me over with that. Usually, I'm the one giving, but this is a treat none the less."

"Chief Maluk. He told me you're an ideal teacher for something like this." Bloodgood's smile quickly dropped to a frown as she heard the name.

"Ugh, that killjoy. He sent you did he. What does that scum filled tribesman want with me now?" Bloodgood said, rolling her eyes in disgust.

"Nothing, only I want something. Chief simply put you down as a reference." Ray explained.

"Well, what is it you require then?"

"I need to learn more about my aura and how to control it."

"Fine, come through," she said, beckoning him with a finger as she walked towards the fog again.

"Wait, what about-"

"Oh, they'll let you through. My babies won't hurt you unless I say. Leave your horse, they'll take care of him." As she finished her beautiful swaying body disappeared into the fog, and Ray soon followed, his eyes shifting back and forth between the two alligators he walked past as they hissed. Ray walked into the mist, and he couldn't see in front of him or behind him, but he heard the shriek of his horse and an offensive snap of the alligators' jaws with the breaking of bones and flesh being torn off. Ray walked further on and begun to see little lights fly around, they looked like fireflies buzzing around zipping from one side to another. The lights buzzed in front of his eyes before zooming off behind him, taking a dive into the ground as he watched. When Ray turned back around, Bloodgood was in front of him, and her soft hands sat on his chest, making Ray freeze in shock at just how cold she was. She rubbed up and down, tempting him to lean forward for a kiss with the slightest flicker of her eyes, before gazing at his lips. The urge to kiss her was so strong, and it was like Ray had no control of his body as he could feel his arms tighten, and his head began to tilt. They two got closer and closer, and Bloodgood's right hand lifted off Ray's chest and gripped the back of his neck. His head went cold, and the warmth of his chest flooded back, and he could hear his heartbeat louder now that she had moved her hand. Bloodgood looked as if she was going bring him in for the kiss, but she moved her head to his side to whisper in his ear, Ray almost felt as though his eyes were about to roll back into his head when she spoke, everything was like ecstasy when she had hold of him.

"See how easy it is. Power is something different to everyone. Mine is temptation. That beautiful light you see that lures you in like a fly. Now I know what you can work on first: Your ability to resist."

Bloodgood released her grip, and her hands slipped back to her side. Ray let out a moan of relief as his eyes came back around and the feeling came back again into his legs. Bloodgood played with her hair as she watched him get his bearings. Ray now felt more thirsty than ever, his lips were dry, and he couldn't think straight, but his eyes were still firmly on Bloodgood's body.

"Do I seem perfect to you?" she asked.

"I feel so guilty right now by saying this, but yes you do," Ray said.

"Why do you feel guilty?"

"Because I would've betrayed the woman I love, and I couldn't stop myself."

"Who this woman?" with a whip of her long hair, Bloodgood transformed herself into Millie as her hair came back down to her sides. Ray couldn't believe how quickly that happened, everything about her was like he remembered except for the hair, but he didn't pay the slightest bit of attention to that. His eyes grew as he saw the woman he had fallen for right in front of him, naked and inviting him over for a warm embrace. The trance was broken, however, when Bloodgood spoke again, "Predictably weak." She said as she whipped her hair back, returning to her original form.

"Stop it," Ray said with a broken voice.

"This will be the first lesson. To resist those like myself who tempt you. Now snap out of it and let's begin."
Ray stood up straight breathing deep and nodded his head to start.

"Good. Now, your aura from the looks of things is still untapped. Maluk may have told you that it learns off of you, but it also plays to the earth. It's an elemental thing."

"Elemental?"

"The natural side of things. The Chief plays to fire as I play to the swamp. Sooner or later, you'll have something. Please tell me if you've been through the ground yet?"

"Couple of times."

"Good, that stuff's child's play; everyone with an aura can do that. Have you done anything else?"

"I guess I heard everything get louder when I stood still one time."

"Interesting. Where was this?"

"In a cave."

"Was it lit?"

"In darkness." Bloodgood snapped her hands in realization.

"Bingo. You are something special. Darkness is your ally, and that's quite rare. Let's see how you handle it." Bloodgood put her hands on Ray again, this time firmly laying them on his shoulders before the two of them sunk into swamp grass. Ray opened his eyes to see where he was, but he was unsure where until he tried to move. His movement was limited, Ray felt around to find it was wooden walls restricting him. He heard Bloodgood giggle again as a small firefly entered the space; he was inside a coffin, and her voice channelled through it.

"Quite tight, but now is the time to concentrate."

As she finished the firefly's glow flicked off and Ray was in complete darkness again. Ray knew he had to remain calm, but his face was only inches from the wooden coffin door and it wouldn't budge and the urge to break it was closing in as he didn't know how long he could breathe inside the wooden tomb. The walls felt like they could get tighter and tighter, but instead of panicking, Ray relaxed, closed his eyes and began to concentrate. He thought of freedom, the air going in and out his nose and the space to move his arms again. Bloodgood wasn't having any of this and broke through the front of the coffin, yanking Ray out.

"You took too long." she said with some disappointment. "You need to act on instinct. Break away from it instantly or you'll stare death in the face like that dopey look you gave me earlier."

"Death was more attractive," Ray joked.

"Funny. You had it before I lifted you out, now get back in there and tell death you've got a crush on her."

Bloodgood, open-palmed pushed the ground with some force and Ray was once again in the dark, trapped inside the wooden tomb again. He didn't miss the chance this time. Ray breathed slowly and concentrated, this time his aura rushed around him with a dark purple glow and Ray opened his eyes again, feeling its power inside of him once again, but with better control. Ray thought about the first thing that he tried once inside of the wooden prison, pushing, and he felt the power go into his hands, the aura responded to him. With more force than any human being could usually muster Ray laid a hand flat onto the wood and with no effort at all, made it splinter and crack until the lid broke and wet dirt fell on top of him. Ray began to climb up, the soil merely brushing past his face with his eyes wide open, starting to glow but not as bright as Maluks aura, his fingers gripped tight into the dirt as he pulled himself up. Soon he reached the top, and one fist punched through the earth, and his hand reaching out before pressing down on the wet grass, soon the other hand came through, and Ray lifted himself out from below the ground while Bloodgood looked on. Her finger rested on her chin as she watched him scrape the dirt off himself, returning back to normal as his aura began to dim until eventually closing back inside him.

"Better. There was a quicker way out of there, but you've got the hang of it," she smiled as she graded him.

"It knew I wanted to punch out. It listened to me."

"It did indeed. Oh it will give you options once you start listening to it more, but at the moment it just likes what you do. Now let's carry on, shall we." She spun with her heels deep in the mud and walked back through the mist with Ray behind her. This time she was still visible at close distance, her smell breezed past him, and it was heavenly. Like being drawn to a homemade pie that was sitting on the windowsill, Bloodgood's smell was that of fruit and hand bar soap, it was subtle at first but got overpowering as they walked on. It seemed to come from her perfect hair more than her body as Ray thought the smell of the swamplands would have stuck on her at some point given that she must bathe around these parts. But she was clean as can be. It then clicked, he stopped walking and waved his hand around to get rid of the smell. He remembered what she said about deception, how the body can be tricked, she had a look, and the scent was part of her game. She continued to walk and without turning her head shouted back, "You prefer the smell of 'gator shit?"

She started to fade from view, but out of nowhere the familiar deep hissing sound came from behind Ray, the three pet alligators were behind him, their faces covered in blood from where they had devoured Ray's horse in a matter of minutes, with some of the horse's flesh still hanging from their jaws. They slowly moved, creeping through the long grass. However, Ray still stood not moving a muscle, he went to turn his back on them thinking of them as nothing but obstacles that wouldn't do anything to him, when all of a sudden as he brought his head back around; an alligator's face was in front of him, and it went to bite him. The jaws opened up looking as if his whole head inside and Ray could see inside the mouth of the creature, for a split-second catching sight of the crooked but sharp teeth before he dropped to the floor in sheer terror. His head knocked back, but as he came back up, he saw the body of it, it was Bloodgood's. Her body was the same gorgeous shape but her head which nested that radiant hair, was now a scaley reptile which was oddly larger than the three that were behind him. It soon started to shrink, the face cracking uncomfortably as the scales began to peel off before eventually returning to a perfectly sculpted face.

"Good in suspecting the smell. If this is what you did in the cave you said about, then you'd be dead. My babies have eaten though so I doubt if they would've done anything. I'm pretty strict about what they eat. So...shall we go again?" she said while seductively bending down. Ray bounced off the floor and readied himself, giving Bloodgood no sign of fatigue from the shock he just had. She playfully giggled again to herself and carried on walking, this time with her pet alligators following her. Ray stood in place, focused before anything could happen, Bloodgood's overall message with every test seemed to be similar to what Ray had been told in his time in the army: Be ready for anything.

The two worked together very well, her tests seemed to be more of a walk in the park once Ray kept on focusing his aura and he remembered his time in the cave with Goida. His senses were heightened, and all the flies in the area sounded louder than ever and the most distant of hisses. That hiss set everything in motion as Ray weaved to one side as one of the alligators broke the silence by launching itself towards Ray, missing him and landing on its belly. Ray didn't wait as another had started to charge at him with all its speed, with its jaw open, he moved out of the way again with his leg nearly being caught between two sets of jagged teeth as he pulled himself away. Now two of them started to pile over each other to feast, and there were more coming. Two or three other hisses came around Ray, and as he made the first two crash into each other, Ray spun round to see three more alligators charging forward in a synchronised fashion. Jaws open and ready to chow down.

Ray was in his battle stance, and his aura was prepared to channel the energy needed for the battle against the creatures. The first attack came from the alligator to Ray's right, it went for the leg looking to rip it from his socket, but Ray dodged and swiftly kicked the alligator's ribs. The middle one lunged forward aiming for his arm, but Ray tucked and rolled underneath the creature as it launched itself over him. Ray landed by the middle one's tail and got hold of it as tightly as he could as the left alligator came around his side and went for the attack. Ray quickly used the middle alligators tail as a shield. The left alligator chomped down on the middle alligator's tail and it hissed in pain, trying to shake off the clenched teeth as Ray scrambled away and he saw the two swinging around each other. The one alligator from the right was coming back around, and it pushed up with its back legs as it got close; its jaws were inches away from just clipping rays nose as his hands caught it. The creature pushed and pushed, frequently snapping to break Ray's grip on the tip of its jaws. However, Ray was still in focus, and after the third hard crunch of the alligator's jaw came down Ray managed to push the creature away and eventually after repositioning his hands shoved the alligator down into the mud, burying it between soggy dirt and long grass. The beast snarled and blew bubbles through its nose as Ray kept on applying pressure. He kept this one down as the two others flopped over each other and Ray saw the opportunity. With the power in his hands gripping so tight into the alligator's snout that the fingers pierced through the hard scales skin of the creature and with another hand piercing through its abdomen, Ray hoisted the near three hundred pound beast over his head. The mud driped down over his head as the two other alligators came crawling towards him looking to leap again to bite. The two jumped together simultaneously, and Ray threw the alligator in his hands, and all three came down hard. The group now lay there after the impact and Ray was itching to get his gun out when a pair of clapping hands stopped him from pulling the six-shooter out of the holster.

"No need for that now. I think that incredible feat of strength is enough for my babies to take," Bloodgood said. She brushed her hair past Ray's face and came over to the pile of wounded alligators to comfort them, stroking their heads as she knelt down by their side.

"Oh, my poor babies. If they were starving, I think they would've had you."

"Thanks. You got any more for me, or you just gonna keep the charade up?" Ray said with a tired tone as he had enough. Bloodgood smiled devilishly. She stood up slowly as she played with her hair as she knew her final lesson had begun.

"What do you mean charade?" she mockingly said with a high pitch.

"What are you? I mean I've already seen people with weird faces and giant whatever in the dessert, so I don't think I'll be surprised when you tell me what you are."

"Persistent, aren't we. I was expecting a dinner before that but if you insist." In a second's notice, Bloodgood's lips hit Rays, and the blood rushed to his head in an instant. His heart beat so fast it felt incredible, and soon Ray was unconscious lying in the mud as he was whisked into Bloodgoods hallucination. When he awoke, Ray thought that nothing had happened. The scene had not changed, the mist still hid the land around him, and the alligators were still in a pile in front of him. But he knew what the difference was, Bloodgood wasn't there. His lips felt warm after she had kissed him, then they began to get warmer and warmer until they started to burn the skin. Ray felt the sting and rushed over to the mud puddle beside him to soothe it, it did not. It stung so badly that he let out shrieks of pain, it was felt real, even though it wasn't. Ray let out a last good shout of excruciating pain before a louder scream, sounding so distorted that it made him cover his ears. It took the pain away from his lips as his eardrums felt the sting now and Ray didn't know where to look but as he did, he noticed the mist had gotten thicker almost fog levels now where he couldn't see anything apart from his feet below him. A smooth voice blew around him; it was hers, enticing Ray to find her in any direction he chose. Bloodgood toyed with him as he began to walk around to his left, belittling him and whispering words into his ear, calling him a cheater or stupid. Finally, something was visible, something small but entirely out context for where Ray was, but this was a dream state, and anything could be possible if it's Bloodgoods. It was nothing more than a sunflower, a dead one. Its head hung down, and a few of the leaves from its stem still clung on. Ray didn't buy the sweet gesture from Bloodgood and gave the flower a swift kick to its head before bringing his boot down to crush the stem from where it had sprung. But as he turned, another sunflower was behind him, this time it was the same height as him, and it looked like this first one he had crushed; dead and in need of being cut down. The head was hung low, and Ray pushed it up with his hand only to find the familiar dotted brown base was a large eye, pulsing and blinking back at him. It made him hesitate for two seconds before Ray closed a fist to swat it away from him. The head didn't come off this time, and the stem fell down to the ground with it still connected. For a second, while it lay there, the stem jerked like a human and the flower head slowly lifting up from laying face down in the dirt. It then turned all the way around, and the petals fluttered as the head was now Bloodgood's perfect face, albeit with patches of dirt of her cheeks, where she landed.

"Bit of a rough one with gardening, aren't ya," Bloodgood said again in that playful manner of hers. Ray then felt stiff as a board, something was stuck into his spine, a small stem had sprouted from behind him by Bloodgood, and it left him in a state of shock so that his hand's and legs couldn't move without hurting. It felt like his whole body was asleep, yet he was conscious as his eyes watched Bloodgood strip away the petals and stem to reveal her body again, walking towards him. But this time it wasn't this seductive. Instead, the jerking motion Ray had seen with her stem body a moment ago was more frequent on Bloodgood, her arms flailed around sharply with her fingers contorting like her neck did side to side. Then more horrifying was the way she now walked, her knees stuck out more and her legs seemed as if they were being dragged across the grass and Ray looked up again to see her face, that once beautiful face was now melting. The skin bubbled as it dropped down into the dirt bit by bit as it revealed the real thing; green, infected pulsating, pussy skin. Her jaw stuck out more, looking like it was broken with her teeth now becoming sharp almost like a cat's and her eyes changed in size and colour. Before long her facade was gone entirely and all the fake love brought on by the witche's presence in Ray was gone and now turned into pure fear. She was demonic, her hair was thin, and her bones were all bent and crooked. She was mere inches away, leaning in closer to his ear, just like before, except all he heard was something that was rotting from the inside.

"Do you still...love me?" Bloodgood said, as her breath leaving her mouth was so strong even when she was speaking by Ray's side, he could smell it. He mustered through the pain that his body was feeling and with a yell of force Ray got his gun out from the holster and shot rapidly into Bloodgoods face causing her to fall back with the sound of many creaking bones. Ray gritted his teeth as he yanked himself away from the stem that was sunk into his back which screeched the tiniest of sounds, before Ray brought his foot down onto its body to shut it up. It left a hole in Ray's back as the fabric of his shirt was torn off with it. The fight was now on; Bloodgood latched herself onto Ray's back as her nails dug into his flesh, he spun round to throw her off him, but her nails felt like nails in a plank of wood that needed some more strength to be released. Bloodgood cackled away as she tried to snap her jaw around Ray's neck, but Ray wouldn't let that happen as he brought the strength of his aura through finally, and with his hands gripped tight on Bloodgood's ears before bringing the witch over his head and down to the ground. The force with which Ray did this, ripped the witches ears off, green and yellow slime poured out from the inside. She screamed in pain as her legs kicked around. Still, Ray brought them to a stop by brining his boots down on her knee caps, bending the witches legs forcing her to stop kicking and causing her to scream even louder before Ray stood above her with his aura finally beginning to shine.

"No, I love my Millie," he said before his boot lifted and was brought down onto her face. But the satisfaction of finally ending the witch right there and then was lost as his boot was only inches away from touching down onto her face, the two were lifted out of the dream-like state, and fell on their backs to the ground. The two lied there, both in pain but the scars had already healed. Ray sat up first to find the alligators circling around them hissing away at him, the threat that had beaten them to a pulp while their mistress began to sit up. Bloodgood was again in her disguise, the perfect woman once more, no puss, no green skin and no sign of age. She simply grinned with delight as she said: "I would've preferred if you lasted longer, but you figured it out, so it's fine." The two stood up and began to talk again. Ray had now brought his gun out to his side, just in case.

"Gosh, you were strong. Yet you still gonna point that thing at me?"

"You knew I could stop you with just my boot."

"Oh, I know, but how else would you learn had I not given up so easily? Darlin', you just showed me that you can handle it. I like that."

"Cut the crap and just tell your lizard pets here to back off, so I can get out of here or I'll put a bullet in you and them."

Bloodgood was now silent and pointed in the direction away from the swamp. No point in provoking him anymore seeing as how she was hiding the fear in her eyes, knowing full well that had she not broken out of the dream state, she would certainly have felt pain or death come her way. Ray walked around to where her finger pointed, keeping the gun trained on her before putting it back in its holster.

"You have it, ya know. A gift. Just make sure to control it better. See ya around," Bloodgood said with a wink in her eye. Ray walked on and didn't look back.

"You ever see this witch again?"

"No, but I did hear what happened to her. Many locals who had lost loved ones to her banded together came her way. Found her, gagged her, drowned her in the swamp lake. Funny how they said there were no alligators in the area at the time they found her. Must've let her guard down."

"Fitting end. More abuse of power but at least you gained something from Bloodgood rather than meeting an untimely end, Mr McCarthy," the President said before sipping again from his coffee.

Both Ray and Maluk sat crossed legged opposite each other around the fire in the centre of the camp with the residents of the Crow tribe gathered around them in a circle as they watched the two auras shining brightly. A mix of both bright orange and purple, the auras swum round each other passing in and out of each other. The two were entwined in each other's powers, and they communicated through each other's minds.

"Bit of hell you went through with Bloodgood."

"I understand why you wanted her to do the dirty work, I couldn't bring myself to hurt you."

"Hold back, you did. Your aura is beginning to brighten more as you speak to it as I am doing with mine. They get stronger each day, so long as you talk to it like was a normal person," Maluk continued.

"So this means I can just storm the gates up north now and take on Waywood myself?" Ray asked.

"Please. The way you conduct yourself, honestly. Yes, I'm sure your aura, that is still pretty much an infant, will cope with everything that Waywood throws at you. Ray, please take this more seriously."

Ray snapped out from the conversation inside the light of the aura and begun to speak normally.

"So you're saying I've got more stinking training?"Ray said, his eyes trailing across the other sets of eyes watching him around the fire.

Maluk continued to speak telepathically to Ray.

"I would appreciate it if you did not startle my people. Now please let us continue as before."

Ray sunk his shoulders down and closed his eyes yet again. The purple light which had vanished as he broke his trance soon again blossomed out from inside him and the purple streaks of light bridged with Maluks orange light once again. The two were linked.

"Not more training Ray, common sense. I've told you what lies ahead of you and your inevitable encounter with Waywood. He has lots of information about where Bazka is and what he plans to do more than anyone. A strategy is always a step in the right direction and for that to work, well I don't think that you can do this purely by yourself."

"So, your saying I need recruits? Like the people of your tribe?"

"No. My people will not be involved in anything like this unless I speak on the matter. Quite frankly, my people have suffered enough. Yes, they may hear the whispers, but I have to be the one who keeps them at ease. This all boils down to you and who you choose, Ray."

"I can't convince people about all this. They'll think I'm crazy."

"If you think the words you speak are crazy, then you begin to question who you are. You must be confident in your words.

Confident in your judgement. That makes a person. And when people see that, they see someone who they can trust. And it could lead to something bigger for you in life down the long road, whether you're remembered or not."

The words sunk in and Ray felt the weight behind them. Maluk knew what the future held for Ray, and it scared him a little with the way he said it in such a sombre tone. What did he know, what could he know? The thought of not dying seemed unbelievable at first, but now the repercussions of living a very long life seemed horrible when drawn out further.

"But how much can you lose in that time, Mr McCarthy?"

"You don't wanna know the half of it, sir," Ray said.

"Ray, with what you have, we don't even know what the half of it is. Does it worry you? About not dying?" the President said.

"It does. But at least I know it's in within my own control. That comforts me because I'll know when the time is right."

"But what if it's never right, Mr McCarthy? What if it gets so far down the road, centuries from now and your mind is still holding out for a moment conceived within your mind that to you is the end, but it never happens?"

"If time gets to me as it does everyone else, Mr President, you gotta just do what we do to dogs when we don't want to see them suffer anymore."

"I understand. Let us pack in for the day, thank you again, and I hope to carry on some time within the week."

"I got the weekend off?"

"You're not a prisoner Mr McCarthy. However, I must remind you that my servicemen will be watching if you head into the city. You understand?"

"Understood, sir. Goodnight." The two shook hands, and Ray left the Oval office again to spend the rest of the day back to his quarters. Roosevelt, who was still sat in his chair, reached for a piece of paper in the left side drawer of his desk. The paper was A5 sized, smaller than the usual A4 size paper for official documents and took the pen from his blazer pocket. The note was short but neatly presented.

By the office of Theodore Roosevelt.

In the event that one individual, Mr Ray William McCarthy, should be in a situation in which he cannot accept or deny the intention of passing peacefully.

He has given authority to the United States Government to enact in aiding of his death. Mr McCarthy is, at the time of writing this letter, discussing his pardoning procedures which will lead to the eventual process and his commitment to the administration's program to use his unique skills in any dark operations that may occur in the coming future.

This act of authority will be used should Mr McCarthy be in line with the countries points of interest or in the event of him becoming a rogue operative.

I am forwarding this letter through the official channels to ensure that this letter will be presented to future administrations.

If any questions should arise, please make sure to contact the branches of government to your disposal and of course Mr McCarthy himself.

He may always be at the countries best interest.

Signed,

Theodore Roosevelt, Jr.

Twenty-sixth President of the United States of America.

VIII.

Ray lay on his bed, flat as he could with one arm behind his head. Deep thoughts crawled around his head with him over-thinking many of them. He couldn't sleep. The thing that was in his head was the day he recruited people for a fight with Waywood up north. It bugged him, the decision he made, the people he chose. The place he would go to first, which would, unfortunately, be unfair to those involved. They wouldn't have done it had he not been a hero to them before. Influence goes a long way through being a good person, but the outcome made Ray squirm uncomfortably as the thought about it. He felt hor-rible, and it made him breathe slowly as he began to sweat in bed, becoming so uncomfortable that it made him stand up to walk around in the darkness of his room. Ray walked back and forth, pacing fast that it took him four seconds to reach on end and then back to his bed. He moved his arms around even though he couldn't see them and before long he stopped and stood in the centre of the room. Ray could hear his heart beating away as he took deep breaths, relaxing his arms to the side before tensing up. He came to for a bit, hunched with his hands resting on the desk. About a minute passed before Ray received a knock on the door, it was very late for incoming calls he thought. He called out to give himself a chance to slip on trousers before inviting the caller in. It was one of the maids, but this time it wasn't like usual, the maid slipped inside the crack of the door before shutting it behind her. The light from the hallway caught Ray's his Rays eyes as it shone through.

"This is really the wrong time to be-".

Ray was cut off by the light being switched on as the face of the maid made him freeze. He recognised her; the hair, the cat-like eyes and the shape fitting into the black and white maid's outfit. Aged through the wrinkles in her face but still as beautiful as ever.

It was Millie.

Bonebag was at its busiest again. Midday with the sun out and everyone going about their merry way. People working, visiting, enjoying a drink or something to eat at different stores with everyone seeming more cheerful after the events that unfolded. Ray stood in the centre of the road up through the town, in the heart of it all. Scouting for the right men. Ones, like himselfwho could handle a war-like environment. Capable of handling harsh conditions with the ability to kill. Some of these men had a military background, Ray had the ideal picture of what he needed basing it purely from whom he had interacted with on the battlefield. In its head it went with the checklist of missing teeth, missing body parts, and an ability to go on and on about a story from just a simple question asked that did not match the time nor situation, such as, like "would you like milk with your coffee?" And just a general look of being unhygienic with the inability to care. Anybody matched this, and they were in. Question of whether they would join or not, was down to whether they were there on the day the Colonel and his men invaded. Ray remembered that some people may indeed be regulars but may not have necessarily been living here, so in the end, it was down to how he talked and persuaded them and for Ray, it felt as awkward as ever. His first place for easy prey was inside the bar, Bostons. He struck luck when he saw the biggest men he could, three of them to be precise, all three strikingly looking of the exact same build. Big and beefy. They were the lumberjacks, the regulars at Billy's. So not only was Ray panicking about how he was going to string up a convincing story to lead them into a life or death situation but he also feared for his own life as it looked like all three, if provoked could each climb on his body and pull him apart. Such happy thoughts. Ray walked over as casually as possible, which in turn made him look very out of place as he came up to them. It started with a casual, "Morning fellas," as all three sets of eyes slowly landed on him.

"Bunch of gators are hungry, I bet." He joked with him only getting the reference. The three men returned to their original conversation, and their axes from work could be seen next to the bar stand. Ray caught sight of them and used it for another opener.

"You boys ever killed anybody with them axes?"

The three went silent again. The one in the middle piped up again after two seconds of silence and broke it with, "We will if you keep talking, mister."

Ray went quiet again and raised a hand up to signal to them; he was of no threat.

"Must be fun driving something sharp into a human skull. I'm just saying it would be quite a messy but satisfying sight."

"Open your mouth one more time, and I'll use this to break

your jaw, got it!" the lumberjack closest to Ray said. The middle labourer pressed a hand onto his shoulder to bring him back into the group as he had gotten right into Ray's face.

"Junior. I already explained to the man what we'd do with him. But I think he should hear it again based on the fact that he put us all out of a job."

Ray lifted an eyebrow at that last comment the next moment, he was being lifted backwards into a set of tables with on-lookers getting up to have a look. The lumberjack lifted Ray back on to his feet, and with his hands gripped together gave him a big clubbing double-fist across his chest, forcing him across the room before stumbling back to the ground near to the onlookers.

"That is what an axe handle can do! Anybody else wanna feel how hard it is?!" the lumberjack growled to everyone. They all shook a resounding no to him in response, but Ray wanted it to continue.

"See... I asked about the sharp bit, not the blunt bit-" With a growl that exited through the lumberjacks gritted teeth he reached and grabbed Ray by his collar and hoisted him up with his feet dangling. The worker then clenched his right hand into a fist ready to strike Ray hard before Keith Boston came out from behind the bar to stop him dead in his tracks with, the now loaded, Henry rifle in his hands.

"You can hurt him all you want, big boy. But I find that this works better for putting down bears like you.," Keith said, lifting the gun above hip level.

"So scared. You really wanna take that risk bar keeper?!"

"Let him go, Junior." the oldest of the lumberjacks said, and the brute dropped Ray back down to the floor.

"You don't know who you're messing with, big guy. That man right there saved this town not long ago, and I'd appreciate it if you'd give him a little respect and answer his questions. All three of you."

"I don't respect the dead," the lumberjack said with a chilling quiet voice before yanking the rifle out of Keith's hand and with ease fired a single shot from the gun with one hand into Ray's head. Everybody froze in shock as the head flopped forwards the floor with a loud thud and the other two lumberjacks chuckled away before the eldest stood up to assert authority. "You see barkeeper, us Bloombergs, we just like to get on with our day as usual and not be interrupted. You say respect him for something we don't know or care about? I think its time you learn about treating your customers with some respect-" Ray sat up with loud intake of air and the entire bar was again frozen in fear. The lone shot from the rifle left nothing but a single hole in the middle of Ray's forehead, and it started to heal as his eyes, which had drifted far apart, began making their way back to the centre even though Ray was not fully conscious yet of his surroundings.

"That was weird. I forgot how to talk. Anyway...what were we talking about again?" Ray spoke with a little bit of dribble coming from his mouth as his wound finally sealed up. Everyone looked on in astonishment at what they just saw. Keith remained frozen, but a smile soon began to break before eventually ending the stunned silence.

"You wait till Millie sees ya again," he said.

"Where is she?"

"We dunno, son. Last time we saw her, she took the Biden fella with her. Tied up and gagged behind her on the backside of her horse. She never came back." One of the old men said.

"How long ago was this?"

"A day or two after you left." Mr Boston said.

Ray couldn't let this go. The fear for his loves life was all he thought of now. Screw the mission, for now, he thought as he got up from the ground to stand up to ask Mr Boston: "Do you at least know a direction?"

North of the town. No roads, open field. Common large spaces to find rogue horses to rustle. There was no indicator that she went through here, Keith was the last one to see her with the supposed Biden who left the town hostage tied down on horse-back. The two stood out their side by side on their horses and looked in every direction.

"We could be out here for a while, Ray."

"Let's split, I'll take the left you take a right." Ray tasked, and the two rode off in their given course. Their eyes were glued to the land, searching every pit of grass that were scattered around here and there. Most things the two would come across were dead rodents to snakes coiled up (usually in the grass). The two searched for a full hour before a gunshot was heard, it was Mr Boston from the far East of Ray. A signal that something was found. Ray rode as quick as he can over to his right until his eyes caught the small blimp that was Keith before getting closer and closer to him. He was off his horse in a shot and walked up to see Keith holding a collection of ropes. They were cut, and about the length to maintain a set of hands or feet together. Biden. Were some of his men still around during the time of the town being hostage? Or was Biden traded? Spared? Either way, there was no horse tracks or human tracks to know what had happened to the pair. In the end, the two knew that where ever Millie and the Colonel had gone too, it would undoubtedly be a long time before anyone could find them. Rays heart went heavy as he tried to keep the thought of her being alive in his head, but the other options bogged it down. But as he stared at the ropes, he had a glimmer of hope as he remembered somebody that could possibly lead him to her. Millie's brother, Thomas. Ray and Keith rode back into town and lead up the hill to find the house where Millie and her brother rested their heads. It was near the woodland and was a log cabin. Small in size but was comfortable. Ray knocked on the door loudly two times before the door swung back open, and Thomas answered.

"Yeah? You're Ray, right?"

"Do you know where Millie went to?" Ray said, sparing pleasantries.

"She was with that Biden fella, showing him a thing or two."

"Did she at least say where she was going with him?"

"No idea."

"Do you have at least a clue of where your sister may have gone after with Biden?"

"Seriously I have no idea. I let my sister get on with whatever. She'd sometimes be gone a month before I see her again. She doesn't really tell me much." Thomas said.

Ray hung his head down. No one had a clue of where Millie may have gone, even asking her brother was pointless. Keith put his hand on Ray's shoulder for comfort as the two walked away from the cabin after thanking Thomas.

"You never know she may turn up, Ray. Think positive."

"I won't be able to."

"Always hold out, son. Now, what was it about earlier when you caused a ruckus in my saloon?" Keith asked. Ray brought his head back with his brain gears as he thought of an idea. Not only would this get him with a crew to Waywood, bound for blood, but it could also lead him to Millie if he was lucky. Back inside the saloon, everyone was speaking so fast that it could've been mistaken for a cattle market. The three lumberjacks once standing in the middle of the saloon, now hidden at the back of the saloon in the corner like outcasts, everyone including them was shaken up. The debate spread around the bar with many of the same questions: 'Is he cursed?', 'Is he a devil?' Or the more comical from one individual: 'Looks like those elixirs actually work'. They were sat down until the doors opened, all jumping up to stand, with their hands inching to their guns. Ray and Keith entered the saloon, their eyes looking all-around the eyes of the onlookers.

"I think you should put him down right there, Mr Boston," one man with a funny eye proclaimed. Another man piped up, saying, "You should've buried him in the dirt out there!".

"I ain't killing no one, you lot! I saw exactly the same thing as you but you forget I know this man. And no type of witchcraft is gonna convince me he's different than the day I met him. Speaking of which, what exactly was that you did?" he whispered into Ray's left ear. Ray didn't want to explain but to get back to the business at hand.

"Look you can exile me if you want, but Millie is missing, and it may be something to do with Biden. If you let me have your attention for just five minutes, I want to propose a grand plan that includes any willing participant." Ray said addressing the crowd in his courageous tone of voice fashioned by his past military profession. No one budged though except the lumberjacks, moving out from their dark corner where they retreated after the two left in search for Millie. All three stood side by side and pulled up a chair in the centre of the saloon while the other two moved tables away. Ray looked back at Keith, who gave him a look of confidence before he walked up to the chair, and the crowd parted for him as he slowly strode through. Ray sat down, legs parted with his hands resting in his coat pockets and began to speak.

"Thank you, gentlemen. The reason I've gathered you all in here, in the worst of ways I'll admit, is to band this town together after what transpired here weeks ago at the hands of Colonel Biden. It was my own doing that lead him here, and for that first and foremost, I am sorry. My own mistakes caused the town to be ransacked and having all of you moved around like cattle and of course, the misfortune of having two members of the community killed by my actions. But that doesn't excuse Biden's behaviour. I believe that Millie took him intending to end his days but may have underestimated of who the Colonel was and who his accomplices were. He had more men, way more men than what you saw that day. The tables turned, and Mr Boston and I found nothing out there, except for these ropes. The ropes that held Biden tight were cut, and no one was found."

"How do we know that she didn't cut em?" a woman said.

"What if she sold out?" an elder woman said.

"In any case, whatever the circumstances may be, one may be dead, and one may be alive, or maybe both of them have survived or died, it does not matter now. What matters is I have the location of the place were Biden's commander may be, the real reason he was given the freedom to do what he did lies with his commanding officer, Waywood. He is held up north, in the mountains, snowy climate and he has men armed to the teeth. Well, right now I've probably lost all of you, but my proposal is that if we can band together and work something out that reprimands this Waywood, think of the funding and treatment, you would all receive. The story paints itself: 'Local town in rural Kentucky subject to violent military conduct, how will the President act during the war?' Imagine it. This town could be a significant player if your stories were told.

Now I'm asking you, who will stand up and let the story of Bonebag continue?" Ray finished with a statesman-like voice as he got up from his chair expecting the town to raise their arms in a defiant and synchronised Yes! It took about ten seconds to pass before the guns started to lift but with more hesitation. Soon, they were all raised including Keith's. Ray looked around counting up everyone before eventually leading them out with the question;

"Alright! Who houses the guns around here?" The people of Bonebag soon made their way to Claude's gun store, who had also been in the crowd at saloon. Still inside the bar were Ray, Keith and the three lumberjacks who, before leaving to join the party all looked at Ray with a grimace.

"Don't think we're in it for you. When this is over, we want an explanation from you. We wanna know what you are scrawny," said the younger lumberjack.

"You won't wanna know."

"Trust us, we do. And maybe, if we're still not happy about it, we can have you be the first person to start our axe count" The middle brother threatened to brandish the axe in his right hand as he brought the sharp metal up to Ray's eyes. The three went outside, not joining the party as from the look of their horses carrying bags they had everything they needed to begin with. Keith was at Ray's side with his rifle he usually concealed behind the bar.

"I think you ought to tell them, Ray. Not many folks can take a bullet to the head and have it grow back magically-"

"No, they can't. And if I tell them then what happens? The story becomes a fairytale. No one will believe them then. The story will be turned into a lie about how the confederates brain-washed them all with stories of people surviving death. They won't get what they truly need in this town. More people like Biden will go to other towns and do the exact same thing leading to more and more panic and disorder. Now you can trust the government all you want, but I've seen how easy it is for them to lead people from towns like this who have nothing. It's better if I leave after this anyway." Keith listened hard to Ray and said nothing in return until Ray was halfway out the door, stopping him and leaving a horrible taste in his mouth.

"Sort of like what you're doing now, right?" Keith said with a cold stare. Ray's eyes were on the floor as he bit his tongue trying not to raise his voice.

"Is this Waywood guy really related to Biden, Ray? Or is he part of something we don't know which you won't tell us about?" More dead silence lay between the two. Ray's hands shook, he was angry but couldn't show it. He had to hold his head high in this, Keith had him right there, stuck in his emotions for what seemed like an uncomfortable eternity. In the end, Ray continued on through the saloon doors and joined the crowd down at the gun shop, leaving Keith standing alone in his saloon, empty like on a Monday morning. Keith closed his doors and waited by the window to see everyone leave together. Everyone at the gun shop had loaded up and began to hitch up on saddles for the long journey ahead with Ray at the front. They all were equipped with handguns, rifles, shotguns, dynamite and knives ready to defend their town of Bonebag to the end. Even mothers with their children were armed to the teeth much to the disgust of their leader, Ray. They all looked up at him, motivated by his speech, half of the people he knew and some he had not seen. Putting on a brave face, he brought his arm up, hand straightened and pointed in the direction they would be heading, and everyone took off while he remained there, looking into the saloon window. His eyes met Keith's again as nearly fifty people obscured his full view of him before they eventually moved out of town.

"I take it you're not coming."

Keith opened the window.

"I don't wanna ruin my day off." he said with a disappointed look like a child's father would, if they had done something wrong. Ray had to be upfront after the brief exchange, he made his way over to get in front of everyone. Keith then closed the window and locked the shutters before turning the sign from 'Open' to 'Closed'. Ray came to the front of his band of followers, and the town of Bonebag was soon riding off up north. All with the intent of revenge, the main ingredient fuelling them, being convinced by Ray's background skills in speech making to lower-tier soldiers in his units. The group consisted of forty-four men and seven women (two of which brought children) All still under the age of ten. Half of the men in the group were workers, regulars of the town and in particular the wood barn. Some had heard of the incident during time off and had joined up with work friends in the weeks after. People attacking your scource of income did mean a lot to them. Others included the inhabitants of Bonebag, Mr Claude, the gunsmith who supplied the majority of the group with the armoury. A man in his sixties, sporting a finely combed black moustache harvesting the odd grey hair or two which were more common on his short hair. He wore a white shirt with a burgundy waist-coat with red stitching. Down the middle of the pack were Ray's former boss, Martha, carrying a double-barrelled shot-gun on her back with a determined look along with the two men beside her. One older than the other but both wearing similar jeans and brown suede hats. The youngest had the longest hair, blonde and straight while the older man's was un-washed and brown in colour. Further down the group were younger women, usually in the profession of seducing men with their "hospitality". Still, today their corset colours of rich royal blue, green and red were covered by dark trench coats, all three with their tangled curly hair let loose, flowing in the wind this time with silver six-shooters resting in holsters by their sides. Behind these three were the three lumberjacks, who had pushed up into the group to get a better view ahead. The three were relaxed but each of them holding a different kind of rifle along with their reins. Women with children were at the back, the least likely to be hit in the case of an attack. They rode close to one another, and the kids enjoyed some jok-ing and playing behind their mothers' back. They had no idea of what was to come, nor did they even understand the situ-ation. The mothers just couldn't bear to leave them home alone with no one else around. They were part of this. It was about midday when the town of Bonebag left out for blood, now the sun was going down five hours later, and the group were in the middle of the state of Iowa, near the borderlines of the unknown territories. Ray had managed to get the group inside a barn for the night, the town sheltering alongside cows and pigs, suffering through the smell. All the horses were out back in a fenced-off area of grass for the night. With fifty plus people all cooped together in a barn, there wasn't much room for movement, so it was more like a human dog pile. Heads rested on people's shoulders, and others were sprawled out on the floor or on top of each other. It was uncomfortable for some and not much sleep to go with it. For most of the journey up until resting up in the barn, barely anyone had struck up a conversation to keep the spirits high or just to make the time go by. That period of silence ended, however, when the more vocal lumberjacks who couldn't get any sleep even if they tried raised a question at an uncomfortable hour. "So this Waywood fella, you got an idea as to why he's letting people like Biden get away with the shit he did?"

"No idea. Wartime makes people make crazy decisions. I was part of the military, and I screwed up that's why Biden came looking for me. Guess they didn't want anyone knowing about their methods."

"You must've screwed things up pretty bad then," a older man said in the right hand corner of the barn with his eyes still closed.

"Still not gonna talk about that though are ya?" the eldest lumberjack said.

"No," Ray said.

"And why the hell not then? Sure you made a pretty convincing speech, and I'm in this to avenge the town, but I, for one would like to hear a reason as to why I was put into all this because of you," one woman said to the left. Ray kept silent.

"Are you some kind of angel, mister?" Came a sweet quiet voice from the right of Ray. It was one of the children who had woken up from the talking in the night.

"What's that, son?"

"Only angels save others. Is that why you can't die? I heard about it in town, but my mum told me to cover my ears when hearing about stuff like that." The child was innocent as they come, round face with a few freckles and bushy hair with eyes that were bright blue. Ray smiled and he played along only to shut everyone up with the questions.

"Yes, son, I am. I guess. You see the problem is that not many people would believe me if I did tell 'em. Angels can be found anywhere not just from the sky when your mummy tells you to pray every night. Do you pray before bed?" Ray asked as everyone awake looked on in silence.

"Yes, sir," the young boy said.

"And I'm sure you've asked them for something from the angels before haven't you?" Ray continued.

"Yes," said the boy now sitting on Ray's lap.

"Well son, why do you think we ask for an angel in bad times?" Ray let the small boy have his minute of think time, playing with his fingers while he bobbed his head playfully. He shrugged his tiny shoulders and Ray continued.

"We ask for angels because sometimes in times of trouble, no one else will come and save us here on earth. And if you believe in the words of God you know that they'll do it without ever having to explain how they did it. I lived in your town for a little while but I saw the people and knew that it was worth saving. Maybe that's how I didn't die when that nasty Colonel put his gun up towards me." Manipulation is one thing, but to do it with a kid was a whole different ball game. Nobody in the group spoke up from then on after the small boy felt comfortable in Ray's arms. However, the familiar looks of distrust hopped from one person to another. Ray was avoiding questions, but he felt that they wouldn't be necessary for leading them on. Instead, the people involved in the conversation merely passed on playful smiles to the child and to Ray. After breakfast was over with, consisting of old cans of beans looking like they have one more good day in them along with some dry crackers, the group set off further North and the far scattered lands inhabited by the natives. The group were soon up in the top part of Indiana before travelling up further to the snowy reaches of the future state of Minnesota. The group still kept their firearms tight and were ready for anything that could hit them at any given moment. The air got more colder the further they went, and the warming sensation from a heavy jacket crafted from animal skin was needed. The crisp crackling of the dry ground under the horses' hooves with the brisk breeze blowing towards them slowly transformed into cold winter showers of soft falling snow that covered the land. Trees had blankets of snow covering their branches, and small lake streams which weaved through the slopes of land were now frozen, some frozen with just the slightest finger poke to crack it while some were thick and with a little bit more force

from a heavy object, you could break through it. Ray was unfazed about the cold as he had done distant travelling before
his days in the military and even when enlisted, exercise done
up in these harsh, bitter conditions were a chore. The journey
had taken them up to the snowy mountains were old base
camps were made, discarded after their one and only use. Waywood was recruiting. This further helped Ray's set up a plan to
lead people to the charge, if he was immortal how else could
they lose. He saw and took the punishment from Goida, who
knew what Waywood could do. The walkway up the mountains had to be continued on foot as the muddy steps up into
the base could only fit very few people. Ray dismounted first
followed by everyone in the pack with the mothers staying behind with the children. The mothers grouped their children together with the horses telling them that if no one was to return, get on and don't look back. With the grimmest of expressions, they all nodded in understanding unaware of what will
transpire as the adult group ventured into the narrow staircase
into the mountains. The steps were slippery with ice and wood
of the structure, moist from the constant snow fall. Everyone
kept as close as they could to make sure of catching anyone
should a slip occur, and it did, several times. Ray leading the
trail of people behind him halted them once they were halfway
up, the sounds of the workmen shouting instructions to one

another could be made out vaguely if you listened carefully while trying to drown out the wind howling in your ears. The entranceway had to be close, and Ray knew it, twiddling his hand he gestured them to move on up the steps which now began to snake around the mountain. The height of the mountain forced the people of Bonebag to bury their heads in the back of the other person in front while they placed their hands on their shoulders to guide them on. The snow at the group's current altitude blew more violently than when they were further down the slope. Everyone's faces were stinging sharply, while their eyes started to water. It wasn't long till they were back inside the protective walls of the mountain and were seeing the reassuring orange glimmer of candlelight, leading them inside towards the base camp. As Ray lead them on, he could see how the mountain base was built as the darkness of the walls vanished, and he was introduced into a flat area surrounded by the broken-down walls created by sharp steel pickaxes. Inside the large circular bases were wooden shacks, averaging from small to medium height, harbouring stolen goods, water, food, money all guarded by one man at each door. There was water pipes, along with food crops, the workmen walked around like ants in a farm. There must've been nearly a hundred men, from the height Ray observed the base made it seem that way. Mr Devlin, the Bonebag butcher, who stood to Ray's right side, said: "There's no other way we can approach this. This is the only way into there," he said as his nerves spilled over. Ray pulled his Winchester rifle from behind his back and cradled it comfortably in his arms.

"Then that means we walk in quietly," he said as he started to walk down. Mr Devlin extended his arm intending to stop him, but Ray was already an arm's length away, he closed his gloved hand and brought it to his face resting it on his mouth to stop the words spilling out. Ray's eyes trailed along to look at the guards, on top of the shacks, they too had rifles watching the hillsides for intruders, he made sure to be as relaxed as possible with his finger on the trigger. The staircase went around in a circle inside the mountain walls, a bit of a journey down but Ray paced himself well, and when the guards had turned thier backs he looked back up to Mr Devlin and signalled for each person to go one at a time. It took some doing but the message was sent, and after another minute of watching Ray slowly descend down the stairs, Mr Devlin told the person behind him. That person did so with the next and so on until the whole group had heard it. They began the walk into enemy territory. Mr Devlin, like Ray, had his gun in hand and kept his eyes trained for anyone acting suspiciously. It all seemed to be going well, the first ten of the group had successfully made it around, spaced out and not looking too out of place but then the calamity began. The silence was gone with one little mistake. By the time the tenth person came down, the lumberjack brothers were next, and the youngest of the three stepped up next. Only he had underestimated how much pressure he put on his gun trigger, and once he made a sharp slip on the stairs causing his foot to bend awkwardly, the gun went off. The group froze, and all the workers' heads shot up.

"Idiot," Ray said with his teeth gritted. Ray's eyes immediately looked over to the guard on the tallest shack, who had only just lifted his rifle to his eyes, when Ray unloaded the second shot, connecting to the side of the scouts head sending him down off the roof into the snow.

"Duck!" Ray shouted to the ones walking the wooden platform as the gunfire began to unload in a hail storm of bullets. The ten people dropped covering their heads, and Ray rolled as close as he could to the mountain walls to avoid as much gunfire as possible. Others followed along, but the rest of the group didn't have it, instead, in a defining moment for the town, all forty of the other townpeople charged in, running as quickly as they can, shooting off rounds of ammunition at their targets. Ray remained flat on the wooden platform, but he could not stop everyone rushing in, their feet stomped past him, and the gunfire continued. On the base ground, the workmen took cover and began to strategize places to move as the walk-round path lead behind them. Sadly though, bodies soon began to fall like dominoes as the second to hit the snow hard was one of the group, one of the mothers, whose child was a little girl of six, got caught with a bullet to the gut. The blood trickled down her skirt as she hunched forward till her body was at a nighty degree angle until she cascaded down onto the snowy floor. Soon many bodies from both sides were hitting the floor one by one, bullets had ricocheted off the steel and wooden structures, and others had pierced bodies, covering them in a red coating of blood as. The effort of the charge paid off as the battle soon was on level ground, it was now at this point seventy against thirty-three. Those in the group who had fallen were workers of the old wood mill while others included regulars such as Cyril Thompson, Bonebag's cobbler and Mr Taylor, the butcher with Mr Devlin, who was clutching his leg in pain as a bullet shot through his knee cap. He screamed in pain. Ray kept crawling past the bodies of his group, the Bloomberg brothers, were now on the ground below, where the workmen had now taken position inside the wooden shacks, popping their heads in and out of the cracks and openings from the windows. As the wooden platform stairs curved down the rest of the Bonebag group took cover inside the nearest shack. The cabin smelt moist but inside was something more horrifying than the men outside. The shack was stacked inside was crates and crates of gunpowder and TNT. One rogue shot and they would be all toast, and it looked like the white flag might be raised as two large men in denim overalls had their guns trained on the crates behind them.

"Drop em, or we light the fireworks," one of them snarled with the only three teeth he had poking over his top lip like a boar. Outside Ray was the only one left on the platform who could still walk leading down to the last staircase, his eyes scanned as much of the place he could be looking for the slightest bit of movement before rushing over to Mr Devlin's aid. Ray took off the wounded man's coat and ripped one of the sleeves from his navy blue shirt, wrapping the fabric around the wound in his knee.

"Just stay there and keep as quiet as possible," Ray said, and Devlin nodded with the smallest of tears running down his cheek as he bit into his fingers.

"Run, run, run, Ray McCarthy! Run, run, run, to the elders who show no mercy!" A voice sounded off down below him. A lonely man stood in the middle of the bloodshed and wreckage from the fight pressing his black leather gloves together as he looked for an answer. He was in a thick blue coat with a beaver fur collar with a black leather belt, keeping the jacket tight around his waist. The folds of his neck fat were hidden by a crudely placed cravat tie, which pushed his collar up slightly while his thin dark hair came past it. He was old, skin sagging, and his posture was just starting to lean further into uncomfortable levels. This was Waywood, Bazka's right-hand man standing at six foot five and he continued to taunt those who had entered the base, under his crooked nose.

"Nice little army you brought, Mr McCarthy. Pity that it did you no good. All it did was make your job harder. How's that heart of yours? Still feeling ok? Not getting the feeling of giving up yet? Bazka has told me to lead the charge and to bring those who live in the right path, the path of the fallen, the path set by Bazka to guide them to a life unheard of. Why keep your guidance under those old fools who are making you do their bidding? They did the same to my master and look what became of him. Stronger than ever. A real army of devotees forgotten during time of war. Can you picture it, Mr McCarthy? Souls who do not see future in those leading the charges of both the Union and the Confederacy. Instead of the faith in a god more powerful than that top hat-wearing fool called the President of the United States. Bazka will bring the land into a future, unlike any other and soon it will convert the world as the way forward and the creatures of the night will come again, and we will be victorious!" The two shacks erupted in cheers at the mention of a promised land in their image, should Bazka's plan be a success.

"But I think you should step on down here, Ray. Let me and the boys get a good look at ya. Or the rest of your so-called family bite the bullet!" threatened Waywood. Ray had no option but to come down, it would be a world of hurt for him but the rest of the town's lives were at stake, he got up from the ground and raised his rifle and hands in the air.

"Pretty boy," Waywood said to himself. "Boys come on out, wait till you see who this man is. He got me all flustered and squawking like my nanny's pet bird!" Waywood and the group of workmen all started mimicking bird calls with some sounding more like an elderly crow than a petite bird taunting Ray as he walked down the rest of the staircase. The Bonebag townspeople, still huddled up together as the brutish grunts keeping them at gunpoint started joining in the squawking, one of the their voices was deeper than the other and the two mimicking sounds moulded together almost sounded like a donkey's cry. Ray's boots touched the ground as he got down from the last wooden step. His feet crunched the snow as he entered the pit of workmen who beckoned him forward, waving their arms around now, like a bunch of friends encouraging you closer to take another drink, only the pain afterwards will be felt all over with what they had in store. The brutes pushed, yanked and screamed phrases that would make a nun crumble, of how creatively strung together they were. Waywood stood in the middle of the circle with his hands out like a father greeting his child. The men pushed him forward and the two embraced in a awkward uncomfortable hug, which rung cheers through the circles. "Oh, how I've longed to see you! Look at ya, not a scratch on you! And to think, men, he's a serviceman! He should have lost something like a limb at least," The workmen piped up again in a chorus of playfully childish, 'ooohhs'.

"Three legs a man has, and I bet he's keeping the third in a box wrapped up for me!" Floods of laughs poured into the inner circle.

"Where is it Ray? Or has it not grown back yet?!" The grotesque Waywood shouted, pulling Ray closer towards his mouth which stunk like the oldest bit of roadkill you could possibly find.

"Oh, it can grow back but how much of a mark can I leave? Rough him up, boys!" The workmen swarmed onto Ray like dogs to a piece of hide. Flurries of kicks, punches, spitting and erratic screaming came from the workmen, showcasing the extent of what they could be like when under a madman like Waywood for a long time in the coldest reaches of the mountains. Like a conductor leading his orchestra, Waywood lifted his hands with palms flat and the workmen ceased their torment. He twisted his hands around with the palms facing up and his fingers curled, with a slight flick the workmen roughly hoisted Ray up and with no effort shot him up into the air and back down onto the cold hard floor. They continued over and over like they were making sure everyone got an equal opportunity to throw their prey around like a piece of meat with the floor being their way of tenderizing him. Waywood waved his hands again and they let him drop one last time. He whistled with his fingers, inside the two big grunts holding Bonebag's people looked at each other in delight, "That's are cue."

"It's like a play," the other said as they pushed the group out from the tight space of the shack.

"Oh, god. I'm gonna die by these fools," said Martha as she and the others looked on in dread, for they were now being pushed into the circle the same way Ray had entered.

"Behold the mighty Bonebag legacy! One of Kentucky's weakest traces of humanity this side of the east! No one's ever gonna re-member them and that's just the way I want it! But let's not waste 'em like they're nothing. Have 'em!" The circle lines broke again, these rabid men had their way with everyone. They beat everyone to within an inch of their lives, clawing and tearing into them with teeth and knives. The screams of the group were drowned out by the loud workmen who got off on their pain. Blood was everywhere, colouring the sheet of snow in a thick dark red which had footprints and hand marks pressed into it. The bodies begun to stack up with Mr Devlin leaving the world, first in unimaginable pain before his eyes began to roll back, they saw his weakness, the knee and they went for it. Be-fore long with enough force the leg was hacked and pulled off while the hounds of Waywood chowed down on him, covering him from sight. Hair was pulled out, tossed around like con-fetti and also worn in disturbing fashion. The lumberjack trip-lets managed to get a bit of offence as they had done the right thing and played to their advantage, staying close together. Like a bunch of bare-knuckle brawlers, fists were thrown in every direction connecting sharply with the chins and cheeks of their foes. Unlike their day jobs, they were striking heavily but uncoordinated which lead to their separation. The carni-vore workmen saw the opportunity and jumped in together on to the largest of the triplets and swooped in on the eldest and youngest brothers. Struggling to keep in sight of one another, the eldest was the first to go, the largest brother at six foot two, watched in horror as he saw his eldest brother slowly slip away into the hands of the psychotic soldiers. In a rush of anger and all the will he had left, the bulkiest brother rushed through the blood-soaked crowd which piled over each other trying to get a piece of their fear laced pie. They tumbled down to the ground, so it created a bit of space for the man in brown-checkered garments to search for his brother amongst the pileup. He found him after shoving away several heads all with staggered expressions trying to get back up, but not the way he wanted with his jaw hanging loose. Still alive but unable to talk properly. His brother's familiar voice had turned into a garbled mess of words sloshing around a blood-filled mouth with a flickering tongue. The man held his older brother's head as the tears left his eyes and in his sorrow, the workmen all rose up, their hands were now on his head pulling him back. The eldest was finished off without his youngest brother seeing him after the middle child was dragged away, held down with all the henchmen's strength.

Martha had fought her battle, she was whisked away from an overgrown lummox, bald with a gut hanging disgustingly over barely belted denim. Poked, bitten, her hands broken from punching the human-bear who groped her before hoisting her over his shoulders. What was a group of thirty survivors had now turned into barely breathing battered soon-to-be corpses and Ray was in the VIP seat watching it from the best angle while Waywood held his knife close to his neck. The conductor of the slaughter raised his hand up, stopping everyone as they all slapped each other to stop themselves. Turning around, Ray could see how deranged one person could turn a group of forgotten souls into a senseless pack of wild animals. Manic-looking, covered in blood and now obeying the lift of a hand from their handler. The few who were alive, like Martha, the two lumberjacks, two elderly men with their eyes blackened and a women with her breast exposed and a chunk of her hair scraped from her scalp were held like trophies for them. Way-wood had a grin that was thin and uncomfortable to stare at for a long time without feeling a shiver run through you. Ray just stood there, lifeless looking, he knew what he would bring this to the group. Nothing but death.

"A feeble attempt sir. All this for what? To feel justified? To feel like the hero you should've been after leaving your men to die like that out in the open!"Ray was stunned.

"How do you kno-"

"What did you do Ray?" Martha said lifting her slouched head up.

"I told you-"

"You didn't tell us nothing! Now for god's sake tell us! There's no one else to tell!" Ray knew they wouldn't live for long so he might as well indulge them with all the worth he had left to them. Like a summons, Ray was ready to present his side of the story.

"I'm part of a tribe. The Crow tribe in the western territory. The Crows took me in before the war and I used my position to keep them safe and provide them with anything they required. I lead the lie for years until it eventually caught up with me. I lead a group of young hopefuls to their deaths, they fought against them and the confederates. I ran and I laid out another lie hoping that no-one would find me. I brought that lie to you and I lied again. I couldn't fight it alone I had to get this dead and buried somehow," he confessed. Martha and the other Bonebag survivors were lost for words. They were weary about their leader and now it came full circle. Waywood loved every second, of it before he carried on for Ray.

"You see here folks, we have a case of a wannabe soldier who thinks of what's best for himself. What you're doing now still is in for the Crow's best interest. I, Gilbert Joesph Waywood, serve the real elder. And as you can see from the few of you still standing and those under my wing prove exactly what dis-organised ethics looks like!" Waywood tightened his grasp on Ray and his essence, ghoulish black in colour, rose up through his arm sending Ray across the circle. The workmen laughed as he landed flat on his back.

"This is what you can achieve once we have banished the likes of this small messenger of the elders for good. Bazka knows you are hungry for redemption and he can bring all that you need. This man says to you that he cannot die like it's some sort of reason to believe him. 'If I can't die no one else will!' He'll exclaim and in the end who will it benefit? Him and him alone. You are all just his little dogs on a leash but with me you can be a free wild wolf in a pack that is hungry for the world around them!" The workmen brought their arms up in support for the mad dogs cry. In unison they chanted Bazka's name, lifting their fists up and down before a gunshot rattled the air and the chants suddenly stopped with a deafening ring. The bullet landed in Waywood's face ripping off his left ear as he clutched it in pain with the blood seeping through his fingers. The shot came from above, Waywoods men saw the man with the rifle, the silver Henry rifle, it was Keith Boston, wearing a large wolf-skin coat and with a few others behind him in similar woollen garments but their identities hidden behind black balaclavas with a wolfs head resting on top.

"You fellas better be bringing the fight cause us wolves ain't leaving without our Bonebag!" Keith shouted down.

"Kill em!" Waywood screamed. But the order to kill was interrupted by an explosion coming from behind the circled gathering. The shack with the explosives shot up into flames and the splintered wood shot everywhere. Unbeknownst to them as they watched in horror of their base of operations lit up into a ball of flame, two men from Keith's group sprung up from behind the crates by the water mill and lobbed Molotov's into the crowd setting them alight. Keith and his men above on the wooden platform, threw Molotov's of their own onto the other side, bringing the workmen to scramble around like panicked rodents. Martha was dropped to the ground and the others were let go as the workmen ran to get away from the spreading fire. Keith and his men then unloaded twenty one rounds of ammunition onto those below and his boys who set off the explosions unloaded fourteen more rounds. Ray sat himself up from the cold snow to see all the carnage happening around him, he sprung to his feet and ran to Martha and the others. "Follow me! Back up to the balcony!" He shouted. The group helped each other as much as they could, Ray lead the two old men through while the lumberjack carried the women who was almost looking to faint from pain in his arms. The screams from the workmen combined with the gunshots being fired in every direction gave the feeling that Ray was back in the war. Ray's group ran as fast as they could, up the curved platform with the two men draped in wolf's skin following them close by, still hammering away at those psycho enough attempting to follow them. They reached Keith and they made for the entrance-way but Keith wasn't done.

"What are you doing, come on!" Ray called back to him.

"Not until after I burn your mess!" Keith growled back. He pulled a Molotov out from his inner coat pocket and lit it from the last bit from his cigarette. He hurled the wine bottle to the side wall, breaking it and spreading the light onto the platform he was on. He scurried up towards the entrance-way, finally, as the whole balcony fire started to spread quickly. The flame's smoke engulfed inside the mountain and from the outside, down below where the kids would be laying almost made it look like a volcano. The sky was a winter fire tonight as the kids sat up from the ground by the horses to see the remainder of the group rushing down the steps. The children cried for their mothers but would never know what happened to them. Everyone knew that when they returned home, everything would be different and some things just won't be spoken about. Back inside, the fire still grew in size as the piles of bodies continued to feed its spread. One man stepped over them all still clutching his ear which had been shot in the beginning stages of the second attack. His blood ran right down the side of his coat as he looked around for anyone but no one was breathing. The army he built from the ground up, slaughtered in a matter of minutes inside the cold confines of the snowy mountain. Waywood was a shepherd who had lost his flock of demented souls. His anger soon escaped as dazed and confused he realised that his soldiers had been massacred and the hate-filled scream echoed out to the sky's as the fires kept on raging and the carcasses filled everything with a wet death smell. That smell blew from one side of his nose to the other, the air manipulated and twisted all around and so too did the flames. The fires contorted, spiralling like mini tornadoes in a dusty open part of the southern regions of America until the sounds of nature spoke to him.

"Don't despair child. My rule is still alive. More like this will heed your words. But this failure cannot be simply accepted.

Follow them, make sure none of them survive."

"Yes, my master. But I am hurt," Waywood answered.

"Oh poor thing. Let me help you with that." As the voice ended, the fires spun round more rapidly becoming thinner and sharper until the two fires shot into him sending him to his knees. Like a dagger it pierced through his heart, his blood oozed out from his deformed ear as the steam rose out from his orifices until another scream escaped him, more deeper and much more demonic.

Coming down the mountain the terrain was difficult to navigate through. Bonebag's group of people wove through the trees while trying to see despite the thick fog, the day got darker since they came out from the mountain and the desperately needed to make level ground before the night crept in and the snow came down harder. They soon stopped in the open field where trees surrounded them, everyone took deep breaths as the threat of danger melted away.

"We ain't out of this just yet. Waywood's coming."

"Well frankly, he's all yours." Keith responded viciously as his lungs took in the cold air.

"No, we need to get prepared-"

"Enough from you! To hell with that! Do you see these people here? This is all that's left, out of fifty Ray! You dragged them and me into a battle that no one should've been part of in the first place! They're coming with me back home where none of this concerns us! And at this point, I don't care whether you live or die; you are not welcome back!" Keith shouted into Rays face with the spit flying from his lips. Ray was frozen. He understood now that nothing he said after that would mean anything.

"But if we find Millie-"

"She's gone, Ray! And she's either worm food or taking some new name and living somewhere far from this bullshit! Just forget anything from us Ray, because soon we're not gonna remember you. But if she does come back, I'm telling her to stay far away from you," Keith said.

"She won't accept that Keith you know she won't."

"Well, I'm gonna damn we'll convince her. You wanna fight me over that, then do it." The two were locked in a deep personal stare-down that had the survivors worried but cooler heads prevailed as Ray turned his head away to face them.

"Guys, I'm sorry. Keith's right. What I have going on right now, it'll hurt you. I got caught up in the moment and brought you lot in because I knew how impressionable you'd be after the town got held up. Just forget me. I'm in a completely different world now and you shouldn't be stepping into it anymore." Ray said with slouched shoulders. Martha and the four others along with Keith's gang kept their eyes on him, standing on his own, as they walked away to his right, in the direction for Bonebag down south. The expression didn't change on Martha's face, who gave him that motherly look of disappointment but with not enough hate to go into full on shout-mode. The two old men held each other up as their impaired vision made Ray out and the lumberjack still carrying the limp body of the female in a blood soaked corset away from them. Keith stood behind Ray as his men were following along with the group and he talked one last time to Ray.

"Don't you dare turn your head around. Keep on looking up there, Ray. That's what you're in now. Hell. And it's following you, not us. I hope God is judging you."

With that said, Ray heard Keith's footsteps crunching over the snow behind him as the wind picked up and he rode off south with the group. He stood there, tense, squeezing his hands into fists as his aura rose from his head and he knew he would have to step back into what Keith described perfectly, and it wasn't just now, Ray knew what it would be like now for the rest of his life so long as the will in him didn't die out. Hell.The ground back up was broken, different now from the first time he walked up it. It was disfigured, the weather couldn't have done this. If Hell was to be painted by a traveller this would surely be quite close to it. The fog got thicker as he walked back up the path into the hill dug wreckage of the former mountain fortress. It was easier to walk up now as it was just him and not a band of people holding on to one another to stay inside the narrow walkways. He reached back up through to the entrance and could see through the crack that the fires burned now immensely. Like a fireplace it was contained, burning upwards into the sky to be blown out. There was no way of making it down without looking like you could break a couple bones in the process. The spiral walkway around to the mountain crater floor was almost gone after Keith burnt it down on the way out. While trying to figure it out, everything went quiet and Ray was rushed off his feet and sent sliding down the the rocky slope as he turned around to a hellish cat-like face roaring back at him. He tumbled down and bounced around before hitting the rock floor with a stiff thud. The flames roared along with it as the creature was seen slithering his arms through the narrow entrance. It broke the rock around him and the creature launched itself out before landing in the fire where it slowly began to be seen clearly as Ray got up with his hand holding his back. Its eyes reflected the burning orange glow surrounding it as it then stepped out, the head was first, the cat-like features coupled with monstrous sharp fangs and wrinkled head that upon closer inspection was the things brain, broken out from the skull. Thin black streaks of hair hung from it and soon the neck and body followed through. The body was also wrinkled and curved like a snake with tiny bone legs sprouting from the sides. It had four crab like legs each with puss-dripping warts which were randomly spread like a fungus. The tips cracked the floor as it lowered itself down with the little bone legs supporting its weight. The head was now on Ray's level as he backed away, pushing the snow down hard with his hands as the creature kept coming closer. Its nostrils flared and the warm breath from its mouth smelt like what ever came up from a stranger's mouth one night around the back of Keith's saloon. It snarled while it looked down at its prey before a deep voice spoke while the jaw hung slightly loose.

"Honourable of you to come back and face me," the creature said revealing itself to be Waywood, now transformed into a being that Ray had seen previously with beings like Goida.

"This should've just been you and me in the first place."

"You thought right to bring an army of your own. But unlike you, I can recruit without my emotions getting the better of me." One of the crab-like legs came down to the side of Ray, it hit the ground hard sending shards of the rock flying over him as he rolled to dodge the oncoming attack.

"More will flock to me and Bazka's word will become stronger!" he bellowed as his other leg came down. Ray scrambled to his feet and now was in a full sprint towards the other end of the crater. Waywood brought his snake-like body back up and was soon crawling along the curved walls around him. Ray was almost there but Waywood jumped down in front of him, eager to slit him in two with one swipe of his sharp legs. The leg came at an angle and by a split second, Ray instantly dropped face down onto the ground before the leg rushed over him, missing him in a split second. Waywood laughed at his efforts and brought the other leg down which connected with the ground, just missing his head by a centimetre. A nice hole ran through his hat now. Ray got up again and this time didn't hold back, he let his aura rise up and he could feel the power surge through his veins. Waywood threw down his leg again but this time Ray leaped up clutching it, climbing up it like a oak tree until he ran past the puss and slime hopping over it like ice breaking beneath him before he bent down and pushed himself hard up landing on the edge of Waywoods cat nose. His two eyes moved into the centre and Ray looked dead into them and said "Come on, Kitty, show me some life before I put ya down" Waywood snarled, his face creasing up in anger before he threw his head back hoping to shake Ray off but Ray caught one of the long strands of black hair which were so void of life that it looked like even the weight of him alone could pull it right out of his head but it held and Ray swung like a monkey around as Waywood violently thrashed his massive cat head around. Ray slid down the black strand of hair, letting go as he reached the end of it landing back onto the creature's front leg, his left food landed on hard exoskeleton while the other landed in a small hole filled with yellowish puss. It was deep, his leg soaked all the way up to the knee and Waywood, like the somewhat cat he was, tried nabbing Ray with a quick bite, like he was a flea and after the first attempt, tried again but Ray had pulled himself out and slid down the crab leg onto the floor again. Looking back, he could see Waywood was agitated, his face look like something was burning, Ray saw from the hole that some mist excreted out with more sticky gooey fluid. Waywoods aura could only be contained from inside, if Ray could damage him from the inside the creature on the outside would break down. He had to find a way to make a hole deep enough to bring just one of his legs down which would incapacitate him enough for Ray to find a way to pull him out from the monster exterior. Purple aura surged up again and this time Ray clenched his right hand into a solid fist, tight as he could and he ran up again jumping right into it and as he landed his fist just below where Waywood was standing. The exoskeleton cracked and Waywood let out a shriek of terror as he saw how close it was to breaking. The creature brought his leg down at a angle which would've crushed Ray had he not let go, he pushed off with his legs as the leg landed flat onto the rock. It wasn't there for long as Waywood pushed himself up again with it and began to bring his other leg up as retaliation. Ray drew both his revolvers and unloaded all twelve rounds into his face in rapid succession, it blinded the creature and the leg was off course hitting the ground. The snow flew into the air and Ray jumped again bringing the same fist into the exposed leg. With a hard crack, the leg casing broke into three large pieces and underneath he saw the flesh inside, looking like he was back in Bloodgood's swamp; it was long, stretchy moss-green muscle with the leg fluid bubbling as the cold environment made it start to react horribly. Like a geyser, the aura mist erupted and Ray was pushed off the leg back onto the floor as Waywood tried to keep his aura inside but his leg just wasn't big enough to cover it. Reloading quick Ray once again shot up into Waywood's face, forcing him to lift his leg up before Ray could use the other six revolver bullets for the open target on his right. The weak flesh broke and puss spurted out before the hard leg casing started to crack even more. A thin crack line went around the top half of Waywood's sharp crab leg and it looked as if he brought any pressure on it, it would snap. Sadly for Waywood, it did and the leg snapped as he couldn't see what was occurring due to being blinded by bullets. With a gargled snap, green blood and puss spat out as the leg broke with the sharp end crashing down into the rock and Waywood fell to one side screeching as his head landed beside his shattered leg. Seizing the advantage, Ray reloaded for the last time and began to sprint again, this time around the hulking body that struggled to stand. If the inside is the weak point, he knew a big enough opening will expose Waywood and drag him out from his auras protective shell. The head, more specifically the back of the head. The most fleshy part it may even take a few shots from a pistol to open it up. Ray ran up the jagged back of the beast, eyeing its weak spot as it riled its head around in pain, but from the corner of its eye the beast saw his prey and Ray stopped. Hook, line and sinker, Ray smiled with glee as he shot one round just down in between his feet and it was all it took to make the creature even more frustrated. Waywood with his one good leg rotated it around with a monstrous amount of cracking from his deformed exoskeleton as his small bone legs on his abdomen kept him in position, the sharp tip end of the leg swung right round like a windmill and connected into a body. Its body, as Ray rolled back at the right moment leaving the creature tangled in its own messed up body like a pretzel. Now to strike, Ray shot upwards into the air and held on tight to the squidgy side of the head. He reached into his coat pocket with one hand while the other held on and brought out his hunting knife, he plunged the sharp knife into the skin as deep as he could and bringing it down was a hard task. The skin while soft was not human and it would need to take even more to wound the creature severely. No use in hanging on he thought, Ray let go and let his whole weight hold on to the knife handle as he and the knife slid in a straight cut down. Waywood roared in pain as he arched his head back while Ray carried on down until he eventually hit bone at the bottom of its neck. As quick as the drop down was the blood didn't start to pour out until a few seconds had passed and soon the green wet blood gushed out of the deep cut. Like emptying out a bucket, it went everywhere, with Ray glad he had a coat that stretched down to his ankles as he got the short stick when being hit by it. As Waywood continued to scream a blood curdling demonic wail Ray thrusted his hands out and the aura, like two pieces of rope, grabbed the open skinned and he began to widen his arms out, pulling it open even more. The same stretchy green muscle was seen, but this time upon opening the skin out to its furthest Ray saw Waywood buried in the muscles covered from head to toe in goo, blood and puss. His mind was deep in controlling his aura's creature that his eyes were tight shut and his head veins pulsed. Ray grabbed his hips and pulled towards him. The muscles began to snap off him as Waywood was being ripped out from inside his monster shell, as he came out more his eyes opened and the horror left his mouth in a scream of realisation that he was being ripped out from his auras creation.

"NOOOOO! STOP! YOU DON'T KNOW WHAT YOU'RE DOING!" He yelled before the final muscle holding him by his back snapped off and he was careening down from the head of the creature. He landed on Ray with a thud and rolled down the spine leaving Ray to chase after him as he soon hit the ground. Rays feet hit the ground and he walked over to Waywood who was now crawling away, cowering in fear.

"You idiot! You really are the elder's brightest aren't you!", Ray got hold of the front of Waywoods thick jacket and landed a strong strike to his nose making it bleed, red and green blood mixing together down his face.

"Tell me where Bazka is!"

"Why don't you ask him?" Waywood said. Ray looked back and could see the aura's creature head bent back all the way looking at the two of them. It's neck was broken from how far it stretched and no pain was shown in how it growled. Even without a host it was still walking and it was still hungry.

"Stop it" Ray said in a quieter tone, before lifting the volume again, "Stop it!" Waywood let out a terrified chuckle at his confusion.

"Don't you get it. The auras of the land find their host and learn from them. They have minds of their own and strength beyond their hosts" Ray looked back again to the see the cat-like creature retract its leg from its back similar to the bug like body it took twisted and broke itself over getting back into shape. The cracking of bones was loud and uncomfortable until it stretched up as high as its long body could, looking down at the two with its head above the mountain ridge. Ray wasted no time in running as far as he could as it looked like the creature would strike, but Waywood lay there, almost in a comforting embrace towards the monster he once inhabited, extending his hands out beckoning it.

"What are you doing?!" Ray yelled.

"If that's you in , master...Do It!" Waywood screamed. The creature then plunged down headfirst from above, and it almost looked that Waywood would be devoured to the creatures open-jaw, but it missed, crashing through the rock floor beside him. The beast hit the mountain floor so hard it sent the two men up into the air as the flames followed down the hole where the creature had buried itself into. Rock shot out across the circular formation, soon the beast was gone, tunnelling through the mountain into the darkest traces of the world below. Waywood was the first to get up, he walked over to the hole and saw nothing, yet he could still hear his aura's faint screeching.

"Great, one more creature loose," he said. Ray got up clutching his right side where he landed.

"Is that what these things are to you? A bunch of dogs? Moulded into killing machines by their careless owners?" said Ray.

"Part of my aura resides in that monster, and I needed to keep hold of the reins, but you stupidly pulled me away from them."

"As far as I'm concerned those... whatever they are, they should be free," Ray drew his gun out from the holster and continued, "and like the people who don't know of this life I have, away from you," Ray said, clicking the safety down on his six-shooter.

"Killing me won't stop Bazka, you know that, right? Sooner or later Bazka will have spread his influence on the unknowingly gullible so it will be beyond your control. Beyond the elders, that they will not know what to do."

"You can't guarantee that, Waywood. Not while I'm around."

"The elders are weak! They want everything to be free in this land. When you let everything be free, too problems arise and your government will see that soon. These creatures will continue to roam, and your precious America will still be in conflict if not one single mind is in control. Don't think it will happen? Watch. If the war comes to an end there will still be problems. Bazka is stronger than any of the leaders in the world, and his word will endure, growing every day for generations." As Waywood carried on, from the corner of Ray's eye he could see hands emerging from the hole, two, twelve then twenty. They were covered in grey paint, the white nails standing out in what light was left, the heads then soon popped up, strange in shape. It was the tribe which he encountered weeks ago in the mountains up west. The disruption from the creature alerted and brought them here, and they overheard everything that Waywood was saying, crawling towards him not making a sound as he babbled on.

All Ray could do was smile as he brought his gun down. It stopped Waywood from speaking as he asked: "What are you smiling at?"

"The free," Ray said. Confused, Waywood turned around, and he was soon pounced on by the eyeless ones. They dog-piled on top of one another as Waywood screamed in terror trying as hard as he could to push them off or get his hands on his gun. He did so and fired the one-shot he could muster onto one of them sending them off the pile hitting the crowd before it was taken away, thrown to the ground as the collection began to part. They had him, hands keeping his hands, arms, legs and feet together as they carried him towards the hole they had crawled out of. His screams were soon muffled by the hands of the tribe as he slowly disappeared down with them into the darkness. Like ants in a colony they all followed in, the last one turned his head around to Ray. The light shone on him and the symbol on his chest was recognised instantly. Workers of the father, hearing his call. He nodded and so did Ray before the man slipped back down until all that could be heard was Waywood's muffled screams echoing out from the hole. As he got closer, all Ray saw was darkness but he knew those people lurked from inside of it. Ray reached into his back trouser pocket, he didn't forget it, the blood bark and he sprinkled it down hoping that it would seal Waywood in these mountains forever.

On the walk back down the flaming mountain top, all Ray could do was frown. While defeating hordes of evil controlled by the hands of a ruthless leader was worthy of celebration, it wasn't enough. Bazka's location was still unknown and his influence would sure be spread. All Ray wanted right now was the warm embrace of the woman he had come to love but never really showed enough. Millie was gone, but that wouldn't stop Ray on his search to find her. He decided that whatever the elders presented him with next, he would make sure that Millie would be located safely and free from anything that he would be challenged with. Trudging through the show, he debated inside his head whether or not it was the right choice to find her. The outcome of them being together would be bleak at this point in the game. Ray could not die unless his spirit was free and ready too. The untold amount of evil that still presided over the young country, the growing responsibility of handling all this, coupled with maintaing a love life, wouldn't play out the way he envisioned initially. Nothing to do but to walk and think, it could be years till he saw her again.

IX.

Millie kept her arms tight around Ray, they seemed to be hugging for a while now. The two of them never broke off how much they held each other. Ray had not been this close to anyone in years, breaking off close contact with people since the early days of him being on the run. It was decades of his personal space being entered. Finally, the two eased the pressure but still kept their hands on each other's waists. Ray didn't know how much time had passed until he looked into that beautifully small face again after all this time. Mille was now in her mid fifties, time had made wrinkles appear but her skin was still as soft as before when she was young. Age spots crept up around where her cheek bones were as did the small bags under her eyes. Her hair was still in those healthy curls that he knew, but there was a shine of white peering through the strands of black.

"I know, I look terrible," she chuckled.

"I haven't seen you in years," Ray said.

"I bet you still fancy me, don't you?"

"You don't know the half of it," Ray went it for a slow kiss but Millie brought her hand up to his lips, stopping him.

"You better come with me to the lounge. I gotta catch you up on everything." Millie lead Ray by the hand out of his room and down the hall towards a large lounge room with a giant fire-place, flanked by newly carved stone pillars with a large paisley carpet, two elegant leather sofas sat opposite each other and the two sat down while the fire crackled and the dawn of the morning breaking behind them through the large windows which peered out into the White House gardens.

"I know this is the thing you don't want to hear but...that day after you left, where I took Biden with me...I didn't kill him. I let him go," Millie told her former love. Ray immediately went into shock from that statement.

"After what he di-"

"I didn't see the point in killing a man who had seen the im-possible not long after that! People would've called him mad anyway. I spoke to him, we both felt like we had seen some-thing we shouldn't have from you. Felt like it was best for the both of us not to be involved. He vowed to trail off and I gave him a dollar from the money you gave me and we both just took off. I rode east and he looked like he just carried on north. I came to Washington after the war, got a pretty nice place to stay in, did a bit of work being a waitress and tending to a place that needed cleaning once a week. I got a bit of luck recently after President McKinley was killed, Mr Roosevelt needed work in this place and I was chosen along with a few other people. Wanted a complete new administration top to bottom," she said.

"Millie, I see Biden's name everywhere now. The bars, the products. You can say he changed that day but I've seen plenty in my time, instances where that's not the case. You need to see it from my perspective-"

"No I can't" she interrupted.

"This is what I'm getting at, Ray. You took bullets to you and didn't die. And you saying about all this stuff you've seen... I-I can't see it. That's why I made the choice not to find you again. As hard as that sounds, I needed to make my life better than what it was. I haven't seen my brother in years. I felt like a burden to him back home and he felt the same. Anything to get away from Bonebag felt like a godsend. You only saw me at

Martha's, you never saw me out of work. Really all I can say to you now is there was no love after that, Ray," Millie said trying to hold back tears as her voice trembled as she spoke. Ray had trouble to not to break down as well. The closest thing to him while on the run, the hope of finding her again, all suddenly vanished.

"I've have a kid Ray. I'm married, I have a life. I don't need to be involved in yours anymore," she continued.

"Then I don't recommend coming into Teddy's office if I'm there," he joked without cracking a smile, trying to ease the tension between the two of them. Millie smiled but turned her head to hide it.

"I still wanna thank you, though. Without that money I wouldn't be here right now. It kept me stable. Lots of folk wondered who I was with all that in my bag. Wasn't common seeing a woman like me financially stable."

"Well at least it went into something you can have and cherish. I won't ever have that." Ray said.

"Nonsense. You will. I'm sure there's girls with a lifespan like yours looking to get all freaky, hocus pocus on ya," Millie joked. The tension left the room and the two were again smiling. They both chuckled quietly and then glanced at each other again. For a moment, locking onto each other's eyes again, the two of them envisioned would life be like had they stuck by one another. Fate not separating them with everything that had eventually lead them both here to the quiet rooms of the White House.

"Did the President ever ask you about...where you came from before?"

"He never-" Millie was stopped midway when a messenger came through the double doors ending the conversation.

"Mr McCarthy. President Roosevelt is ready to continue when you are." Ray got up from the couch and walked to the maid who would lead him up to the President's office, he stopped at the door and faced Millie the last time of that day.

"I would welcome catching up better, Millie. You know where I am." Ray said and Millie exchanged a smile with a nod. With luck would have it, Roosevelt was seen coming down the hallway in a very brisk power walk, carrying his umbrella and suitcase tucked under his arm with all the confidence in the world.

"Ah Ray good to see you. I thought I would bring you with me today on one of my rallies today. I think you'll find it rather good to interact with other people rather than me questioning you all the time. Come along, our coach is waiting," Roosevelt said as he continued to walk with Ray catching up by his side.

"Shouldn't your Vice President be doing something like this?" Ray asked.

"Well that's the thing, I don't have one. Not yet anyway. That's why bringing a normal human being rather than some 'Yes' man would be all the more enjoyable. Come, you can sit with me in the back seat," The President excitedly said extending his arm out to the coach and horses near the White House doors. The two secondary coaches with protection were nearby, one at the front, one at the back. "After you," and Ray hopped in through the other side of the coach and sat down on the leather seats with the President following him in. Roosevelt gave the command and the coaches were soon away.

"I thought I'd give you some time off today Mr McCarthy, as I feel like I've not given you much hospitality. I've merely questioned you to death and given you a room to sleep in. I thought today you'd like to see the outside world without any pressure of being hunted down by us and I also have a proposition for you."

"Proposition?" Ray said with a raise of his eyebrows, curious to what he may get also from this long week.

"Yes, one of great interest but all in due time. Today, I've taken the liberty of inviting you to a rally I'm holding. I'll be bringing up some of my administrative declarations as well as some things that will need seriously addressing like this miners strike going on. There may may be some people there you've heard of before like Morgan and all that," The President continued.

"J.P Morgan?" Ray asked in astonishment.

"Oh yes. He's one of the heads trying to calm it down but I don't trust him."

"Why's that, if he's trying to stop the strike?"

"Corporation gain, Ray, my boy. They may be spearheading the talks like a bunch of hungry lions but it's all for show like a peacock attracting its mate. They're out looking for gain out of this situation, no matter what. I'd like to put the people at ease and give them reassurance that this will not continue," Roosevelt said, slamming his hands on his leather tied case that sat on his lap. On Ray's side was sitting one of the Presidents men on horseback conducted a hand signal to the President after tapping the side door window of the black coach. Roosevelt nodded at the signal and got ready to step out of the coach as the horses slowed down.

"Presidential protocol. It's actually quite easy. Right out we get," Roosevelt said in excitement and Ray followed suit, being escorted by the President's men surrounding them. The group arrived at the Southern railway station and it was deserted aside from the workers manning the station. It had been cleared for the presidents arrival and a group of men were huddled together in discussion. The group all parted as one of the collected heads caught sight of the president walking up, all standing accordingly with their postures upright while others adjusted their clothes. Roosevelt shook hands with everyone and discussed the trip ahead as the train sat waiting to sound off.

"Mr President, Senator Pritchard will be waiting for us in Asheville when we arrive and the stage in the park will be set up, per your request."

"Excellent. It'll be a nice seed for what people will soon see of my administration as it continues to grow. Right enough standing around, let us discuss in a moving train instead of standing here like lemons in the cold." And the men all followed behind the President and Ray as they embarked for Asheville, North Carolina. As they came up to the train, everyone followed in through a carefully organised procedure to ensure the President's safety on board the presidential coach. Once inside, Ray could see the royalty design inside that carried on from the decorated halls of the White House. A rich dark mahogany brown covered the walls with a deep blue carpet floor. The windows along the coaches had netted drapes with the same blue as the curtains with a golden rope cords to pull them across. Ray saw the other coaches with their plush duck egg leather seats with a table sturdy enough to have the finest China on it without spilling a drop should the train bump along the tracks. Continuing on the President's men, Ray and President Roosevelt made it into the second and final carriage of the train. Complete with armoured plating around the outside, inside the tables were formally aligned like a standard seating row in economy class, the President's desk sat at the back, bulky but not as regal as the one in the oval office. Roosevelt sat first then allowed everyone to sit at their designated areas with Ray standing as awkwardly as possible at the back near the door with the two guards giving him a slow glance over their shoulders. Roosevelt smiled, he beckoned him over and Ray did so with his hands behind his back.

"Gentlemen, this was the man I informed you about. Mr Ray McCarthy. A wanted man now in the midst of becoming a free man again." A small applaud came from the men in the carriage.

"He is accompanying me as a reward. Anything we discuss today that I have underlined in your packages must not be spoken on these premises until he is escorted out. You understand the procedure, Mr McCarthy it's just all for securities sake," he went on.

"I understand, sir," he replied.

"Unfortunately, Mr McCarthy, we are starting this now, so I'm afraid you're going to have to walk straight on back through there."

"I'll go up front. Help out the driver," Ray said.

"Yes, of course, by all means," and Ray walked on till he was hit with the scent of burning coal and the whistle whistling in his ears.

Roosevelt turned back round with a serious expression, which had been masked by his previously upbeat smile he presented when Ray was by his side, turning to face his group.

"Now. You've all seen the file on Mr McCarthy. I am making this perfectly clear from now until the end of my presidency to a hundred years from now. Beyond us. What that man possesses cannot be compromised. Very soon, I will end Mr McCarthy's pardoning procedures with a deal. A deal in which he will be bound by a government document, his signature will ensure that his loyalty is to this country and to the people he protects under the flag. Make no mistake about it, as I see the man for who he is, I do not doubt in the slightest that in this group some of you see him as a weapon. To an extent he is but only for those forces that are not bounded by the realities we as men face. That is why under the witness of the lord and the minds I see in this room, this administration will put into effect, the creation of a unit who will oversee this fiendish world Mr McCarthy has informed me about. It will oversee Mr McCarthy, the forces of those who are lead by, from what

Mr McCarthy has told me from previous sessions the "fallen angel" of the native elders, known as Bazka. The unit's intention is merely of national surveillance. This unit is not to be seen or used in anyway by those who have not had the correct authorisation by that of the acting President. At this time all of you, as am I, are the founding members. The founding fathers if you pardon the pun." Roosevelt documented as he spoke to the wondering eyes of those inside the carriage.

"Mr President. With the rate our government is moving, not only on a global scale surely this program must be held off?" said the oldest man in the group.

"This unit will be set in stone before my administration can unleash the full potential of what America can do. At this point in time this is merely the inception. You all will be given titles and your roles will be performed under the sworn secrecy this unit is built from. No other unit created before us or from those in the future will know about this." The president explained.

"So what do we call ourselves, Mr President?" a younger gentleman asked.

"You men will simply refer to each other as Eyes. Fitting

for a unit called H.A.W.K. The Human Administration of Worldly Keepings. You are this great nation's watchful eyes, gentlemen. Now please, open the brown envelopes I've laid out for you to make yourself acquainted with what your roles are." And the rustling of paper notes all collectively opening started. Meanwhile, at the front of the train, Ray rested against the side of the train, looking out at the open fields that passed him by like clouds. The train driver was shovelling away at the coal that piled up in the corner to Ray's right, as the train carried on straight down past large open fields populated by only a few trees. The train driver glanced back at Ray over his shoulder while he was shovelling.

"The President doesn't usually make exceptions to people on the outside. What's so special about you?" Ray looked at him sombrely and said "Just special."

"No one's just special for no reason."

"Well I am," Ray said back quick, hoping he wouldn't hear. The driver rested his hands on the shovel handle, sitting his chin on the top as he looked Ray up and down from his boots to his hat. His eyes scaling him to try and put a description to the image like a painting in a gallery.

"You look like the adventurous type. You hunt? Mr Roosevelt is a prime hunter," he asked.

"I've noticed. I'm not one to kill something for no reason so no."

"Well, the damaged gear and the stern expression tells me you like to hide in plain sight if there's a crowd sooo.... bounty hunter?"

"I was the bounty," Ray indulged him as the driver's eyes widened.

"Like Jesse James and Wesley Hardin?" Ray chuckled.

"They wish they were me. I outlived all of them. And I met a couple of 'em too."

"You aided them? Worked with them even?" The driver pressed on with more intrigue growing on his face.

"No, nothing like that. But I have a pretty good story of how I met Sundance."

"Butch Cassidy and the Sundance Kid!?" the driver said in excitement like a little kid.

"No, no, just Sundance. This was when they separated for a little while. Nothing much to it, I happened to be walking into some old town, I forget what its called, but Sundance was piling up his guns, looking set for a new crusade by the way it all sat on his horse. Looked like he was prepared for a storm that was chasing him anywhere he went. I simply offered him a hand with his gear. Poor sap looked in a state, dropping everything. Calmed him down a bit but I could see in his face he was scared of something. He wasn't all what he looked like in those dime novels which happens with most people telling stories about encounters with outlaws. He wasn't ready to take on the world, he was running from it. He'd aged. Like most folk. He thanked me and was on his way."

"Damn, if that was me I'd be too nervous to even go up to him," the driver said.

"You wanna know why I outlived everyone?"

"How?"

"Unlike Sundance, I didn't choose this life. And they couldn't handle a storm to save their lives. When you're thrown into something you gotta think, prepare and act. And they all acted day by day. Didn't plan ahead. They thought they were untouchable. I am untouchable and it's hell living through it." On that note Ray walked back in through to the President's coach.

"Mister! What's your name?" the driver asked just before Ray could put his hand on the door.

"Whatever you want it to be," he said and Ray went through the door, not knowing if he was allowed to or not. The chatter inside was now jumbled as multiple conversations were taking place while the President kept his head down on his writing. Roosevelt lifted his head up when he saw a shadow cast out on the floor behind him.

"Ah Ray, very good timing."

"I take it everything went well in here?"

"Indeed. Please let me walk with you for a bit while they all collect themselves," Roosevelt said as he got up away from his less impressive desk.

"You must've set something pretty hard on them." Ray said.

"Oh well, when you're in my administration the last thing I'm having are slackers. It's merely a new system we are putting into place. A boring one at that." The two walked down the following carriage as the train whistled and the smoke rushed past.

"Mr McCarthy, I feel like I have neglected you."

"Neglected me? Mr President you haven't left me alone for the past week," Ray said.

"No, I've pestered you long enough with questions and all that. Sometimes people are not given a second chance. Previous administrations have made it clear that you are not to be trusted. That you're dangerous, unpredictable. And now I stand and feel like I know the real you. And with what you've presented to me I see you as someone who can help give back to those in this country. Mr McCarthy after you will be pardoned, I would like to make it my personal pleasure to have you join us as one of the country's founding members of a new branch," Roosevelt said, letting the notion sink in for a few seconds before continuing.

"This new branch will be yours and yours alone. To reign

and be an important part of any administration. Bazka is still pretty much a threat is he not?" Roosevelt asked.

"He is," Ray said.

"Theodore, I couldn't possibly. After all I did, I'm not fit to help anyone."

"Yes, you are. I see someone who who cares about people's well being. The United States is growing, Mr McCarthy. More people will be at risk from these other worldly forces that you have dealt with. You were a different man back then. You've had time to grow, to think. You don't look like you have but inside you have. And that will help you in the future," Roosevelt said in a reassuring tone. Ray knew from the moment he lead that group of boys into a battle zone he thought he would never be inserted back into the frame till the day he died. Dying wasn't much of an issue now and perhaps had he died he may have been pardoned later on. Who knows but that mattered now that he was considered in the country and to the President now as a humble servant. Respected again in the eyes of the people, but a past and future hidden for maybe generations to come.

"Do you accept this?" the president asked.

"I'd be honoured sir." The train pulled into the station at 13:45 p.m. The sky was clouded grey over Asheville and Senator Pritchard waited patiently by the tracks, awaiting the President and his entourage to step out. The guards disembarked off the carriages first, standing guard at the doors on either side. Out came the first man. To the Senator's surprise, he wasn't wearing the usual suit and tie worn by the entourage of advisors, law makers and so forth but instead stepped out Ray, wearing tattered clothes with his long long coat and duster hat. Like the guards he too kept a mask of disciplined expression across his face before breaking it with a quick smirk as he saw the senator giving him a look of confusion. Breaking the confusion Ray simple pulled open his jacket to reveal a pinned seal of service on his waistcoat. The Senator lifted his head and nodded before Ray stepped to the side to let the President step off the train.

"Senator Pritchard. The clouds look like they will break away today." Roosevelt said gripping the Senator's hand in greeting.

"Mr President. The crowds are beginning to pick up. The horse and carriages will take us up Depot towards the square. You'll arrive through the back way unbeknownst to the crowd, like you popped out of thin air," Pritchard said.

"Excellent. I like to give them a good show."

"Who might this be to your side may, I ask?" Pritchard said.

"This is General McCarthy. Former leader during the Civil war and now commanding general of the newly formed task force H.A.WK. I will brief you later on it," he leaned in to the senators ear.

"Very good. Uh, let's move shall we," Pritchard said pulling away from the President's grip. The two followed him while the entourage followed up out of the train. As protocol the guards surveyed everything first before Roosevelt and Ray could step in and the did not pull away until the President's men pulled away. The carriages made their way around the small town through a weaving route over the park hill before making their way down towards Patton Avenue and the court square. The President caught eye of his stage and buzzing crowd filling the atmosphere with cheers and the red white and blue flying high behind them. Roosevelt's energy to speak was making him twiddle his thumbs in anticipation. He asked Ray before the carriage stopped;

"What do you think? Pince-nez on or off?"

"On I think," Ray said amused. "You ready?"

"Ready and waiting," Roosevelt said, before thrusting the door open and stepping off the coach to power walk over to the stage before his guards could catch up with him. The wide crowd which spilled almost now around the stage, caught sight of the President and the cheers rung out louder. Ray and the President's men rushed to his sight before a flood could obstruct him. People waved and reached out to catch the President's attention but they were pushed back while Roosevelt smiled and waved, before walking up the stage steps. He was now centre stage, Roosevelt thrusted his fists in the air as he was now in good sight of everyone. The crowd roared with excitement waiting to hear from the President. Roosevelt as the showman he was, kept on moving around the stage, surveying everyone, pointing back and screaming with excitement back before eventually standing dead centre of the wooden framed stage waiting to speak. The noise from the crowd slowly died down and Roosevelt began to speak.

"Americans. I see all around me. To the left of me, to the right of me, right down to you sir in the middle at the front. You are all Americans and as your President, I humbly thank you for me into your town of Asheville." The President's words were greeted by a loving response from the crowd.

"Now, as you know, I was thrust into this position after the tragic events that happened to our former President, the man I had the pleasure of being by his side for his four years in office, Mr President William McKinley. He was taken from us, by the selfish act of one individual, whom I shall not name nor give time or energy to because my energy is in full flow for you all this afternoon!" The president rose in passion as he pounded his hand down on a flat palm while the flags waved in the crowd enthusiastically.

"As you all know, I take no exceptions. I make sure my authority is firm and reassuring at the same time, like a father thrusting his young boy into the outside world for the first time. Encouraging yet directive. That is my aim for my administration, to keep the people at home like all of you today, encouraged and optimistic for the future changes of this country. In particular, a town like Asheville should not go unnoticed, the land as I stand...above all it should be fully protected. Many different towns, cities, they all hold a level of meaning to this country, every state is different. And as we continue to expand, developing communities like this one it will inevitably lead to great progress. I carry the same traits as my predecessor, this nation of people I see from far and wide coming together, stronger, faster than any other nation on gods green earth. We can only hope to succeed in making this country what it can be. We shall not be made until we work together, not primarily as Northerners or Southerners, East-erners or Westerners, nor primarily as employers or employ-ees, townsmen or countrymen, capitalists or wage earners, but primarily as American citizens. As American citizens to whom the right of brotherly friendship and comradeship with all other decent American citizens, comes as the greatest and first of all privileges. Your privilege is that you are, under the lines written by our founding fathers, have the voice that leads our men behind the desks pushing the laws and juris-dictions to every home in America as they see fit. You see what is right in this nation and should you be displeased with the way that I or any other servicemen like me in a fancy suit, well you should be the one whose voice is heard and listen too. Never let your voices not be heard!" President Roosevelt exclaimed. The crowd following his every word cheered in sheer delight as the President touched their hearts with his words. Roosevelt shuffled around taking it all in, adjusting his sleeves he continued."It is unacceptable, and I, as your President, will not stand for that. You all have voices, opinions and above all else, characters. Personas shaped by the places you inhabit and the people you've met. For a citizen to be worth anything, what you need is character, and into character many elements enter. In the first place, decency and honesty; if a man isn't honest, isn't decent, then the brighter he is, the more dangerous he is to his community. Asheville is a collection of people who stand in front of me today as a collective unit of proud townspeople ready to have their say on the governing bodies. And I am all ears to you. But let me indulge you on what my administration hopes to bring you in the coming years of my term and maybe even my second term. I will for one, like I had stated earlier, will make sure that the governing bodies and those of banks and businesses will not speak over and rule you on what you can and cannot do in this country. Their tight grip will not hold you, for you outnumber them. My administration will make sure that the rule of big business and those in our government, will have their savage, greedy hands kept to themselves." Another round of applause echoed around the President as he drove home his first point."Furthermore, your rights as workers will not be forgotten. At this moment in time there is a strike happening. To the coal workers, who work so hard to provide minerals and valuable goods down south of North Carolina, are being strong in their will to have their voices heard over those who control their wages. I wish not to see this ever happen again. I want to give you the management, resources and trust. Your passion for work, to commit is my highest priority, so is mine on communities and everything the land has to offer. To my next point, the land itself. I am a firm believer in treating the land with respect. This is the land of opportunity and for it to prosper as you all soon will, we must keep the land of ours protected at all cost. The mistreatment from co-operations using this, our land is poor, inexcusable actions such as these must be accounted for. My hope for the future is to make sure that these lands, these beautiful mythological sites that capture the imaginations of hundreds if not millions of Americans. This is our home. Yours, mine, the people driving me in my carriage, I will not stand to see such exquisite angelic beauty be besmirched by those who do not see what you all see. So as I leave you today, I simply say to you, you must trust your instincts. The words you heard from me today may not always represent you the people. You must be heard. You are the government, you and I, and the government will do well or ill according as we, he spoke. And we must make up our minds that the affairs of the government shall be managed. I thank you, Asheville, for having me and accepting me." And with that final line, the President was greeted by a large round of applause. Roosevelt was completely engrossed and thrust his arm with a close fist, pounding the wooden barrier in front of him. He waved his hands up towards the crowd and was then escorted off the stage by his personal guards. Ray remained downstairs, tucked away resting underneath the wooden staircase, he heard the footsteps above him and shot up to greet the President.

"Brilliant speech, Teddy," he said.

"Thank you, dear boy. Come along now. I need you by my side. Time to hear each and everyone of them, up close and personal," Roosevelt said, and the pair lead the group of the President's men through into the crowd. The people of Asheville almost threw themselves over atop each other to catch a chance to greet and say hello to the President. Climbing over each other like ants, the President looked like he couldn't breathe with the amount of space he had between him, his entourage and his guards. They swarmed around while Ray followed close behind. Roosevelt was enjoying every moment of it, and so was Ray. Knowing that he would be seen as a force for good in the eyes of the government he was now serving under again Ray would never get an audience like this nor did he expect to ever have this kind of appreciation. And he loved it. Back in the White House, it was dusk, and the candlelight inside was dim. Only Ray and Roosevelt entered through the front doors as the guards remained at their stations outside by the stairs and entrance gate. Roosevelt shrugged his shoulders and let out an exhausted sigh as his arms drooped to his sides, his briefcase still in his hand.

"What a day," Roosevelt said.

"So, what happens now?" Ray asked.

"Sleep I presume, it is gone eleven after all."

"No, I mean with me, sir," Ray said.

"Well, you don't need me to tell you anymore, Mr McCarthy. I presume you understand the responsibility you carry now in your new position."

"I understand that, but I meant with me. You definitely guarantee me safety when I leave?" Ray asked.

"My boy, do not panic. You are fully secure to roam this country without fear of reoffending," Roosevelt reassured.

"Good. I ain't no lap dog though, Mr President. You may call for me but as I understand it, this new department is mine to control correct?"

"Correct."

"Right, so my rules. If I have to operate of my own accord, I will tell you-"

"Mr McCarthy. It is late, let us talk about this after we sign the decree that you will be pardoned," Ray's frown disappeared, and his expression was relaxed.

"Agreed."

"First thing in the morning. I will be up earlier than usual," Roosevelt said patting Ray's back as he began to walk in the opposite direction. "Good night, Mr McCarthy."

"Good night, Mr President." The two started to turn away, but Ray had one last thing to know. "Mr President. Was Millie the one to tell you about my misfortune?" he asked. Theodore swivelled back round with his heels from down the corridor to answer.

"She was, yes. Mrs Adams told me everything from her side. I was sceptical, of course, but she convinced me to hear it from you. I pieced things together pretty quickly. Must have eaten her away seeing your face on every desolate street corner with reward money hanging on it. She was your guardian angel Mr McCarthy, remember that. Angels can be found everywhere, and they help out at the right moments.

Roosevelt said. Ray answered back with a two-fingered tip salute, and the two went back to their rooms to settle in for the night. Ray went inside his room and quietly closed the door behind him, his table light burning an orange glow as he entered. Ray sat on the edge of his bed, feeling more relaxed than ever since being here. It felt like a new lease of life after today with President Roosevelt. Finally, after years of running, carrying a secret which he thought could pose as a threat to everyone around him, it could now be used for good that could be controlled under his own will. The thought of this brought a humble smile stretching across his face. Tomorrow would be the start of something new.

X.

Ray had a very good night's sleep. The anxiety that would cloud his mind and vision at night with thoughts of death, despair and loss seemed to have vanished as if they were never there. After yesterday, Ray felt like he had been reborn, this time, with a purpose. It was like joining the army again, when his family were at their lowest point and all he wanted was an escape. He woke up feeling like he had slept on the finest mattress imaginable. His head was clear and he was ready to sign the paper that would free him for good and become a saviour for the American people, a hero who could walk around in the public, with no fanfare just like an average joe. Ray wondered what that would be like, while he got changed. The possibility of just grabbing a beer without having to look over his shoulder in fear that he would come cross a pair of eyes amongst a group of strangers chatting amongst themselves, staring deep into his with the intent of choosing the opition of dead or alive as the more appropriate option. He did up his waistcoat and made himself a little bit more presentable than before, his shirt's top collar button was done up with a polka dot neckerchief wrapped around. His sleeves were rolled down, still with the worn-in creases after having them turned up all the time and his trousers were straightened out as much as he could by running his hands over them them when placed on the bed. The effort was perhaps not good enough for meeting the head of the country for a pardoning procedure. At this point though Theodore would not even bat an eyelid after the countless hours that he and Ray had spent together, recalling Ray's life leading up to this point. There was still much more that Ray could've told after the last chapter had been told but the President had heard enough, his mid was made up and it was in Ray's favour. Ray stepped out from his quarters and made his last walk up to the Presidents office. He would be back to that same office, possibly some time in the future, and he knew for sure with the way he was loving life at this point, that he would not give in and let the spirits take over. Who knew what the future held beyond this. The double door into the President's office was left ajar, letting the bright dawn sunlight creep through making Ray squint as he walked up to it. As he stepped in, Ray not only saw Roosevelt but a whole collection of people in flashier suits than him. These could've been the same people from the train but they were much more distinguished, members of the President's administration that were cemented in congress during the McKinley administration.

Fresh faces for Ray with different backgrounds, young and old, they were obviously there with the president for the publicity shot as the photographer was seen to the left of the group setting up a camera stand.

"Here he is, the man of the hour. You sleep well, Mr McCarthy?"

"You have no idea, Mr President," Ray said.

"Is this all for me?"

"Indeed it is. Certainly have to commemorate it for some personal memories and what not." The President's desk had what looked to be a single sheet of paper on it. Not piled up with unimaginable amounts of paper work like the last few times Ray had been at the desk. Neatly squared with Roosevelt's hands and the signature line was empty, the room went silent as Ray gazed upon it. One of the men handed Ray a pen from their pocket during the silence. One signature to start a new life and end the old, this was it. His scribble was quick and the air left his lungs once the pen was given back and the President went over what was on it.

"Congratulations, Mr McCarthy. Under article two, section two of the constitution, I, Theodore Roosevelt Jr, President of the

United States of America, do hereby pardon one Ray McCarthy for crimes that had been under investigation by the United States government and the Pinkerton National Detective Agency spanning thirty seven years." Roosevelt read while the group of men gave him a round of applause. The pleasantries were done and now it was on to the photograph. The photographer moved the equipment to the centre of the room, calling for all men to gather together, Roosevelt stayed sitting while Ray was instructed to stand to the President's left side.

"I think you should show it off," said Roosevelt, giving Ray the pardon paper to display. The photographer now draped over with a black hood from behind the wooden camera and his right hand raised out with the flash.

"Alright everyone. One...two...three." and the flash went off with a blinding, sizzling flash. A little bit of smoke raised into the air as the photo was captured with the process of developing the picture due to take weeks. Ray shook hands again with Roosevelt and the others of the administration after the photo was taken and some left the room in a hurry, possibly to get back to their posts in the office. Roosevelt got up from his chair to shake the hand of the photographer, before walking back behind his desk to look out to the field through his window. Ray simply walked around, like a child does at a family gathering, hands in his pockets and just kicking his legs about wondering what will happen next. It was only him, Roosevelt and five other members of the administration while the other eleven had left the room. Now that the room was a lot less crowded, Ray actually recognised one of the faces from the train journey to Asheville yesterday. He was the youngest on the train and still the youngest in the room. The other two men were older than Roosevelt and just about getting to Ray's, despite him looking a great deal younger. Both sprouted small tufts of white hair from their scalps, one of the men had very thin hair which he combed to the left as wet as he could, and the the other gentleman, had his swept back which only just lined up perfectly where the tips of his ears were. Like the youngest, they wore black suits, white shirts with polished black shoes and black ties. The younger man's tie was a little bit longer, like a cravat which he had tucked into his shirt opening. Roosevelt heard the door close and then turned around to Ray.

"Right now that that's out the way perhaps we can discuss the business of your branch, Mr McCarthy. These gentlemen here will be the ones explaining the laws and requirements that we have in the establishment of such a branch. To my right is Alan Banks, he is one of the interns of the Home Security department; he took up the role as the advisor. To my left is

Frank Grimshaw and Gerald Harrison, they both are expert surveillance tacticians, and served during the Civil war. They of course take the role of this branche's chief operators." Ray stood confused.

"Operators? I thought I was the one man wrecking crew," he said.

"You are Mr McCarthy, you are, but the gentlemen are only here to help. You don't need to see them but they could prove to be very useful should you ever need them. They work under the shadows as much as you will now," Roosevelt answered.

"We merely wish to see you grow, Mr McCarthy, from what we understand through the President's briefings, it will provide you with a good sense of knowledge in the use of intelligence and perhaps strategic skills in times of crisis," Gerald chimed in.

"The last thing the President wants is for a unholy amount of catastrophes brought about from the demons of the world you have encountered, to spread. With you getting back to us it will simply let us have a close eye on them and to plan out ahead of things," Frank added.

"I was a General, gentlemen, I do know how to plan out missions-"

"And to run from them," Alan said abruptly. That sentence stunned Ray, making him scowl at the young intern. "You wanna say that again?" he said raising his voice slightly.

"Gladly, but I do think you will regret it if you should get rid of me."

"Why's that then?" Ray asked.

"Simple. It's like what I just did then. As an advisor, I'm a voice of reason, Mr McCarthy. I can also calm a fire in a room like this. Let's face it and I have to be blunt with this, you need the opinions of others, rather than just your own. With the intel we can achieve through you we can all come to our own conclusions about things. Make missions more complex rather than it being big brush strokes which you've done throughout the decades," Alan continued.

"He is right, Mr McCarthy. As sharp as his tongue, is he brings up good points. Throughout your entries in the period leading up to Waywood's defeat and his army being diminished I did notice a particular theme with them all. A lack of certainty. Unpredictability in one's choices. It seems to me that most of the time, you've merely been working it out as you go along. But you're not on the run anymore, Mr McCarthy, you're one of my men now. And even though you are free to do as you wish as part of this branch which is based around you entirely that doesn't mean you can ignore over the fact that you now have others on your side. You need to stop this stubbornness," Roosevelt said. Ray looked down at the floor for a moment before bringing his head back up. The President was right. He took all of it in, made him think for a moment to himself that this was the better option. Roosevelt had listened to the stories and just painted the picture that Ray was hesitant to observe and think about. It was time now to put the past aside and do what was best for his own interests. "I understand," he said.

"Good that we have our understanding," Alan said, giving him a smile.

"So, tell me what's the name of my branch?" Ray asked. Roosevelt smiled and said, "H.A.W.K"

The room looked and smelt like a boiler room. It was damp, decrepit but strong in its construction with the brick only harbouring slight remnants of mould growing on it. The trail to the inside of it walked you out of the White House and underneath to the garden. It was empty and the floors were wet and dirty. Large in size but cold, possibly used as a storage unit but had been forgotten about. This was to be H.A.W.K's base of operations, separate to the White House, were no staff inside would be allowed to venture, unless they hade the correct permissions given to them by the President. The five people looking into it were the only ones who knew of its existence, and it was intended to stay that way until the right successors were chosen in the future. Ray knew he can out live everybody in that room but Alan, Frank And Gerald would be easily forgotten about. As the leading man Ray knew people would come and go but something stuck with him when speaking to President Roosevelt, a connection, almost like a father and son bond. Like they could talk to one another about anything. Ray wondered what future administrations would bring once Roosevelt was out of office, would he strike up a friendship with them? Or would he be hesitant to speak? He didn't even know if he would even last one year, one month or even a week doing this. Either way who ever was in charge he would have to serve. In the grand scheme of things it wouldn't really matter given that Bazka was still out there and his influence would crack communities, put people's lives at risk and perhaps bring the world down and rebuilt into the hell he desired. He may serve the president but his sworn oath to the natives was far more meaningful.

"Looks like we need a few desks," Alan said jokingly.

Ray had put all of his things together in a bag for the journey. He had informed Roosevelt today after seeing his new workplace that he needed to see someone before he could put his mind to work. Roosevelt accepted and Alan, Frank and Gerald all began to work in the underground office space below the gardens. He put on his hat, along with his duster coat and stepped out from the bedroom. A carriage was set to take him to the train station, where he would be travelling south west, back to Kentucky. The home of Bonebag and where the Crow tribe had been established. Before he exited the front door, he heard the sound of shoes running on the hard marble floor behind him before a loud, "Wait!" was heard. Ray turned to see Millie catching up to him, lifting her maid dress in her hands, as she ran.

"I only just...got wind your leaving," Millie said as she took in some air.

"Yeah. It's official. I'm off the hook now."

"You mean it?"

"Yup. Got the letter sealed with a signature," Ray said patting his bag.

"Oh, that's good. So where you going now?" she asked him.

"Well, I'm heading back down to Kentucky, there's a few things I gotta see to first and then after that, I really don't know to be honest," Ray said remembering that he had to keep his position here as secret as possible.

"You're not going back to Bonebag, are you?" Millie said worryingly.

"You kidding? It's just west of the town I'm going. The trains gonna take me straight past."

"Oh well, that's different then. What do you think you'll be doing then now that you're a free man to live as long as he wants?" Ray laughed.

"That's a pretty good question. Maybe I'll come back in a few years and have a catch up with you," he joked.

"Don't you go pulling my strings again. I'm old as it is, I don't need you bringing down what youth I have left," Millie said with a playful wag of her finger. The two expressed a chuckle between them, before both their eyes locked up again in a familiar loving fashion.

"It was really nice seeing you again, Millie. I bet the President thought you were madder than any street beggar when you told him what happened in Bonebag," he said. Millie was about to follow that up but she stopped herself. About to reveal what she said and then her eyes dropped back down. She didn't feel the need to go over it all again. But she had a gesture that made Ray remember the good times.

"Here, I have something for you." Millie's hand went down between her breasts and when they came back they had money crumpled up in them. Her fingers flicked through, counting up the dollar notes before she handed it to Ray, cradling it in his hands.

"Hear. It's the same amount of money you gave me when you left me that time, just in today's money. Had a bit left over from my work days. Just sitting there. Thought you could do with a roof over your head as well," Millie said. Ray smiled.

"Thanks, grandma," and they both chuckled again before hugging and saying good bye.

"Listen, while I head down maybe I could come back and visit you some time?" Ray asked shrugging his shoulders.

"Sure. Maybe we could catch up properly when you finish down in Kentucky? Let's say...two days from now?"

"I'd like that," Rays said.

"But don't go expecting a cherry pie or something when you get there, because I ain't no cook!" she said giving him a playful slap across the neck.

"I'm just down south of here. A small barn over on the hill. Just follow the green."

"I gotta find me a woman like you," Ray said with a warm smile and Millie smiled back. As the two finished their conversation, Roosevelt was heard down the hallway shouting out Ray's last name hopping to catch him. The President came around the corner to say goodbye, playing it off to Millie as it would be the last time the two would see each other.

"Mr McCarthy I do hope you have enjoyed your stay, even if I've put you through an entire week of all these recollections and all that."

"No, no, it's fine, Mr President. Thank you for hearing my side of things. It feels good to finally get all that off my chest."

"I suspect so. Mrs Adams, you would not believe the stories I've heard, this man deserved that pardoning."

"I can imagine. I hope he tells me a few when he visits me." All three chuckled but Ray and Roosevelt put on their best fake laughter when doing so together while eyeing each other.

"Anyway, mustn't keep you waiting, Mr McCarthy you have a train to catch. Pleasant journey." Roosevelt shook Ray's hand and made his way down the hallway.

"He's a character, isn't he?" Millie said.

"Must feel weird having him as a boss," Ray joked.

"Right, well I must be off. Lots to do, lots of places to go and a lot of stress left behind me." Ray got his hand to the door before he turned round to view Millie again.

"Two days time."

"Two days time," They both said before Ray walked out the doors of the White House and made his way down the stairs to the horse and carriage. He got inside, sitting in the middle of the seats and the horse pulled away leaving Ray to look out the side window, keeping an eye on the door just in case he could see Millie. Not there. The doors were still shut as they pulled away towards the gates with the carriage going up the stone pathway Ray had walked through only seven days ago. The carriage journey was only ten minutes up through Washington, the city more lively as it was the middle of the day. All the people rushing around chatting amongst themselves in their groups, men drinking early and school kids running around the street as normal. Ray felt normal again, for the briefest moment when looking out to them. Instead of a wanted criminal, he was a free man and an unknown. Nobody knew of him and for all the ones remembering a face on a wanted poster, the thought would surely fade with the price tag disappearing from bar walls and store windows. He hadn't felt this relaxed in almost thirty seven years. He thought the train ride down would be more enjoyable as the thought of a nap after a nice snack would be most welcome. The carriage stopped at the station which stood near the post office and Ray waved to the driver as he pulled away again. Inside the station there were a lot of people waiting reading the newspapers, families took up the benches while others stood resting their shoulders on the walls while they waited for that eventual train whistle to signal the train's arrival. Ray paid for a newspaper after purchasing a ticket from the clerk behind the barred window. He slid down and rested himself on the floor with his back against the wall opening up the paper to digest the news and stories from the state newspaper. It occurred to him while his eyes trailed across the columns of tiny print that he had not caught up to speed with what had happened over the years. The last thing really that stood out in his mind while running across the map of the states was the assassination of President Lincoln, a year after defeating Waywood and his army. He couldn't really escape that one, he caught wind of it while escaping a bounty hunter down south in rural Texas. Soon after, he just brushed off anything new that was happening as evil was around every corner, both in the spiritual world (the real world) and the new world (this one he was sitting in right now). He read about the affairs surrounding the coal miners strike, new construction, and of course the illustrated cartoon version of President Roosevelt in the small sections at the bottom of the paper. Just skipping a few pages ahead, Ray came across something that caught his eye but it had to be left as the sound of the whistle was heard and everyone scrambled to their feet to wait outside. It was but a small column, detailing about a storm in Missouri, with what the locals say was brought on by a "witch's curse". Curious, he thought but he folded the paper and walked out with the rest of the busy families looking to cross states. The train pulled up with a slow screeching of its wheels hard on the brakes and the smoke of its engine lifting up into the air. Attendants raised their hands asking the people waiting to step aside for those getting off to not cause a grid lock. Men and women both embarked and disembarked the train and Ray just watched and waited before stepping on last. He was in no rush really, it was just a nice feeling to do something normal again. He walked through, checking the carriages to see if there was a seat available, luckily a mother and her daughter allowed Ray to sit with them. Ray sat down and unloaded his bag from his shoulders as the daughter continued to scroll along the pages of her novel with her finger with her mother saying the words for her. The final whistle sounded and the train was away again with a loud honk. It pulled away slowly, picking up seeped after a few minutes then it was away at regular speeding leaving Washington. He could see through the window that the city of Washington was growing in size. Buildings under major construction large and small. The turn of the century incited a new age in America, much like President Roosevelt envisioned.

It came with a grungy grey look from all the fumes spilling out through the clouds. Fields were still rich with green, soon that was all Ray saw which was much more pleasant on the eyes. While the mother still read on with her child, casting her imagination in a loving romance between a prince and a princess, Ray got out a book bound in leather. Scarred, the leather worn in as well as its pages, it was the journal Ray had kept on his travels. As he flicked through the dates had been recorded on each top right corner, the years flipped by before he landed on a clear blank page, ready for the graphite of a pencil to hit it.

September 13th, 1902.

I have just been pardoned by the current President of the United States of America. It doesn't seem real.

Not only have my unjust descriptions of so-called "Crimes" been eradicated from my name but the President has also approached me with the proposal of officiating a new branch inside the government that will aid me in the eventual capture of Bazka. Again, it doesn't seem real.

After all, what I had done in blind panic all those years ago, my clouded mind suddenly has some sunshine coming in. Mother always said it shows up when you need it the most.

I am currently taking the train from Washington back down to Kentucky. I have a few loose ends to tie up with the elders. They will want to be informed of what has happened, as I have not made contact with them in fifteen years. I feel new again. Reborn.

Loose ends have been resolved, and old friendships have been rekindled. Millie has invited me to visit her place outside of Washington after my two day period away from the capital. This is the new lease of life I need.

The words left him through the pencil, words encompassing his thoughts and memories formed onto the page which telling from how thick it was and how bent the spine had become that Ray had written down every single step of his day to day life since Waywood's defeat. The feeling of isolation from the world after Mr Boston and the remains of who was still breathing in Bonebag, turned their backs on him after what they had witnessed, was enough to make Ray feel that he could help nobody. But in that time, from then to now, he felt like he'd grown in what must be done to keep the forces of Bazka at bay. But in reality, he was hoping for a gust of wind to just blow it away so he could eventually die in peace. But it was like the elders had said, the aura of the one individual who drinks the vial of the spirits will not find solitude in death until his mind is at peace and his troubles are gone. No worries, no actions, Ray will know when his time was up and the spirits grant his request when they feel his work was done. As they train rode on through the American countryside, Ray took a few moments to walk through the carriages to get the feeling back into his legs. A lot of people during the afternoon were in their seating areas enjoying a relaxing cup of coffee, while the journey got shorter and shorter. Kentucky was only half an hour away, it would be an hour to go before the sun started to set. Ray ventured into the last train carriage and it was the most basic after coming through the finer carriages. This one was the basic one; two wooden seats in front of the other in two rows of eight. While the floor was also plain, pale brown wood flooring the wall decor was still similar to the royal green tone of the higher end carriages. A few eyes met with Ray for a split second, before returning back to either the floor or out of the window while Ray continued on down the path to the end of the train, where the door leading to it had a curved metal barrier for protection. Behind the train the tracks stretched on and on to the horizon, the open land was now drier and more humid. From where Ray was standing, it was like leaving all his troubles behind. The land remained the same but society was changing rapidly without his notice. The door had opened again and someone had come through to stand in the last bit of space the small platform had. Ray moved to his side but didn't really catch sight of the person standing to his right, someone just catching some fresh air like him he thought.

"I recognise you from your poster," the person said, feminine and sweet sounding. Rays heart dropped and so did his face, loosing its relaxed expression and was now showing fear again. His eyebrows straightened and his mouth drew downwards. He prepared for the worst. As he turned he saw that the voice matched the face perfectly. It was the mother of the daughter in the carriage he sat in.

"I must've seen your face everywhere I went. What did you do exactly?" she asked. Ray didn't want to answer. If she was in for the kill unbeknownst to him then anything he would've told her wouldn't be enough for her to not be convinced to whip out a sharp pocket-sized blade drilling into the side of his neck finishing him off for a bounty that had now been lifted. He also thought that being said to have been pardoned by the President, wouldn't do him any favours also, when you're on the run for so long away from police, bounty hunters and anyone who's desperate to go the mile to be rich, wouldn't want to hear anything from you. They'll either tie you up and drag you to the authorities or just simply put a bullet in your head. Ray was quite partial to the small knife idea that came to him.

It would fit this lady's character. He thought of it, The Ray McCarthy who had outrun the most sinister of villains from the spirit world, to dodging crafty bounty , to the local drunk at the nearest saloon in the area, would be taken out by such a sweet face who would nest your head while you died like she did her daughter in her arms, once that blade was in the side of your neck. But sometimes evidence is always the best thing for a case to be finished. Ray pulled out the paper which had not only his but President Roosevelt's signature on it, indicating that what was on the paper about his recent pardoning was genuine. He gripped it tightly with two fingers on the top corners and with all the toughness he could muster said, "What ever you wanted it to be darlin'."

The mother in the long pink dress gazed upon the letter with the Presidential crest inked onto the page. Her eyes widening as she read through it. She simply smiled while nodding and then walked back inside. A sudden rush of relief went down Ray as he rolled the paper to fit back into his coat pocket. That was all it took now. No fights, no one-on-one duels of who had the quickest draw and no skirmishes which would lead him to fleeing wherever he was. Even though she may not have been a killer and was just an onlooker, the sensation would've still been the same. Had it been a large man who's frame would've crushed him into the tiny corner he had left of the train, who with the slightest of ease could've snapped his neck with one finger and a thumb pinching tight the feeling would be delightful. Again, Ray looked on out to the vast land that quickly rushed by him and shed a single a tear in joy.

Back in Kentucky the locals were just as friendly as he'd remembered. This was just as he was coming off the train and walking out from the station. It was busy and crowded, the paper boy shouted out the news with its captivating headlines to sell the issue, people filling the air in conversation with their parties and the clip clop of the horse's hooves walking up stone roads. The evening would set up to become very lively tonight as the sun started to set, but Ray was looking for a quieter setting. As he passed up through the streets, Ray could see multiple different routes as the road weaved through in different directions. The idea at first would've been simply to just keep straight and avoid everything but it was becoming much more trickier nowadays, more people meant bigger development in construction and that meant more traffic. Before long, Ray stopped for a moment, slouching his back onto a wooden pillar of a food store to wonder where his next step should take him in order to find the elders gathering. The people wouldn't be getting any quieter he thought until his eye caught something which he hadn't seen before. Something very new for the time, but still in its infancy. It was the first time he saw one up close and there stood a man next to it, he wore a long tweed jacket with a matching tweed waistcoat and a black hat. His beard was grey and strangely, thin but long while he puffed away at his cigarette. Ray brought himself upright again to walk towards it to have a look for himself."

"Excuse me. Do you mind if I take a look at this thing?" he asked him.

"Sure thing," the man said taking his cigarette out briefly to speak before putting it back into his mouth. It had a mix of old train-like qualities going from the colourfully painted side plates which were a fiery red and the outline being in a shimmering gold. The wheels were like the ones on a stagecoach, somewhat small but could accommodate the weight of its two passengers who would sit comfortably on its red leather seating. To its side by the front wheel it had a funnel which was connected to a piece which linked to the inside mechanics of it. "Does she run well?" Ray asked again intrigued.

"Does for what I do to get by for a living. They're saying these things could stop us using horses all the time should they make more of 'em," the man said.

"They want to make more automobiles?"

"Yeah, gonna make 'em bigger and faster they said," Ray had finished looking the machine up and down and came to the mans side while he continued to smoke.

"Do you think this thing can get me outside of town across to the hillside?" Ray asked.

"Sure thing, if you've got the cost of travel covered," the man said with the smoke blowing into Ray's face. Ray's hand fiddled around inside his coat pocket and dug out a good amount of green notes and placed them into the mans hand.

"Sure thing I do," Rays said. The man finished his cigarette with a flick of his fingers and adjusted his cap before hopping over to the driver's side. Ray followed suit jumping on to sit the other side while the driver cranked at a handle in a circular motion. The automobile shook and roared as the sound of the engine got to work. The machine was away with the driver being careful of the pedestrians walking through the town as he drove through, past the many shops and saloons which were open at this time. On a sharp left the automobile drove past a set of gates which looked like the entrance way into the town because Ray could now see ahead of him the open fields going up to the hillsides as the automobile jiggled around while going across a wooden walk-on bridge which stood over a small river stream. It was just beginning to get darker, a few stars' dim lights were starting to seep through the deep dark sky while a slightly fading orange glow from the horizon had at least ten minutes left before vanishing. The driver had taken Ray as far as he would go before packing it in for the night, he had got him through town and up the first flight up one of the hills. Ray got out and thanked the man who again was cranking down on the handle which made the machine purr a mechanical roar before turning around to head back to town. The sound of the automobile drifted away as the hillside got quieter till the only sound Ray could really tune into, was the breeze blowing past his ears. He was only up the first hill, the second would be his destination for the meeting with the elders. It was steep but the ground was not hard to walk up, purely just grass with the occasional dry spot of dirt. Ray got higher to the point where the glow of the small town by the train station looked how a single gas lantern would look like from afar, like a orange pimple of light. The wind was much more heavier now, it rushed past his ears faster and it was much colder than a second ago but it didn't bother him. But then as Ray stood still with a big slow intake of air through his nose the wind shifted in direction hitting Rays back instead of his sides. The grass rustled around and the earth started to vibrate. Before long Ray's feet soon begin to sink through like it was sand and then his shins were next to be engulfed by the grass which looked normal but wobbled around like perfect water being disrupted by a single stone. Next to go was his body, his hands, his arms, his neck and then finally his head. After the dirt from the underground brushed past him leaving him with some dusty brown marks he was back again on the solid ground. On the floor was dirt and on the walls was dirt, he had sunk through to the part underground which was square shaped and had a passageway covered in roots. The earthy smell was strong but Ray went through like he had done many times in the past. Along the walls the roots started to slowly rise upwards as he walked along past them, they had been embedded in those dry dirt walls for so long that maybe even the slightest touch could make them crumble into a powdery mess on the ground. The walls then started to open up to another room, much wider in size but no one was inside except for Ray. He stood there shrugging his shoulders impatiently as he looked all around, waiting for one of the elders to arrive. "Am I early or are y'all just playing with me?" he joked out loud. No response. Not even a rumble in the ground. Seemed like they were fooling around with him by the way Ray cracked a small smile from the left side of his mouth. Just then the roots on the wall started to crumble, some into dust and some just breaking off in small parts. The side of the wall to his left had its roots break off in different places until it started to look more like a shape. It was like rubbing out the guidelines to drawing a face, as more and more came off, the roots soon formed a face. An old wrinkled face with the roots shaping the definition of its skin. The crackling sound from the roots stopped for a second and then the face zoomed straight off from the dirt wall, floating inches away from Ray's face. They both stared eye to eye as then the other roots behind him formed similar faces and thrusted off the wall to circle around Ray. He looked round, puzzled, like he wasn't meant to be there but instead of showing fear he turned to the first face that scared him with how quickly it jumped out at him from the wall and cracked a smile."Your scare tactic needs a little work." Ray said. The root constructed face then shifted downwards to make a frown and as the roots brushed together as it spoke, "You're good, young one." The voice familiar yet aged so much. Behind the roots, an aura pressed out green smoke trickling down from where its mask was and shaped into a body. Forming first the outline and then becoming more detailed in skin and bone structure. As the shape of the elder formed, the roots all finally crumbled away, the revealed elder took a step back and raised his hand up, palm flat above his head as the other root mask began to take shape with their red and yellow auras. Soon there was one body with three spiritual ghosts standing in the ground below the surface. Ray spun around to see everyone in the room before turning back to the first elder who was now joined by the other at his side.

"And on time too. This reunion was obviously important to you. It better be to us." The green elder spoke.

"I have good news for you elder ones. I have others now to my disposal. I'm sorry for not making contact with you in a while-"

"Fifteen years is, as you say, a while," the red elder spoke in a sharp sarcastic manner.

"Alright. I haven't made contact with you in fifteen years and you obviously are concerned that if I am fulfilling my duties in which your gifts have given me. I have now become part of my Government. They requested that with me at the helm of a new branch Bazkas actions will be monitored and they will come about his destruction," Ray explained.

"So, you have learnt from your mistakes. The recruiter becomes the recruited," the red elder said.

"The fearful becomes the determined," the yellow elder said.

"The follower becomes the leader," Green elder said, concluding.

"You've done well, Ray. But it is far from over should Bazka remain hidden in the shadows. His words have grown in strength, people can be turned and they could become something that may be hiding in plain sight. Evil like Bazka should not become this difficult to track, Ray." the red elder followed on.

"The President has given me a full range of resources at my disposal. I have associates who will pinpoint and keep record of should his influence become prevalent," Ray said. The three elders all looked at each other sharing stares of thought before turning back to Ray.

"I am not certain you should've gone this route, young Ray. The Shaman's people have a network underneath the land stretching miles. For what you did up in the mountains all those years ago, bringing them light was enough for them to help you with anything." The blue elder said.

"I'm telling you, I have the highest power my country has to offer. I am as much in the shadows as Bazka is. That's why I didn't speak to you. The connection was lost because I had to go off the grid in this world. If Bazka had found me back then when I had skin frail as week-old roadkill, then everything would've gone wrong. For you and for the land. For all we know, he may have got into my head and then...well the worst may have happened," Ray said courageously. The elders paused leaning back a little by the sudden information.

"A fine point, but nothing we hadn't thought about all ready." the yellow elder said.

"We always knew the possibilities should that...outcome were to have happened, Ray. You attach yourself too much to what could happen rather than what should happen, even after decades of running. If we can leave you today with something to meditate on then it is this. Train yourself to let go of your worries. Not physically but mentally," spoke the green elder as he approached Ray closer with slow steps.

"I think it would be best if you do this with us now" He finished placing his right hand on Ray's shoulder. Ray nodded and the elders circled around him again placing their hands on Ray's shoulders. They were hollow and Ray couldn't feel any physical pressure but he felt it on the inside as they all began to chanting an ancient native language together, closing their eyes as they brought their heads down. In a crackly string of words the words of the forgotten passage echoed through the walls and into the chambers, continuing on from this room. The roots lifted and shook softly like the wind was blowing them but as they did they grew thicker, stronger and more youthful as the green colour was brought back into them. The dirt was clearing with more grass now covering the walls with flowers popping through. The elder's auras shun bright, Ray squinted harder as the room became brighter than before. The three elder's were now pure white orbs in a last flash of light as they became dim again, they again started to float like their initial disguises were when Ray entered down from above. The exercise was power, left Ray reeling a bit, shrugging his shoulders but the sensation afterwards was rewardingly relaxing.

"Now young Ray. This will be the last time we meet, until Bazka and his peers are eliminated, we will meet again for the last time," all three orbs said together in a calm breathy voice.

"That could be...a long time," Ray said catching the air back into his lungs.

"We are the land. And time for us is nothing. You will find your true swan song. And you find the peace in the most unusual places." As the elders spoke their last words to Ray they evaporated into dust that sparkled down to the floor. Ray knew the elders would live on, seeing him in some sort of fashion but this was like the last time ever he would see the faces of those who brought him into this world. His teachers, prophets till the last breath. However, there was one more talk to be had as the sound of footsteps were heard to Ray's right with the daylight from it to reveal a silhouetted figure. Ray knew it instantly from the shape alone. The wide frame, the stubby legs and head dress that was large enough to hold a bird's nest in with the whole family sitting comfortably as he walked. He stepped through and the face though familiar to Ray's eyes, had aged dramatically. His face though still the same size was much more longer now. The skin showing it wear and tear through the years. It looked full still but the signs of death were clearly visible from his sunken eyes to his last two teeth. He spoke

"Nice to see you again, McCarthy," his voice was dry, sounding as though it could break apart like his body in a matter of seconds but there was warmth still there. Still life through a decaying heart that was slow in rhythm. Ray extended his hands out and gave the man a hug. Maluk still smelt of the stench that was inside his smoking pipe and it made Ray choke up a bit once his nose was within smelling range. The jolly old man let out a laugh of joy once his hands were around Rays neck patting him on the back. A warm embrace compared to the elders.

"Did they give you a hard time, like old times?" Maluk asked.

"Actually, I think I gave them a hard time for once," Ray said.

"Nice change. Definitely has been a long time. Please, catch me up to speed." Maluk said extending his arm out to sit on the floor with him. The two moved over to the centre of the room and crossed their legs together on the floor. It took Maluk a little longer than Ray as his knees creaked with enough strain that Ray brought his head up in a quick glance of the fear that they may break. As the two sat their they brought their auras out into the open, extending their arms outwards with the smoke of both their auras colours rushing out to the sides of the grass walls. It rushed under them, covering the whole floor before the smoke rose up lifting the two men into a cloud-like comfort. Maluk reached into his head piece and pulled out a smaller version of his pipe much to the delighted chuckle of Ray across from him. He placed his thumb onto the hole, covering where the smoke would exit, his thumb fat enough to cover it whole. He blew hard into it forcing his big cheeks to go as red as his partial body paint on his open stomach. Ray could see the wrinkles in his eyes even more and he was about to see something very familiar to him once the smoke emitted a fire which shot straight up from the pipe. It shot around the ceiling circling around the two before dropping down to float in the middle of them. Floating like an orb Maluk emitted the familiar smoke that would become his body scent blew into the flaming orb which in turn shot up and spread all across the room. The smoke was dull grey at first but then slowly turned a shade darker, flowing down the walls like a waterfall as Maluk was more relaxed while he hovered.

"So young Ray, what was the meaning of this visit?"

"Well, for one to smell that good stuff again," Ray joked. Maluk gave a hearty chuckle which broke down into a coughing fit before Ray carried on seriously.

"Just a regular update. Everything is in my hands now, the government has granted me a full branch of tools at my disposal to stop Bazka and all his baskets of tricks."

"The New Americans know of the real lands false prophet?" Maluk said, leaning forward more intrigued with a slight sign of worry in his eyes.

"Yup, in full detail. I explained to the President...the chief...that Bazka is a force to be reckoned with," Ray continued.

"This is most strange of them to be heeding the words of my people after all they've done to many tribes, good and bad. If I knew I needed an interpreter, I would've called you back years ago."

"Well, that was the thing Maluk, wasn't it? I just wasn't right after what happened in the mountains. I shouldn't have shunned you; it wasn't the right thing to do." Ray said. Maluk showed a small smile. A smile like a father would give their young son or daughter for warming encouragement.

"Things can always stay with you, Ray, for a long time. It is in the past now, trust me when I tell you, you will have. A. Past." He was right, Ray thought. What happened then was only a small portion of what he may see in the future.

"As much as I don't trust who you are working with, I know you will have the common ground and do what's right for this land that we call home. So long as you respect that which brought you into it," Maluk said.

"You want a medal? That was a fine speech," Ray joked, making the big man laugh.

"Ho, ho, I don't need one of your peoples' trinkets. My peers praise, and the respect the spirits give me for my service is worth more than that," he said. Maluk once again brought his smoking pipe for one last puff before his auras smoke faded away, lifting him down gently to the floor. He got up in a struggle, pressing his hand on his knees to push himself up while Ray quickly hopped off his smoke-filled chair. Ray helped him up and adjusted Maluks headpiece as he stood upright.

"It was good seeing you again, big man," Ray said.

"And you too, young one. But I think you are more than ready to carry out the mission that I and the elders entrusted you with. All on your own, may I add," Maluk said.

"What?" Ray said puzzled with his eyebrow raised. Maluk put his big meaty hand on Ray's shoulder and guided him out from how he entered as the grass in the room started to shrivel away again back into the wall. The way Maluk had come in was only a few steps away, now the bright light from the outside was blinding the two men. It couldn't have been morning now,

Ray thought. He was only in there for about ten minutes. But it wasn't his mind, perhaps it was Maluk's smoke, but it was shaping to become morning outside. They had come out the steepest side of the hill and Ray and Maluk could see the beautiful open landscape Kentucky had to offer.

"Yours to own now. To protect. This is where the land thrives Ray. On sights like this, where the spirits roam free and let everything grow. It will last longer than what you will, what I will."

"You sound closer to it than I do," Ray said.

"Indeed, I do. But it's been like this for some time. With my last breath, I said to the elders, that someone comes over and obeys by the rules and sets the world in balance. That with all the faith I have left in the natural order I select him, I said." Maluk went on, with Ray piecing it together more and more as his head tilted towards him.

"No. I surely can't," Ray mumbled.

"Death is a happy occasion, Ray. You will know it when you set in stone what you want to grow in your place." Ray gripped the chiefs big hand as he started to walk back inside the earthy room, keeping it tight with his other hand covering them.

"Thank you, Chief," Ray said.

"You too, young one. Take this, I made this before you arrived. Look to it in the darkest of times. My last bit of faith of my word is inside this. Look at it, study it, and above all else, love it," Maluk said, slipping a small dream catcher in Ray's palms. Delicate when handled and holding the simple but prettiest of purple flowers in its woven centre consisting of string, with the Crows native hymn written around its circular frame.

"I bless you, young one. Now leave and let me be free." Maluk said for what would be his last words to Ray as he turned and headed back inside the hill from which they both came.

Ray stood there watching him walk slowly inside as the light began to leave him until he was submerged by the tunnel pathway's darkness. Perhaps this was the greatest gift that the vial bestowed upon him, the ability to choose death with the spirits granting your release, felt satisfying if Ray had to go on from what he saw with Maluk. The chief was calm, at peace, and felt that his mission on earth was complete. This world's wisdom that Ray fell into brought to him some real joy and also fear. The fear being that should such a being like Bazka dominate it, would become a terrible wasteland of filth and suffering. Not just the real land with the elders and other natives, but America in general. He also wondered while he walked back down the hillside if he could trust his government and if they believe him to respect the word of the elders without using it for their own needs. It would feel like a betrayal, but it wouldn't be catastrophic, he thought. But as he got down further, he just reflected on what Maluk told him for the final time. He looked back up the hill, and as he did, he saw something rising from the hole Maluk had walked into. It was the same smoke again from his pipe mixed in with an orange, dusty aura smoke, spiralling together as it rose into the air. It was like a fire burning, and it was uncontrollable. Maluk's aura almost clouded the morning sky as it continued to rise up until the last puff of smoke lifted up from the hole. For a moment, like a cloud, it just sat there as the only thing in the sky as the morning sun beamed up from the hills while the blue sky was empty as can be. Ray watched in astonishment, seeing the two colours flow beautifully together, as it started to sparkle, soon shooting out across and then finally falling down to the ground giving the grass a shine like it had been raining but landed slowly like snow. Maluk had taken his final breath of existence and exploded into a ball of spiritual wonder which filled the air and took shape around the land he called home. Ray tipped his hat to his mentor, and he carried on, leaving behind him a hilltop with a small hole to walk in and a flourish of lush green wild-life growing at a rapid rate.

XI.

Ray stayed in the small town near the Kentucky train station that evening. He had walked back and found a small apartment to lay his head for the night. Cosy but the noise from the towns night life was something to get used too. He got out of bed with a huge stretch which made his back click with a deep moan. He had slept with his clothes on and the creases were prevalent. After moving his legs around, Ray went for a sip of water before crossing his legs up on the bed to meditate. He blew in and out very slowly as he let his purple aura to rise on its own, soon his eyes opened to reveal the purple light shift from his pupils while the whites surrounding them pulsed red. As his eyes opened, his face stayed the same, an emotionless mask of concentration to which the aura around him grew thicker and deeper in colour. The aura flowed through the room across the floor and hitting the sideboards of the wall with a gentle tap of smoke. Soon the concentration started to make the veins in his head pulse, the muscles around the sides of his head tensed as his eyes started to water, while he squinted tight to stop it. He said it to himself over and over, quietly like a whisper to himself to stop it. His mind projected scenes of death, screams of innocent people crying out his name in unison while the land burned, cities crumbled, trees burned and the creatures of hell rose from the ground. Images flashed before him before they finally stood still on a image, more horrifying than the rest; it was Millie. Grey skinned, her eyes sunken in, pale with no pupils and she was being held up in the air by her spiralling hair. The vision of her spoke but the body was jerked around to just make her jaw move, giving the image of her as a wooden puppet being moved by what was sitting behind her. "Let his word in." She said. His word was what was holding her up as it leaned forward close behind her, the background was dark in the vision but the outlines of a face with two ghostly cloud-like eyes beaming in from behind. "Let...me....in" it spoke in a deep rumbling voice like an erupting volcano, spewing saliva.

Ray shot out from his meditative state and scuffled back on the bed with his back to the wall. Whatever it was in his head was surely Bazka. The telling of his word, the harrowing presence which looked over your shoulder, it was surely him he thought. Was this what people saw when they were taken over? Ray didn't have time to think it through. He got up quickly, packing up everything, before shooting out of the hotel room like a mad dog. His footsteps quickly banged down the staircase down to the lobby of the hotel. Ray quickly asked for his bill and the clerk behind the counter did so in very cool slow fashion that made Rays blood boil as he was still in a panic. He finally brought the bill and Ray started flicking through the notes in his pocket to the exact amount. As he started counting the clerk was not the only one watching him; in the corner by the door sat a man with a bushy brown beard, with a beaten up trench coat and bowler hat. He twiddled his fingers in his cigarette paper making a fresh one to go. He got up once he had finished making it, struck a match and let the smoke lift into the air, filling it with that strong tar smell.

"You should know partner, you're a big deal right here," the man said. Ray turned to see him, the last bit of money in his hand he put down on the counter for the clerk to carry on counting.

"Listen buddy, don't know if you've heard the news but that bounty has been lifted now," Ray said.

"Oh, I'm not talking about that man, I'm talking about the new one. The one the man has put up for your head. It's pretty big, but the hunt ain't starting yet."

"What do you mean, hasn't started?" Ray asked as he relaxed his shoulders hoping that this wouldn't end with one person hitting the floor.

"The man with all the money said no one's to touch you until he says, and if I remember correctly, he's given you till tomorrow."

"And just who might he be?"

"The man who runs Bidens. Said it's a bigger sum than what the government had on ya." The man said. Ray just rolled his eyes, stepping back resting his arm on the counter and looking at the clerk's nervous expression as he finished the bill receipt.

"Good to see that family name is still covered in the shit he stepped in long ago. Look buddy, you're not gonna get anywhere being attached to that man's name. The real Biden built this whole business of his, on murder and theft. Now he's dabbling in the likes of mercenaries and racketeering. He knows his ship is sinking. Poor men just looking for a drink would always be tangled up in his web, families got ruined and their name got tarnished. Now if you would do me the honour of going up to who ever this snot-nosed brat of an inbred grandson is running his business like this, tell him I ain't scared and I hope he puts up a decent fight, because I ain't bending over backwards in fear at his name again!" Ray yelled definitely as he snatched the bill from the clerks hand and brought his rucksack over his shoulder, storming out of the building. As the door swung open however, he froze. He had never had so many eyes trained in him as he did right then. He came out to a see of different coloured eyes, all focusing hard on his face, the face plastered still on posters with a bounty greater than what he previously had. Everyone stood still like scarecrows in a corn field, not budging but looked intimidating. The man in the bowler hat walked out and stood behind him with his hands in his pockets looking up to the sun rather than what was in front of   him.

"Oh, I'll tell him. But he won't like what you said just then. Course as you can see, word spreads like a wildfire. I hope that money's decent. Good luck to ya." And the man just walked down off the wooden staircase as if this was normal, passing through everyone else who all remained still like statues. After his eyes met everyone, Ray as brave he could took the first step down off the hotel step, and then the other till he was on ground. He stepped slowly through everyone, there must've been a hundred plus men and women all with the same intent; of capturing or taking his life. But they abided by the rules. Not lifting a finger as Ray slithered past them trying to not budge one by accident in the hope that it wouldn't start a chain reaction in making them dog pile on him. As he carried on through, Ray noticed something in everyone's eyes, all different coloured and yet all had that crazed look. Like they all had a disease, suffering from the same illness. This kept going until he reached the town's gates again, it seemed never ending, even people in their houses were peering through the windows to watch him. The whole town was a part of it. A pocket of desperation yet some dedication in the state of Kentucky really wanted that prize on Ray's head and they sure as hell weren't going to muck it up. Ray went through the gap in the rusty barred gate of the town and started to pick up speed as he walked off, still glancing over his shoulders to see the same townspeople watching him. After five seconds, Ray started to run, he took what the man in the bowler hat said as hallowed gospel and ran as far as he could like it was the second coming of the apocalypse, time was scarce and he had to prepare for it. The road ahead was just dirt but he knew he had to find a horse and fast if he was ever to get back to Washington quickly. Business in his new department at the White House would surely have to start now. Already he could sense Bazka's hand in what the town had become. Nobody was normal back there, too many already seemingly under his influence through greed and manipulation in his deadly voice which lured any desperate man or woman to bend to his will. The promise of a profit would only increase Bazka's hold on the innocent. Ray continued to run and run and run until he became tired. He had been on a full sprint for ten minutes now and the Kentucky land still looked the same. He was panting, ringing his arms up over his head to let the air in. He was lost...from the town at least. He checked around, moving around in a three sixty swivel, nothing. With one sharp intake, Ray held his breath, concentrated, let his aura flow through till his eyes opened, and sunk through the ground. He rose up, this time not through just dirt but gravel too. An alleyway, dark grey with washing lines hanging from windows above him. The smoke of chimneys funnelled up then down and the sound of daytime chatter rung through the streets rang through as Ray got his bearings and walked on through towards the White House. Washington would not be a likely place for Bazka to infiltrate at this stage. Too much of a gamble. Bazka seemed to only prey on the weak through others, playing Chinese whispers, letting the word spread. The structure of the organisation changed but Bazka was still the centre piece of it. Washington was too crowded, everyone seemed to be fine, not letting their guard down while the hopes of prosperity filled their optimism in any room while Roosevelt was in charge. Small towns forgotten seemed to be the likely place. Slowly building before the eventual target would be where Ray was walking through. Ray had paced through the streets whilst clutching onto his rucksack, his hand fondling around to find his clearance pass that would allow him through the gates again. The procedure in, had to be stealthy to avoid attention but it didn't seem like it would happen. Ray was in too much of a panic at this stage to even worry about a thing like protocol procedures on going through a door. Coming up to it, he simply pushed his hand through the bars with his paper in hand and the guards hurried to unlock the gate, squeezing him though. Ray ran up to the White House door and pushed it open while the guards tried to apprehend him, he showed them the paper and they backed off, quietly muttering to themselves wondering who Ray was to have such a clearance. Inside it was empty. Perfect he thought. Roosevelt had laid a perfect trail towards the underground base that would avoid suspicion amongst the administration workforce, should the bookshelf be too much of a walk. Keeping at the same pace he used on the streets, Ray weaved through the hallways, avoiding contact with the two people who were both cleaners sweeping the floors. Then he saw it; the junction at the end of the hallway, one way to go left one, way to go right. A huge portrait of the ninth president, William Henry Harrison, stood in full view to Ray as he got to the junction, he looked both ways, no one in sight. Not a sound. Beside the portrait were two small wooden tables with lamps atop of them, underneath the table to Ray's right was a small button, tucked away just at the back of it. It clicked and the portrait lifted up, only a small space, big enough for someone of Ray's height to crouch under it and then the portrait slid back down again closing him in. He saw nothing but darkness for a second before the lights on the wall slowly illuminated until they were as bright as can be. They highlighted every small crevice of the stone paths narrow hall into the H.A.W.K base, it had a plain door at the end with a US flag pinned to its centre. Ray knocked the first part of the agreed sequence then followed it up with and ending thud on the door with the tip of his boot. He heard some footsteps and Frank's skinny frame greeted him.

"Earlier than I expected-" Frank tried to finish but Ray had pushed past him into the boardroom. It was different now then when Ray was in here last, there were tables at least, and a swivel chair he hoped was for him.

"Bazka is already showing signs of territorial dominance in the southern region. I went to where I was needed in Kentucky but the town, it was off, when I was leaving." Ray stated to all three men who dropped what they were doing, turning to face their commanding officer.

"What do you mean by off?" Gerald asked.

"The people...they all watched me, like a lion that hadn't eaten in weeks. But they did nothing. That's when I was told that outlaws inside the Biden family company have put a price on my head. Whoever is running it, we have to find them."

"You presume Bazka is in connection with these crime bosses?" Frank asked finally sitting down at the desk.

"He's used that scum's name before, but never to this extent with just ordinary folk. While I was on the run, men who were recruited by that bastard, were the obvious so and so who would be involved in dodgy dealings, these people just looked possessed. Using the reward money is just a factor in the spell. I have until tomorrow before they hunt begins for me again." Ray said as he sat down, pulling himself tightly into the table, rubbing his fingers through his hair as the others studied and thought.

"We'll need to scope out areas. Scouts should be the ideal way to go about this. We bring in the recruits, falsify the information given to them, they return in a weeks time with which are safe zones," Alan started with, grabbing a notebook, jotting down names and places before tearing them off to stick to a board which had the state map pinned on. The notebook slid across the table between the three men as they all chimed in all the while Ray was still sat back in his chair. He watched the men at work, his men, his information given and they were hard at it setting the sail in motion to start a long haul mission which may take years to achieve, Ray was overwhelmed with the dedication. They took him seriously and the confident smile started to stretch out. His confidence grew and he soon joined in. The crew worked for a solid four hours, covering every aspect that need to be taken with such a task; the state coverage, the ways in which infiltration units had to be handled, Ray's involvement, Ray's missions, protection of civilians all the while the amounts of paper work started to stack on top of each other and the map board was soon covered in notes. It had now gone late in the day, four thirty two in the afternoon and the sun was starting to set. Inside a base underground can leave you forgetting the time of day. The time was used correctly but Ray remembered in the midst of all this that there was still one thing left to do, see Millie. It could well be the last time Ray ever saw her before the mission started, possibly stretching out to years of operation.

"Gentlemen, we did well. The scouts will have to be taken into effectively at dawn tomorrow. Gerald, you think you can handle the scouts at that time?" Ray asked

"It will be no problem, sir," Gerald said.

"Good. At the moment, a likely excuse for them would be that foreign agents are establishing camps in towns and are recruiting through the black market. We can't let anyone know of its true nature."

"I'll alert the President before sundown today. He'll get them sent for and then the operations will begin come tomorrow. We should begin the discussion about your safety Mr McCarthy, I know you'll be our boots on the ground but really we need to keep you hidden for a while." Frank said.

"I could do with a week's holiday. Good start to the job." He joked.

"The scouts will secure the southern territories first before we make progress over the western side of the country. The scouts bring us floor plans, group numbers and we'll try to find the whereabouts of the the Biden residence. Oddly enough their base tends to change frequently."

"Backtracking, knowing them."

"When things become heated, the king has to move. We'll have have one scout infiltrate the company records. There may be a pattern as to where the base shifts over time." Gerald said.

"Who's exactly is in charge of the Biden residence?" Ray asked. Alan pulled a sheet out from a leather bound folder and slid it over across the table. Ray examined it while Alan filled in from the opposite side of the table. "It's Bidens supposed grandson. Henry Jack Biden. Mid-twenties, has a degree in finance and business studies-"

"Could be forged." Ray interrupted.

"Started the business after a small fortune was found left over by his grandfather, whom you've encountered. From there the company sought after the saloons and through Pinkerton reports and from your word of mouth, the insertion of the Biden name took over with racketeering, armed robbery and murder."

"That small fortune is the reason they have a strong hold on things. Bribery should be added to that list, it's hard trying to convince the law whilst you're on the run from it yourself. Can

GEORGE A. THORN

I see his photo?" Ray asked. slid the photo down and when he saw it, a photo small enough to fit inside his wallet but it gave Ray such an emotion kick to his stomach he thought he might be sick. The grandson was identical to Colonel Biden in every aspect. Hair, shape, jaw line, eye colour, the similarity was almost too perfect, but Ray noticed something about the picture which completely shocked him. Biden's grandson had a scar on the left side of his face. Not just any mark, a burn mark. Ray instantly made a run for the door and slammed it shut loudly behind him. The officers behind him were stunned and confused wondering what may have cause such an exit. Ray continued to run as fast as he could up though the corridor then up through the secret portrait opening. He charged through the hallways once again and got round to the front door, bursting through them before rushing down the stairs screaming for the gate to be opened. The guards obliged and Ray was once again running through the streets of Washington, shifting through the oncoming traffic of people walking in the opposite direction to him, whilst running he felt the occasional bump on his shoulder now and then but he couldn't stop, not now. Like his movements, that picture raced in his head. Thoughts of what could happen should he not succeed in arriving in time. Confusion, doubt, fear. He couldn't brush past this. How could it have been done? There was no indication of this from the elders nor from Maluk. Were they hiding something from that he did not know about? Was this Maluks way of teaching him about how to handle his actions because if it did then it made him regret everything even more. He felt like a teenager again, thinking not of the consequences later on down the road before ending up at that road and then instantly regretting that turn towards that path. He remembered the place, the place he said he'd visit before another long journey to destroying Bazkas world but he didn't know if this was the end of his. His heart was pumping fast, fast like at in a moment he would be clutching it in pain and the air rushed through in and out his lungs. The number of people going by was startling, Washington was in it's rush hour, now Ray could see hordes of people coming through a road he had to trail through to get near the outside of he city. They all moved in the same walking direction with little space for anyone to squeeze through like a pack of cattle. Ray, squishing his arms as close as he could to his chest, burrowed through the multiple bodies and tried to weave through. Everywhere he turned he was bumping, sometimes face-first into someone's stomach to then be shuffling sideways as an arm caught him on his shoulder. It was so tight Ray wished he could just seep through the floor and be there in a matter of seconds but the elders loophole made him wish he could alter it now that they were gone with the spirits. In the end Ray had enough and barged through, shoulder first, pushing people to the side up against the wall as he finally managed with a small bump to the floor get out from the traffic. He shot up and continued to run, almost slipping as he got to his feet. He hopped the fence that gated out the lush green fields with its black painted bars and dashed straight forward, but as he could see further on past the green horizon he noticed it, smoke, thick black smoke. The worst had happened and Ray screamed his frustration out as he went to do a full sprint. Millie's small home was on fire. The word had spread and the deed was done. Ray scrambled up the top of the hill towards the burning wreckage of charred wood that once was a home; up close it worse. The walls were crumbling, the windows were broken; shattered remains all over the ground from where the panes buckled from the heat. The thick dark smoke gushed out from the open rectangles, violently spinning up into the air as the wind blew it up. The most horrifying scene of it all was what was on the front porch area down from the stairs, Millie laid there, lifeless and burnt. Ray came to her side trying his best to get the breath back into her lungs but to no avail. He compressed down onto her chest, one, two, three, four but nothing. He tried again in that order, the tears rolling down the sides of his cheeks for the worst had happened. She was gone. Millie's eyes were closed yet relaxed, her skin scorched but she felt nothing and her body was limp with her dress just barely still together from catching on fire and she was at peace. Ray couldn't contain it, he burst into tears and nested his head onto hers, the tears dropping onto her cheeks leaving little lines from where the tear cleaned the soot from her face. The two just sat while the fire raged on behind them, the wooden embers of a promising catch up was now the burning fuel for haunting nightmares to come. A hidden relationship now just a pile of ash. Nothing in the home was salvageable beyond this point, the fires had been alight for at least fifteen minutes before Ray had arrived. As he held her for the last time and whispered, "I loved you. And I wish I could've saved you." As he finished Ray let her head sink down and laid her down flat on her back as he rested on his knees still looking down at her beautiful soot-covered face and burns. In the midst of his grief, he could feel something, his aura lifting from him ever so lightly in his left shoulder. It felt warm, comforting yet it was not him doing this. Like someone else was stood there beside him. Ray's aura felt a presence and just before the wind blew the aura away he could make out the slightest outline of a hand on his shoulder, then it was gone. But as something goes, something comes. Behind all the crackling of burning wood, lightly paced footsteps rustled behind him, Ray heard it but did not turn his head until the person had got right in front of him. His eyes moved and he saw the figure, now his heart was racing again. The fear was in his eyes and his body was tense in so much anger that it made him paralysed. As he looked up, the man wore a black jump suit with a white shirt, his cuffs ridiculously large protruding from slim sleeves. His neck was covered in a royal red cravat tie and around his waist sat a cutlass in a dark silver lined holster which ran down near to his ankle. Finally his face was like the picture. Not aged, frozen in time yet still held the same sensation as Ray raised his eyes to see him. Biden. Colonel Biden. Thirty severn years past and still alive. How was he here? The questions kept filling Rays mind as he stood over him with that smug toad like grin on his face. But as Ray's mind kept asking, the answers made more sense. The constant barrage of people out to kill him, the establishments across America with his name plastered on them with big bold lettering and the stories he heard of the Colonel's name ringing through the criminal underworld. From that day Millie showed the slightest bit of pity he took the opportunity and rode with it in a direction she didn't expect until it was too late. Biden had repaid her the only way he saw fit, to further tor-ment the man who had stunned him and made him a fool. He was now standing over him as the victor, but for how long this moment would last would be another thing as neither man spoke nor moved. Frozen in time which felt like hours, while the fires of their new reality would rage on for years to come.

NATION WILL CONTINUE...

COMING SOON:
GRAVESTONED

ABOUT THE AUTHOR

George A. Thorn

George Thorn is a first time writer who has had a passion to create stories since his early school years.

George wishes to continue bringing imaginative stories to his peers in different genres. NATION is his first book.

FACEBOOK: George A. Thorn
INSTAGRAM: geronnie95
TWITTER: GeronnieBeGud

Printed in Great Britain
by Amazon